THE
LINGERING SCENT
OF WRONG ASSUMPTIONS

Jensen Siblings Book 3

Todd H. Davis

Todd H. Davis

The Lingering Scent of Wrong Assumptions
Copyright © 2022 by Todd H. Davis

Name:	Davis, Todd H. (1963)
Title:	The Lingering Scent of Wrong Assumptions / Todd H. Davis
Series:	The Jensen Siblings: book 3
Summary:	"New school. Confusing relationships. Mean girl. Assumptions and accusations. You know, typical high school stuff. Except for the skunk and the umbrella-wielding Japanese grandma. Those aren't typical." – Author.

ISBN:	978-1-7373413-4-5 paperback
	978-1-7373413-5-2 hardcover
LCCN:	2022905187

Subject: Sexual harassment; [BISAC: **FICTION** / Christian / Contemporary | **FICTION** / Christian / Romance / General | **FICTION** / Family Life / Siblings | **FICTION** / Friendship | **FICTION** / Romance / Clean & Wholesome | **FICTION** / Literary]

Rev. 1

Independently published, Cypress, Texas, USA
For information, contact www.toddhdavis.com

Cover design by Todd Davis and thekidgraphic

Contents

Prologue

Early June – Jentler family vacation day two

As the Jensen/Butler family – or Jentler family, as Alia liked to call them – was exploring the Texas Tech campus on Sunday morning, Sophie's phone buzzed with a message.

> Alia:
> I left

> Sophie:
> What do you mean?

> I walked out. I packed my
> stuff and left. I'm at a gas
> station now

> Calling u

"What happened?"

"I already told you they put me and Andy in a room with one bed, right?"

"Yeah. That was Friday night."

"It was just weird, and I felt awkward. I must have looked surprised at the arrangement because Andy's aunt said we don't have to pretend that we never sleep together. I mean, a year ago, I would've assumed everyone slept together, but over the last few months, I learned a lot of people don't, maybe most people don't. So, I don't know if it's normal for most people to assume Andy and I slept together or was it because they assume certain things about *me*. When we first got there, Claudia – that's his aunt – said she'd heard so much about me. I don't know what she heard, but they put us in a room with one bed and a box of condoms. At the time, I thought I was just being too sensitive, so I didn't make a big deal about it."

"Yeah, that sounds bad. But maybe it was just a misunderstanding of your relationship with Andy. Is it bad enough to leave?"

"Andy's cousin Brody is a pervert. When he found out Andy slept on the floor, he seemed disappointed. When we were at the pool in his backyard, he tried to take off my bikini top. He said he was just helping me with sunscreen, but I didn't want his help and he gave me the creeps."

Sophia moved closer to her husband Ty as they walked through the campus. Sophie's younger siblings, John and Emi, and Emi's friend Annie were a few steps out of earshot, engaged in a discussion about the merits of attending Tech over the schools they had visited the day before.

"Alia, Ty's right here. Do you mind if I bring him into the conversation?"

"Sure."

Sophie put her phone on speaker mode and summarized what Alia had told her.

"Hi, Ty," Alia greeted. "I hope your trip is going better than mine."

"It sounds like there's more than what you told Sophie so far. What else happened?" Ty asked.

"People here – not Andy's or his parents, but his uncle's family – make comments about my 'background' or my 'experience' or whatever. Like, once a prostitute, always a prostitute. It's like they just expected me to be a slut and Brody was even hoping for it."

"I agree, that's pretty rude," Ty said.

Sophie asked, "You don't think it'll get better when they get to know you?"

"If that was all, maybe. But it gets worse. Shelby invited me to stay at her house last night and that would have been better. But Brody started making a big deal about it like he was offended. And I didn't want to cause trouble between the families, so I just kept with original plans. But this morning, everything changed."

"What happened this morning?" Ty asked.

Chapter 1
The birthday gift

Mid-August

The young man confirmed that the address on the sticky note attached to the box matched the address on the mailbox before walking up to the door. The box contained a hair trimming set. It was a returned item from his recent venture into online selling. He was at the house to trade it for a used computer monitor that he saw listed on Facebook Marketplace, for sale or trade. The owner provided her address in the chat message, and he transcribed it to the sticky note which was now attached to the package. He removed the note and put it in his pocket, brushed his wavy brown hair out of his eyes, then rang the doorbell.

Ty opened the door to see a teenager holding a box.

"Hi, I'm Joel," the boy announced.

"I'm Ty, Emi's brother-in-law. Come on in. We're just about to cut the cake." Joel could hear the last lines of "Happy Birthday" being sung. The monitor owner's last name was Nguyen and Ty didn't look like a Nguyen. He was White, not

Vietnamese. But he said "brother-in-law," which meant he married into the family.

"Let me take care of that for you," Ty said, taking the hair trimmer box before Joel could object. Ty placed it on a table with a pile of birthday presents. Most of the presents were wrapped in festive paper or placed in decorative gift bags. A few, like the hair trimmer, were unwrapped. Had anyone looked at the name tags, they might notice that the non-wrapped presents were from boys.

"Come on back and let me get you some cake."

"What about the monitor?" Joel asked, but Ty had already moved towards the kitchen and didn't hear him above the chatter. He returned momentarily and handed him a plate of cake.

"The monitor?" Joel asked again as Ty headed back to the kitchen. Ty began distributing the birthday cake slices that had been placed on paper plates by a young Black woman with light brown hair pulled back in a puffy ponytail. *She doesn't look like a Nguyen either.*

Why would they want to do a trade in the middle of a birthday party? Joel asked himself. Not to be impolite, he began eating the cake while looking around at the other people in the living room. A sign attached to the wall above a row of teddy bears on the fireplace mantle said, "Happy Birthday, Emi." Most of the guests appeared to be about his age. He spotted who he assumed was the birthday girl; she was wearing a cardboard crown that had "15" printed on the front, fitted snuggly over her tight curls. *Okay, a year younger than me*, he corrected himself.

She bore a strong resemblance to the young woman cutting the cake. *She also doesn't look like a Nguyen.*

The girl looked directly at him and started walking his way before she was distracted by a friend wanting a selfie with her. He set his empty cake plate down on an end table, pulled out his phone, and opened the Facebook Chat app before reaching into his pocket for the sticky note with the address. Upon comparing the address in the chat with what he had written, he saw the mistake. He had reversed the last two digits of the house number.

I'm at the wrong house, he realized. He looked around the room. Selfies complete, the birthday girl resumed her walk towards him. *Crap!* Joel quickly started for the door and exited before the girl reached him. In his embarrassment, he left the hair trimmer on the gift table.

Chapter 2
~Heading out~

Previous June — Jentler family vacation day one

"Do you think Alia misses us?" fourteen-year-old Emi asked her fellow passengers as they pulled out of the driveway for their trip to the Grand Canyon.

"Probably not yet since it's only been a day. It's good for her to develop other friendships," Sophie stated. "The only thing I heard from her was a text message last night saying they'd arrived at Andy's uncle's house."

"Any details?" Emi asked.

"The drive was boring. The house is big and looks like a hotel. And Andy's aunt is the shortest grownup she's ever seen in real life."

"I'm sure she'll have fun in Arkansas with Andy and Shelly," Ty added.

"Shelby, not Shelly," Emi corrected.

"Right. Shelby."

* * *

At the gas station, a white Volkswagen Atlas was parked at the pump on the other side of the one Ty used to fill the family's Cadillac Escalade. A young woman with long blonde hair smiled at Ty as she filled the tank of her vehicle.

"It looks like you're going on a trip," she said. After setting the nozzle to flow automatically, she stepped closer to Ty. "I can tell by the luggage in the back."

Ty noticed her brown eyebrows didn't match her hair, reminding him of Daenerys in *Game of Thrones*. The loose-fitting jeans and short-sleeve yellow blouse gave her a take-me-serious-I'm-not-a-teenager vibe. Her outfit was a big contrast to the T-shirt and cargo shorts he wore.

"Yeah, we're heading to the Grand Canyon," Ty explained.

"Vacation. Nice. I've never been to the Grand Canyon, but I want to go there someday."

Ty noticed a young man, possibly a teenager, sitting in the passenger seat of the white SUV. The fact that the vehicle's fuel tank opening was on the passenger side allowed Ty a close view. Close enough to see the young man roll his eyes at the woman.

"How long is the drive?" the young woman asked.

"Well, we'll stop at Lubbock tonight, Albuquerque tomorrow night, and plan to be at the Canyon by early Monday afternoon."

"Going up Highway 6?"

"Yeah. With stops at A&M and Baylor along the way."

"Ah, the college campus tour. I'm a Baylor girl. It looks like we're both headed in the same direction for at least a few miles. My brother and I are visiting family in Bryan."

Ty's family had been listening to the conversation from their seats in the Escalade. Emi may not have been able to see the young man in the white SUV roll his eyes, but she shared his sentiment. The others had been watching with amusement, especially Ty's wife.

"He's married," Emi called out to the woman.

"Oh? How long have you been married?" she asked Ty, without skipping a beat.

"A little over a year."

"Oh, you're still newlyweds. Is that your wife," she asked, nodding to the young Black woman in the front passenger seat.

"Yes, that's my wife. And her sister and brother in the back."

"Is that other girl your sister?" she pointed with her chin toward Emi's friend Annie, whose light complexion was more similar to Ty's than to the siblings.

"No. She's a friend."

"So, it's both a family and friend trip," the woman observed.

"Yep."

"Hi!" She waved to Sophie. "I hope you enjoy your vacation." As she spoke, she nodded to each of the front, middle, and rear rows of the Escalade. Turning her attention back to Ty, she added, "I'm still working on my boyfriend. He just needs a little more time to commit."

The woman's gas pump signaled its completion with a click on the nozzle handle.

"Looks like I'm done." She put the nozzle back in its place on the pump. "It was nice talking with you." She looked to the Escalade and waved. "Y'all have a good trip."

After she drove away, John asked, "Was she flirting or just overly friendly?"

"That was flirting," Emi opined.

"I think she was just being friendly," Ty said, putting away the fuel nozzle. He looked at Sophie. "Jealous?"

"I don't have to be," she stated. She looked back at the other occupants of the SUV, then back at Ty. "You'll be sleeping with me tonight." She began humming.

Ty smiled as he recognized the song. At the appropriate point in the tune, Ty joined in with the lyrics, "So don't forget who's taking you home and in whose arms you're gonna be. Oh, Darlin', save the last dance for me."

"Y'all don't forget I'm sharing the room with you two tonight," John pointed out, curling his upper lip.

Ty and Sophie both laughed.

After they reached the highway and the vehicle was comfortably positioned in the center lane, Ty asked, "Does everyone understand today's schedule?"

"My college tour," John stated without enthusiasm. "A&M, Baylor, and Texas Tech."

"I thought you'd be excited," Sophie stated.

"Well, it's not a real tour," John complained. "We're just driving around."

"And walking around," Sophie pointed out. "It's still important to get a feel for the campuses. Then you can decide which ones to visit for a formal tour."

"Look, Jock Head," Emi stated, "we're going out of our way so you can see colleges. At least try to act like you appreciate it; act mature."

"Emi, don't call him Jock Head," Sophie scolded.

John took that moment to add his own criticism. "Oh, look who's talking about maturity. I'm seventeen and you're only fourteen."

"Only for two more months," Emi stated.

"I'm excited to see the colleges," fifteen-year-old Annie interjected, trying to diffuse the situation. "Mom said I need to send her pics and give her a report."

"See, John, Annie wants to see the campuses," Sophie emphasized.

"Ant Bites, you're not even in high school yet," John responded.

"Don't call me that," Annie stated with a tone that indicated her dislike. "Where did you hear that term?"

"Ant Bites? I heard one of your friends say it when I picked y'all up from Paolo's Pizza the other day."

"Whoever said it was not my friend."

"Jock Head, …."

"Emi!" Sophie warned.

"He just called her Ant Bites. *John*, you can't go around talking about girls' boobs. That is super inappropriate. Especially to her face."

"Huh? Boobs? What are you talking about? It's just a cute nickname: Annie Bates, Ant Bites. Nicer than what you call me."

"Ant Bites is not about my name. It's about …." Annie placed her hands flat against her chest. "It's about how small these are."

"What?" John looked confused. His moment of clarity was signaled by an exclamation of, "Ohhh," followed by, "Sorry. You should have told me back then. I could've roughed up that guy."

"I'm sure we can find better ways of handling insults than roughing up someone," Ty responded.

"Well, Ty" Emi interjected, "I recall that you got in a fight with someone for insulting Sophie."

"I don't remember that."

"I was in sixth grade. That was the night Sophie told us she…um…. It was the night you gave us the sex talk. Your nose was swollen."

"Oh, yeah," Ty mumbled, having lost the high moral ground about fighting.

Sophie smiled and reached over and rubbed Ty's arm.

"Okay, y'all. Let's just focus on the schools," Ty commented, to move the conversation to a more appropriate topic. "A&M's first. You can wave to Aunt Ruth and Uncle Ayo when we pass Navasota."

"As if they could see us waving," John replied.

* * *

The white Volkswagen Atlas had followed the Jentler family after the family passed it ten miles into their journey until they exited onto Texas Avenue in College Station to visit A&M. The Atlas continued on Highway 6 for another seven miles before finally taking the exit for FM 158, also known as the William J. Bryan Parkway.

"How can you talk to strangers like that at the gas station?" the boy asked his sister after an hour of silence.

"It's memorable."

"It's embarrassing."

"Why would it be embarrassing?" she asked. "People like to be acknowledged. That guy will remember me for the next few days. He might even tell someone about the overly cheerful girl he met while pumping gas."

"Is that what you do for your job? Flirt with people until they buy stuff?"

"It's not flirting," she defended. "It's just being friendly. Then they remember me next time I see them."

"Some people don't want attention. They just want to be left alone."

"Deep down they do, especially if they know you're not judging them."

"Whatever," he stated, signaling the end of the topic. "I hate coming here."

"I don't like it either. But this is the situation we're in. Mom wants to see us, and I want to tell her about my new job. At least this place is closer than Dad's. And the guards aren't as handsy."

"Yeah. I hate that place more. I miss Mom and Dad, but I'm still mad at them."

"Me, too."

* * *

"Next stop, Baylor," Ty announced as they left the Texas A&M campus. "So, what did you think of A&M?"

"It's super spread out," John stated. "You could probably fit four Prairie Views onto the College Station campus."

"Yeah, well, I guess I can count that as an advantage of my school over the big TAMU," Sophie observed. "Everything is close together, so I don't have to walk as much. What do you think, Annie?"

"I haven't seen many other colleges, so I don't know how to compare them. But my mom says A&M is the best."

"Your mom must be an Aggie," Ty observed.

"Yeah. She's happy for us to visit other schools, but she wants me to go here. Today, when we were walking around, it took a long time to get from one building to another. And we even had to drive to that part on the other side of the train tracks. If they only allow five minutes between classes, you're always gonna be tardy."

"College is different than your school," Sophie responded. "You might only have two or three classes on one day and the times can be spread out."

"Why didn't we drive through your college, Sophie?" Annie asked.

"Well, our family is already pretty familiar with it, and I don't think you'd be interested."

"Why not?"

"Prairie View is a Black college," Emi explained.

Annie's eyes widened. "They have separate colleges for Black people? I thought Martin Luther King ended – what's that word? separation? – no, segregation."

Sophie laughed. "I think you got your history a little mixed up. But yes, segregation ended a long time ago. *Historically* Black colleges were founded when schools were still segregated, but nowadays anyone can go there. But still, the student body is mostly Black."

"Like how you're mostly Black?" Ty teased.

"Ha ha. So funny. You know what I mean. And maybe I'm mostly Black as to looks, but I'm half-and-half and proud of it."

"They do let me visit the school, though, Annie," Ty stated.

"Stop," Sophie said as she reached over and squeezed his thigh. "My friends like to see you at the games."

"And they like when I grill hamburgers for them. Annie, I bought a Prairie View shirt for myself so I could show support for my beautiful wife." Ty looked over to see Sophie nod in approval. "You should've seen the confused looks from some of the PV guys when I wore it in Galveston during spring break. One guy seemed to have a little attitude about me wearing it, but once Sophie and her friends finished explaining the facts of life to him, he went and hid behind a car in the parking lot until our group left."

Chapter 3
First day of school

Late August

Alia Jentler pulled her aging pink Ford Ranger into the parking space next to fellow Senior John Jensen at Cypress Grove High School – affectionately known as Cy Grove to the students – after having followed him from home to school. She thought they were early, but cars and trucks already filled two-thirds of the parking spaces. She felt nervous excitement on her first day of the new school.

At least I know John and Lizzie, she thought, referring to John's girlfriend, Lizzie Abboud. *And Emi, of course.*

John's sister Emi waved as she exited the battleship, as John called the Cadillac Escalade ESV, the family vehicle that was mostly his. She hurried off to the front entrance of the school to wait for a friend. John walked over and stood in front of Alia's truck waiting for her. He noticed others staring at the pickup, likely due to its unusual color and black swirling vine patterns that Alia had painted herself. Students paused at the sight as they made their way to the entrance.

"How're you feeling?" John asked Alia.

"Good. Maybe a little nervous. How do I look?" A wide pink ribbon held her dark hair back in a ponytail. She wore a sleeveless pink shirt, a gray skirt, and white sneakers. It was a similar look to the outfit she wore last January on her first day of school at the Bauman Center – the school that helps students catch up on missed credits. Between the Bauman Center and summer school, she had caught up enough to attend a regular high school. This time, her outfit excluded the long sleeves and leggings needed for the cooler January weather. Feminine, but not overly revealing. Still, her mother would have been appalled at her for betraying her conservative Syrian heritage by showing bare arms and legs.

But Mama no longer has a say in what I wear.

John clicked the remote key fob to lock his SUV. "You already asked that at home. You look good. Fantastic. Beautiful."

"Thank you."

"For an introvert, you sure like attention."

"No I don't," Alia protested. "I only asked you, not everyone."

"Did you bring extra clothes for your shop class?"

"I doubt we'll be doing anything dirty on the first day. But I've got an old T-shirt and jeans in my backpack just in case. I may buy overalls later."

"I'm guessing there aren't many girls taking welding. So, whether you change or not, I'm sure those welding nerds will be drooling all over themselves to get your number."

"I don't know if that's good or bad." Upon further reflection, she added, "Do you think many people will already know about me?"

"You asked that at home, too," John noted. "My friends and Lizzie's friends know your story. Probably no one else does. Even if they did, their attention spans are too short to remember anything that happened before the summer." Changing the subject, he said, "We both have third lunch. If you haven't met anyone to sit with for lunch, text me. You can join me and Lizzie. We usually sit with my basketball buds."

They had been walking down the hallway from the main entrance. When they reached the first junction, John stopped.

"Your first class is down that hallway," he pointed to the left. "Mine is further on. Good luck."

"Thanks."

* * *

As Annie Bates stepped out of her mother's gray Lexus RX350 at the drop-off lane in front of the school, Emi greeted her. "First-day jitters?"

"A little," Annie responded as they began walking into the building. "We were at the top of middle school; now we're at the bottom as ninth-graders."

"Freshmen. You should say 'freshmen' not 'ninth-graders'."

"Oh yeah."

"I'm nervous, too," Emi admitted.

"How did you get here? The bus drop-off is on the other side."

"I rode with John. Seniors get the good parking spots up close."

"Hey, Emi, Annie" They turned to see a girl with light brown hair and clothes that looked like they came off a mannequin at a high-end boutique, including the high heel sandals.

"Hi, Sienna," Emi replied. *A bit overdressed for school*, she thought. *Even if it was the first day.*

"Annie, I see you're still on the Itty Bitty Titty Committee."

Annie glowered at Sienna Zamora as she walked on. Annie flicked her long brown hair as she complained, "I got highlights in my hair, curled it this morning, got my nails done on Saturday…"

"I was with you for that."

"… and put on a cute new outfit, and all she can comment on is my chest. I have three White grandparents, but I just had to inherit the body of my Asian grandma. I should have worn a baggy shirt."

"You look great. Ignore her. At least you're not named after a minivan," Emi offered in consolation.

Her face brightened as she asked, "Meet you for lunch?"

"Of course. But how will we find each other? Each lunch period has, like, a thousand people."

"Let's meet at that pillar," Annie said pointing. "By the way, you look great, too. I like the crown braid with the puffy curls behind it. But then, all of your hairstyles look great. Did Ty help with that?"

"Not this time, but he offered. See you at lunch." Emi took a step and then turned back to Annie. "And don't let Sienna get to you. This is gonna be a great day."

* * *

A white Volkswagen Atlas pulled up to the curb taking the spot just vacated by the gray Lexus, and a boy with wavy brown hair and wearing a dark blue polo shirt opened the door and stepped out. He leaned back in to get his backpack and get parting advice from his older sister.

"I know being in a new school sucks but try to make the best of it. Be friendly and meet people," his sister told him.

"Be friendly. Got it. Thanks."

"It's better than sulking in a corner," she replied.

"I don't sulk. See you tonight." He started to close the door but stopped and opened it again. "You're not picking me up after school, right?"

"Right. You can take the bus or walk. And this ride was a one-time deal. Tomorrow and after, you'll have to take the bus."

"I'll take the moped. Good luck with sales today." He closed the door and turned towards the school. The Atlas drove away.

Chapter 4
~Brody's house~

Previous June — Jentler family vacation day minus one

Alia awoke to Andy's nudges. She lifted her head from the pillow she'd placed against the window of the SUV's door.

"We're almost there," Andy said, pointing to a Little Rock city limit sign up ahead.

A few seconds later, his father stated from the driver's seat, "We are officially in Little Rock. Just a few more minutes and we'll be there."

Alia had stayed awake for most of the trip from the outskirts of Houston to Little Rock with Andy Crenshaw and his family. After lunch at a Dairy Queen in Texarkana, the vibrations of the road and the warmth of the afternoon sun beaming in through her side of the vehicle brought on drowsiness she couldn't shake. Andy had watched her head droop and then jerk upright a couple of times before he had pulled a pillow from the back of the SUV and handed it to Alia. No request; no statement; just handed her the pillow; with a smile. If he was disappointed that she leaned against the window instead of against him, he kept it to himself.

"We're already in Little Rock? How long was I out?"

"Well, you were snoring for about two hours," Andy's father stated.

Alia's eyes widened. "Oh, sorry. I didn't know I snored."

"Stop it, Jerry!" his mother admonished. "You were not snoring, Alia. It was more like purring."

"Don't listen to them," Andy stated, patting Alia's arm. "You didn't make any sound at all." Turning back towards the front, he scolded, "Mom, Dad, she's not used to us. She can't tell when you're joking."

"Sorry, Alia," his mother apologized. "We'll try to behave."

"Remind them of the plan, Tiff."

"Sure, Honey. We're staying with Craig and Claudia tonight and tomorrow night, and then Sunday we'll caravan to the lakehouse," Andy's mother explained as they exited the freeway. She pronounced Claudia's name like 'cloud' with an 'e' and 'a' at the end. "We'll see Maribell and Jeff tomorrow. I think Craig's planning a barbeque or something."

"Aunt Maribell and Uncle Jeff are Shelby's parents," Andy explained. "We're staying with Uncle Craig because his house is big and has a pool." Andy pointed out.

"With a waterfall and a slide," Alia added.

"Oh yeah. I already told you."

"Will Shelby be there tonight?" Alia asked.

"I don't know about tonight," his dad said, "But they'll be at dinner tomorrow."

"I think she'll come hang out with us by the pool in the afternoon," Andy said. "Brody, too. Uncle Craig's his dad." He lowered his voice. "Shelby doesn't care much for Brody. Probably because he tries to be funny, but just can't pull it off."

"Not like you," Alia stated.

"Right. Wait. Were you being sarcastic? You don't think I'm funny?"

"You're funny most of the time," Alia replied.

"Sometimes when you're not even trying," his dad added.

Before Andy could reply to his dad's dig, Alia spoke up again. "I've got a question, Mrs. Crenshaw."

"I told you to call me Ms. Tiffany. And you can call him Mr. Jerry," Andy's mother pointed at her husband.

"Okay, Ms. Tiffany. A minute ago, you said *Cloud*-ee-ah instead of *Clawed*-ee-ah. Is that how she pronounces her name?"

Mr. Jerry decided to answer before his wife could. "She's from somewhere in Central America. I don't remember which country. Honduras, El Salvador. One of those," Jerry said.

"Buzz! Wrong answer," Tiffany screeched. "She's from Guatemala. Come on, Jerry! How many times do we have to tell you?" She turned her head to look at Alia, sitting behind her husband. "At Christmas, he said she was from Costa Rica. She threw a cookie at him."

"At least I don't say Mexico anymore. But maybe I will if she throws more cookies. It was good." Alia could see him smiling through the rear-view mirror.

"You'll like her," Andy's mother stated. "And she's a great cook."

* * *

Andy's dad honked the horn as he pulled into the circular driveway of his brother's house, passing a four-car garage. He stopped under the portico.

It looks like a hotel, Alia thought. She half expected to see a bellhop at the door. Instead, three casually dressed figures emerged. The woman was significantly shorter than the two men, even in high heels.

"Jerry, how was the drive?" Uncle Craig asked his brother.

"Boring as ever, right, Tiff?" Jerry answered and inquired of his wife.

"At least we had a new passenger to keep things interesting," Tiffany said. "Hi Claudia, Brody. Good to see you."

"You like her because she hasn't heard your jokes before and laughs to be polite," Andy added.

"That's not true," Alia defended. "Your parents are funny."

"Hey Brody, I didn't think you'd be here 'til tomorrow," Andy greeted the younger of the two men.

"I don't want to miss family," Brody said as he clapped Andy on the back. "Besides, it's just across town." Whereas Andy had a thin physique, Brody looked to be a few pounds heavy – not in the unhealthy range, but certainly a noticeable contrast to Andy. Although his hair was closely cropped, his face and neck sported several days of beard growth.

Alia wondered if the growth of facial hair indicated he had started his vacation early. She had shaved her legs for the trip. *It's not fair*, she thought. *Girls shave for a vacation and guys stop shaving for a vacation.*

"And you are Alia?" the petite woman asked in a distinctive Spanish accent. "I'm Claudia. We hear much about you."

Alia smiled politely at Claudia before turning to Andy and raising her eyebrows in a questioning expression. He shrugged his shoulders in reply.

"You stay in room of Valeria," Claudia stated. "I hope you be comfortable."

"It was Clarissa's room before it was Val's," Brody pointed out to Andy in a low voice.

"Brody, help your aunt and uncle with their things and take them to your father's 'man cave' by the pool," Claudia instructed before turning and heading into the house. Looking back at Alia and Andy, she said, "You come with me."

With her backpack slung over one shoulder and pulling a small suitcase, Alia followed Andy with his duffel bag, who followed Claudia.

"This was room of Clarissa before she moved out and married," Claudia explained to her nephew and Alia at the doorway to a bedroom. "Then it was room of Valeria when she come back from college. Now she live in apartment with boyfriend, uh, fiancé. Now is another guest room. We paint and change decorations to make grown-up style." She paused and chuckled, "I say 'we', I mean me. I guess decorating now is my hobby. Come in."

"So, all the chicks have left the roost," Andy said. "You'll have to give my parents tips on managing an empty nest."

"Well, Brody come many times, the nest no is empty yet. I think he just not like cook for himself." She lowered her voice. "Or maybe he just not grow up yet."

Andy followed Claudia into the room and set his duffle bag down in a beige cushioned chair on the far side of the queen bed, which was against a pale green wall, the only wall of that color; the other walls were white. The green was the same shade as the drapes and complimented the beige bed covering. The red decorative pillows on the bed and side chair stood out in contrast to the rest of the room.

Claudia turned around to see Alia still standing in the doorway. "Come," she said, taking Alia's suitcase and rolling it to a spot next to the bed. Alia noted that, even in heels, the top of Claudia's head only came up to her eyes. "Bathroom here," she said pointing to a doorway. "Closet there," she pointed to another door. "So, anyway, I hope you two like the room."

Alia finally stepped into the room, more or less following her suitcase. "This is for both of us?"

"Yes. No need to pretend nothing going on between you two. We are all adults. Valeria live with her fiancé. Dinner will be ready in about an hour. Until then, you can settle in," she said with a wink.

"Well, that was unexpected," Andy said after Claudia left the room. "Did you notice she winked after saying we can settle in? What's that supposed to mean?"

Alia stared at the bed before answering. "Look on the pillow. Does that answer your question?" She pointed to a box of condoms.

"Oh."

"She's heard so much about me? What did she hear? That I used to be a prostitute? That my father tried to kidnap me?"

"Remember after Christmas when I found out what your tattoo meant? I talked about it with Shelby and my brother Bryan. They may have told others. Alia, I swear I didn't put them up to this. I didn't know the sleeping arrangements. I kind of envisioned sleeping bags on the floor."

"Andy, I like you. I appreciate you inviting me on your family vacation, but I'm not ready for this," she said pointing to the condoms. "A year ago, I might have gone along with it. But I'm different now. I feel like that old me was not even me at all. This is the third me."

"I understand and I'm with you on that." He opened a drawer of the nightstand, placed the box inside, and closed it. "I can sleep on the floor."

"You don't have to sleep on the floor, you can sleep on the bed, too. But just sleep. I'm sorry if this disappoints you."

Andy held up his hands. "Stop. You don't disappoint me. I admit I was hoping we could be more than friends. But I was not – am not – expecting to engage in any activity that requires those," he said, pointing to the drawer. "I'm just happy you came."

"Did you tell them I sometimes sleep with a teddy bear?"

"I don't think it ever came up. Why?"

She pointed to the teddy bear positioned on the armoire across from the bed.

"He must be the spirit animal of the room. His sash looks like it goes with the curtains. Besides, you won't need a teddy bear. You've got the Andy bear."

She took a deep breath and let it out slowly.

"Come on! They told us to settle in, so let's settle in."

"We just talked about…" She stopped when Andy hopped up on the bed and stood up.

"What are you doing?"

"Settling in." He started jumping on the bed, producing squeaking sounds from the box springs and bed frame.

"Come on up."

"No."

"Oh, baby! This feels so good!"

"Stop," Alia stated sternly but, she hoped, quietly enough not to be heard outside the room. "Everyone's gonna think we're having sex."

"So?"

"This is one of the times you're not funny."

Alia slammed the door as she left the room and walked down the hall. She found Claudia in the kitchen.

"Can I help with anything?" Alia asked. "Andy's settling in without me."

* * *

Alia awakened a bit later in the morning than expected. She attributed it to the thick curtains over the windows keeping the room dark long after the sun rose. But it could also have been partly because she took longer than usual to fall asleep due to a late-night conversation and an unfamiliar bed.

When she finally got up to get dressed in the morning, Andy was still asleep on the sofa cushions he had arranged on the floor by the window, still covered by the bath towels she had placed over him after he fell asleep. In the dim light, she lifted her suitcase onto the bed, then turned on the bathroom light to better see her clothing options. She stared at Andy's sleeping form as she changed from her oversized T-shirt and "sleeping" shorts to her "daytime" clothes.

Alia wandered down the hall past a bedroom that had been converted to an office and another full of exercise equipment before arriving at the kitchen where Brody was finishing off some pancakes.

"How'd you sleep?" he asked.

"It took a while to fall asleep. But I guess I made up for it by sleeping late. That room's pretty dark with the curtains closed."

Brody continued, "Yeah, those are blackout curtains, the kind hotels have. I should have put a nightlight in that room to give you at least a little light."

"It's probably why Andy's still sleeping."

"A lot of late-night activity can also make you sleep late," Brody said with a smirk. "Anyway, our parents are done with breakfast, but Claudia left a stack of pancakes out. I'll warm some up for you."

* * *

"Knock, knock," Shelby called out as she entered the house.

"Hi. Come on in," Brody called out. "Claudia and Aunt Tiffany went shopping for groceries for the lake house. I don't know where Dad and Uncle Jerry are. They may be out getting supplies, too."

"Where are Alia and Andy?"

"I think they're changing into swimsuits. I hope you brought yours. We're gonna chill by the pool."

Shelby held up a tote bag. "Got it."

"Is it that skimpy little bikini you were wearing in that Instagram post from Spring Break?"

"No. And you shouldn't sound so interested. We're cousins and that's just pervy."

Brody shrugged his shoulders.

He lowered his voice, "I think Alia and Andy may have gotten into a fight last night."

"What happened?"

"I don't know, but when I checked on them this morning, Andy was sleeping on the floor. I think Alia kicked him out of bed."

"They were sleeping together?"

"At least to start with."

"Was that their idea?"

"Well, we just assumed they'd be together so we put them in Clarissa's old room."

"They've never slept together before."

"You mean, she gave other guys the good stuff and Andy just gets leftovers," Brody stated sarcastically.

"You're a douchebag. Alia didn't choose that life and she got out when she could. You need to treat her like any other girl."

"Is Andy gay?"

"You know he's not. The more you talk the bigger a douchebag you become."

* * *

The Jentler family left Baylor University on their way to Lubbock.

"Baylor looks a lot nicer than A&M. But the town, Waco, looks old," John observed.

"Mom would probably kill me for saying this," Annie added, "but judging by the feel of the campus, I like Baylor a lot more than A&M. Maybe I have to see the schools when all the students are there."

"I liked the bear place," Emi stated, referring to the habitat for Baylor's mascots. "I wonder if they let students take care of the bears."

* * *

"How far to Texas Tech?" Emi asked as the Grand Canyon crew got back into the Escalade after lunch.

"Lubbock's another five hours from here," Ty answered.

"Five hours!"

"We can trade books," Annie offered.

"Did you bring a library?"

"We can do car karaoke," Ty suggested.

The Jentler family responded unanimously with "No!"

"Maybe I'll just do it myself," Ty stated.

Sophie reached into her backpack and pulled out a plastic bag full of little green objects shaped like bullets. John and Emi each extended a hand toward Sophie.

"What're those," Annie asked.

"Earplugs," Emi explained. She leaned over to Annie's ear and whispered, "You haven't heard Ty sing."

An hour later, everyone but Ty had dozed off.

* * *

As the group arranged the lounge chairs around the family swimming pool, Brody pointed with his thumb to Andy and joked to Alia, "If this guy's not giving you what you need, just remember my room's right down the hall."

"Ugh," Shelby groaned. "Brody, you need to knock it off. Try to be normal."

"Is there a bathroom in there?" Andy asked Brody, pointing to a door just off the patio where his parents had spent the night.

"Yeah, that's Dad's man cave. But why don't you use one in the main house and then get us some drinks from the kitchen when you're done?"

"Sure thing. Don't do anything fun without me."

Alia sat on the edge of a lounge chair and opened a tube of sunscreen. She wasn't going to repeat the mistake she'd made during spring break and let herself get sunburned to the point of blistering.

Brody watched as she rubbed the white lotion over all the parts she could easily reach. When she contorted herself to reach her back, Brody stood up and walked over.

"Let me help you with that; I'm good with my hands."

"Thanks, but I've got it."

"It doesn't look like it. You're gonna end up with burned patches all over your back. Let me help. Then you can do my back."

As Alia hesitated with a response, Brody grabbed the sunscreen tube from her hand, squeezed a large dollop onto his right hand, and began rubbing it onto her back between her shoulder blades, skipping the strap across her back. Then he applied the sunscreen to her lower back, all the way down to her bikini bottom. Alia gritted her teeth at the unwelcome contact. *He'll be done soon.*

Brody slid her shoulder straps down off her shoulders to apply sunscreen there.

"I already did my shoulders."

"Not under the straps."

Yes, I did, she thought. *Surely now he's almost done.*

He smoothed the sunscreen across her shoulders and shoulder blades. "Just one last area in the middle." Brody began unfastening the strap in the back.

"Hey!" Alia jumped up and stepped away from Brody, holding the front of her swimsuit top against her chest to prevent it from falling off.

Shelby witnessed the interaction from her chair next to Alia's. When Alia stood, she also stood. "Move away, pervert. She doesn't need you for the sunscreen."

Shelby refastened Alia's strap and grabbed the sunscreen from Brody. "You've got to tell him 'no' more forcefully. He doesn't understand a polite 'no'."

"She was supposed to do my back. Since you ran her off, you get the privilege," Brody said to Shelby.

"I'm not touching you, creep. You can just keep your back away from the sun."

"What did I miss?" Andy called out as he approached with an armload of drink cans.

Chapter 5
The new guy

Still the first day of school

"How were your classes?" Emi asked Annie as they walked with their lunch trays to find seats in the cafeteria, which was a large open area that formed the hub between the two academic wings and the short administrative hallway at the front of the school.

"So far, so good. But there's gonna be a lot more reading than I expected for English and they're not the kind of books I would have chosen myself. Why can't they have books like *Geek Girl* or *Percy Jackson* on the list?"

Just as they reached an available table, they noticed a table of freshmen boys watching them. The boys were from the same middle school as Emi and Annie.

"There's a table full of trouble," Emi whispered to Annie.

"Don't say it," Annie muttered to herself.

"Hi, Ant Bites," one of the boys called out to Annie above the murmur of hundreds of conversations.

Annie took a breath and shook her head. *He said it. I don't have boobs; I have ant bites.*

"I see you still haven't hit puberty," another said, getting chuckles from his friends.

"At least *our* brains have matured," Emi retorted.

A boy with wavy brown hair and wearing a dark blue polo shirt stopped at the girls' table and set his food tray next to Annie's.

"Hi, Babe," he said, looking at Annie. "It seems like I haven't seen you in forever." He emphasized his affection with a side hug and a kiss on her cheek. The table of freshmen boys looked on with surprise. But not nearly with the surprise that Annie felt.

"Uhh," Annie sounded, unable to think of how to respond to the stranger's affection.

"Can I join you?" the wavy-haired boy asked, sitting down without waiting for an answer. "And, you're welcome," he whispered.

Annie took that as her cue to sit down next to him. Emi walked around the table to sit across from them. The boy rolled his shoulders in a stretch before picking up a fork. Both girls couldn't help but notice his broad shoulders and toned arms. He looked like someone who worked out but didn't overdo it.

"What was that about?" Emi asked.

"It looked like a table full of a-holes needed a lesson in respect. I thought it was my duty as a good citizen of Cypress Grove High School to demonstrate proper behavior."

"And proper behavior is to kiss a girl you don't know?" Emi asked.

"That was a bonus," he smiled.

"Can you come with me to my classes for the rest of the day?" Annie asked.

"That probably won't work, but I can kiss you again if needed."

Annie giggled.

"You look familiar," Emi stated. "But you're not from our middle school."

"I just moved here during the summer. My name's Joel."

"I'm Annie. Annie Bates. Are you a freshman, too?"

"Sophomore."

"Wait. I know where I've seen you before," Emi stated. "You came to my birthday party and then left suddenly."

The smile disappeared and his eyes widened in recognition. "Emi, right?" He popped a baby carrot into his mouth, trying to look casual.

"Yeah. It's actually Emily, but I go by Emi. Thanks for the hair trimmer, by the way, but why'd you even come since you don't know me?"

He finished chewing the baby carrot before answering. "It's kind of embarrassing. I was at the wrong house."

"So, the hair trimmer wasn't meant for me?"

"I was supposed to trade it for a used computer monitor at a house down the street from you. But I wrote down the address wrong and ended up at your house."

"I guess the trade didn't work out."

"Not the way I planned it. I ended up just paying cash for the monitor."

"I haven't used the trimmer yet. I can give it back."

"No. Keep it. After all, it was your birthday."

"Where did you move from?" Annie asked.

"Briarwood Estates. It's close to Memorial City Mall."

"Okay, I know where that is," Emi stated. "I mean, I've been to that mall, but I really couldn't tell you how to get there. It has an ice-skating rink."

"Yeah, I had a skate party there a couple of years ago for my birthday," Annie added. "See, we know malls. We don't have a good mall in Cypress," Annie stated.

Before Emi could respond Annie added, "The outlet mall doesn't count."

Turning back to Joel, she asked, "So what brought you to Cypress?"

"My parents had to move away for… uh… for an assignment, so I moved in with my sister. She was a teacher at an elementary school somewhere around here. But she hated it and now she does medical sales. We live in an apartment behind H-E-B."

"I know where that is," Annie offered. "Emi lives with her sister, too, without parents."

Joel looked at Emi for confirmation. "They died four years ago," Emi explained. "And now my sister and her husband are our legal guardians."

"My sister travels a lot for her work, and she stays with her boyfriend a lot, so I'm still figuring things out. Such as buying groceries and cooking."

"I know what that's like," Emi stated. "It was hard for us at first, but we figured out how to make things work, and now we sort of take care of each other. When we're not arguing, that is." She paused before asking, "What kind of assignment are your parents on?"

Joel looked down at his food tray and took another bite of the barbeque pulled pork that covered the baked potato. The girls glanced at each other. When finally Joel looked up, he said, "It's complicated."

When it became apparent that he did not want to elaborate, Emi stated, "Okay. Sure."

Joel pointed back at the freshmen boys at the nearby table. "Do those guys act like that all the time?"

"At least since eighth grade when the other girls started filling out," Annie answered. "That's when they started calling me Ant Bites."

"Does that bother you?" Joel asked.

"The boys or having a flat chest?"

Joel hesitated. "Either."

"I don't like their comments, but I think the more they talk, the stupider they sound. If I never fill out, I could get a boob job," she said, pointing to her chest. "But they could be stupid forever."

She looked over at the table of boys again and back at Joel. "It still bothers me a little. Last week, I posted a topless photo of myself on Instagram."

"What?!" Emi exclaimed.

"Don't worry, I set up a secret account no one knows about. And I hid my hair in a baseball cap and wore sunglasses. I just wanted to see if Instagram would ban it for violating their nudity rules for women."

"And?" Emi asked.

Annie sighed. "The photo's still up. The Instagram people think I'm a boy." She looked over at Joel. "I'm a girl," she clarified.

Joel looked into her brown eyes and paused the fork that he was lifting to his mouth and chuckled. "I never doubted it."

Emi cleared her throat. "If you two are done flirting, maybe you should exchange numbers or Snapchats, or something."

Annie turned red. "We're just having a conversation," Joel stated. He held out his phone to Annie. It was open to his contact list, specifically to the screen to add a new contact. She smiled and took the phone from him. After she put in her contact information and returned the phone, Joel sent "Hi" messages to her by text and by Snapchat. He then slid his phone across the table to Emi.

"You, too."

"Okay. We'll let you sit with us tomorrow," Emi said jokingly, taking his phone to put in her information.

"Do you think I'll get tainted by hanging with freshmen?"

"Not the cool ones like us," Emi replied. When she finished inputting her information, she used his phone to send herself messages so she would have his contact information.

"Tomorrow, we'd better eat first and talk later," Joel said. "Lunch is almost over and I'm only halfway done."

When the bell rang to signal the end of lunch, the three stood up. Joel looked over at the table of freshmen boys and then back at Annie. "See ya later, Babe," he said to Annie before kissing her again on the cheek and gathering up his tray and backpack.

"Hey, what about me?" Emi stated, with her hands on her hips.

"I'll catch y'all tomorrow. Don't want to be late to class," he said with a wink, walking quickly to take his lunch tray to the conveyer belt that led to the kitchen.

"I like high school," Annie told Emi, giggling.

* * *

Sienna walked from the food line with her lunch tray and looked around the cafeteria for people she knew. Most of the freshmen had the first lunch period, but she recognized several in her second lunch. However, no one from her circle of friends. She finally spotted a table of guys who used to hang out with her ex.

"Cody, do you mind if I sit with you?" Sienna asked, nodding to an empty seat.

"Oh, sorry. We're saving that for Audrey," Cody said. "How's Hunter? Do you still talk to him?"

"I guess he's fine. We talked a lot when he first moved away, but not so much in the last couple of weeks. Have y'all heard from him?"

"Naw. But he's probably taking charge and getting all the girls. Oh. Sorry, Sienna. I just meant he always makes friends easily."

Audrey arrived with her lunch tray and took the empty seat that Sienna had been hoping for.

"Good talking with you, Sienna," Cody said, effectively ending the conversation and dismissing Sienna.

Her smile dimmed as she walked further through the cafeteria in search of an empty seat. She ignored the table with a boy wearing a shirt with the periodic table on it and a girl wearing a NASA shirt. *Too nerdy.* She bypassed the table of kids with questionable fashion sense. *Why would anyone wear sliders and socks on the first day of school?* Sienna thought.

At last, she found a seat at a table with a girl she recognized from one of her classes that morning. *At least she's decently dressed*, Sienna thought.

"Can I?" Sienna asked, pointing to the empty seat.

"Sure. Aren't you in my algebra class with Mr. Q-tip?"

"Yeah. Do they call him that because he's so skinny and has fluffy white hair, like a big Q-tip?"

The girl laughed at the image, a laugh that reminded Sienna of a braying donkey. "I think it's 'cause his name is Quincy Tipton," the girl explained. "But now that you described him, I'm seeing a giant cotton swab. You don't see many old White men with an afro. I'm Charlotte."

"Sienna." Sienna sighed as she sat down. *This is gonna be a long day.*

* * *

Although his turn for cooking would normally be a few days away, Ty volunteered to prepare dinner that night since he was the only one who had not started a new school year. He cooked steaks on the outdoor grill and potato wedges in the oven. Sophie brought five cups of banana pudding from the Buc-ee's in Waller on her way home from classes at Prairie View A&M.

"Alia, how was your first day at Cy Grove?" Sophie asked.

"It was good. I felt a little out of place because everyone else seemed to know each other. There was a girl in my English class who came up to me after class and asked if I was the girl from the news a few months ago."

"We talked about that; that someone might recognize you from the news last May," Sophie pointed out. "Did you give her the answer we discussed?"

"Yeah. I admitted it was me, but that I didn't like to talk about it."

"How'd she take it?"

"She just said 'I'm sorry. That sucks.' And then she went on to her next class."

"Good. Anyone else?"

"No one asked me about it, but I got a sense that several of them knew."

"Like a spider-sense?" asked Emi.

"Spider-sense? Really? You're such a nerd," John stated to Emi.

"No," Alia said. "Like, they would glance at me, then say something to a friend, then glance back at me. I could tell they were talking about me."

"But no one else asked you about it," Sophie reiterated. "That should be a relief."

"I'm just afraid someone will treat me the way Andy's cousin did; just assume things, expect me to be a certain way, and then get mad if I don't, like, act the way they expect."

"Most people who remember the news story will probably just remember the part about your father trying to kidnap you," Sophie responded. "I doubt anyone remembers that quick statement about sex trafficking. If they bring it up, all you can do is tell them that's not you anymore. Don't assume everyone is as rude as Andy's cousin."

"Yeah, okay" Alia acknowledged. "No one else talked to me. That's another reason I felt out of place. I sat with John and Lizzie at lunch. One of John's friends from lunch was in my government class right after that. At least he said 'hi' to me."

"How was welding?" Ty asked.

Alia smiled wide at the thought of her welding shop class.

"Every guy in the class asked for my Snap."

"See, I told you," John laughed.

"Did you give it to them?" Emi asked.

"Well, I didn't mind for some of them to have it, and then I didn't want to be rude to give it to some and not others…"

"So you gave it to everyone," Emi finished.

"Yeah. I just don't know what they expect from me. There was only one other girl in the class and I gave it to her, too. So everyone has everyone else's Snap."

"Were they asking for her Snap, too?" John asked.

"Uh, no. I assume they already had hers."

"Who is she?"

"Her name is Gretchen. But I didn't get her last name."

"Black lipstick and fingernails? A little on the heavy side?"

"You know her?"

"Gretchen McKinney," John replied. "Sort of a goth emo tomboy. She's generally nice. I had a history class with her last year."

"I also told them I was dating someone, so they won't expect too much."

"Would that be Griffin or Andy?" John asked, facetiously.

"I didn't say who. And I'm still undecided about Griffin and Andy."

"Okay. I don't know much about Griffin," Sophie said, "but I know Andy likes you."

"Emi, how was your first day of high school?" Alia asked to steer the conversation away from her dating life.

"Good. Remember that guy that crashed my birthday party?"

"Yeah. He left a hair trimmer," Ty recalled.

"He sat with me and Annie at lunch. And – get this – he kissed Annie before he even met her."

"What did Annie do?" Ty asked, intrigued by the teenage drama.

"At first she was shocked, then she giggled like a little girl," Emi explained.

"So, who is this kissing stranger?" John asked.

"He just moved to Cypress from somewhere by Memorial City Mall. He said his parents are on an assignment, but didn't want to talk about it, which is kind of mysterious. He pretended to be Annie's boyfriend 'cause some boys were making fun of her. His name is Joel…" She pulled out her phone and looked up her contacts. "Joel Vaclavik."

"Did he say why he came to your birthday?" Sophie asked

"He was at the wrong house. He meant to meet someone down the street from us. He lives with his sister like we do. But in an apartment. He said she's gone a lot."

"How did everything else go with school?"

"Fine. Meeting Joel was pretty much the highlight of the day. Especially for Annie."

Chapter 6
The first week

Late August

"My name is Alia Jentler," Alia began, standing in front of her first-period class in one of the summer dresses she bought just before school started. Her face went red, and she felt the heat in her cheeks, but she couldn't back out of her speech now. "Yesterday, I could tell many of you were wondering about me. So, yes, I'm *that* girl. If you don't know what I mean, ask a friend, because I don't want to talk about it. Besides coming from a messed-up family, I wanted you to know a few other things about me.

"Some of you probably know John Jensen. He's on the basketball team. Well, I live with his family. They've been very good to me and made me part of their family. My favorite color is pink. You may have seen my pink truck in the parking lot. I mowed lawns and power-washed driveways to earn enough money to buy the truck and fix it up. I also work at Bullseye, but mowing pays more."

She realized she had deviated from her planned speech and was babbling. She took a breath and went back to her intended topic. "I'm eighteen years old and I still like Harry Potter. I read all the Harry Potter books over the past year. And I like frozen yogurt. I don't have a favorite flavor. I like to get a different flavor each time, or sometimes get two kinds in one cup. There are lots of things you can talk with me about, so don't be afraid to say hello. Thank you." She looked over at the teacher to signal that she was done. The redness in her cheeks had already dissipated.

"Wait, I've got a question," stated a boy on the third row. The teacher checked her roster.

"Yes, Garrett?"

"Alia, do you have a boyfriend?" The other students chuckled.

"Go on and take your seat, Alia," the teacher instructed, ignoring Garrett's question.

"Hey, it's a legitimate question," Garrett whined.

"I'm dating a guy in college," Alia replied, stretching the truth. The term 'dating' is a little vague.

"Ah, the old 'out-of-town-boyfriend' story," Garrett stated. He looked around the room. "That means she doesn't want any of you losers to ask her out."

Alia looked around at the class, unsure of how to respond.

"That's enough, Garrett," the teacher said. "Let's all turn our attention to college algebra."

* * *

The family sat at a long booth at Chili's, waiting for the waitress to bring their drinks. It was a delayed celebration of the start of school. Cy Grove was new to Emi and Alia.

"How did the speech go?" Ty asked Alia.

"I only did it in first and second periods. I chickened out after that. But later, a girl came up to me to say she'd seen my pink truck around the area and thought it was cool. And others said hi in the hallways throughout the day. So maybe the speech worked."

"Did you sit with anyone at lunch?"

"One of the shop guys asked me to sit with him, but I decided to go to John and Lizzie's table."

"Are the shop guys too nerdy for you?" John asked with a grin.

"Well, that one was. That reminds me, I need to buy some things for school, so after dinner, can we go to Bullseye?"

"What kind of things," Sophie asked.

"For one, I want to get a new insulated lunch bag. I'm not sure I want to eat the cafeteria food every day and my old lunch bag is falling apart."

"Is the cafeteria food not up to your standards?" Ty teased.

"It's not that. The lines take so long, there's not much time left to eat."

"I need one of those, too," Emi added. "And we're almost out of toilet paper upstairs."

"Sure. We can go to Bullseye," Ty said. "You know how much I love shopping with the family."

Sophie smiled at his sarcasm. "You didn't mind when it was just you and me," she pointed out.

"Yeah. While y'all are shopping for your stuff, maybe I'll check out the umbrellas. I could always use a ninja umbrella to keep in my truck to fight off bad guys."

John unconsciously touched the scar on his chin while the rest of the family laughed at the reference to a misunderstanding involving an umbrella during their summer trip to Arizona.

The conversation was interrupted when the waitress came with their drinks and asked for their food orders. When she left the table, Sophie returned to the topic of school.

"Emi? Anything new on the freshman front?" she asked.

"We sat with Joel again. He didn't kiss Annie today. I could tell she was disappointed. Did I mention he's a sophomore and he can drive? He has a moped, but also gets to drive his sister's SUV when she's out of town."

"Is that important to know?"

"He mentioned that he could take us to Chick-fil-a after school one day."

Sophie looked at Ty. "I don't know about you going anywhere with him," Sophie stated. "We don't know anything about him; what he's like; his character."

Emi stared at her for a moment. "It's like you're channeling the ghost of Mom."

"You said yesterday he lives with his sister and she's gone a lot," Ty pointed out. "I agree with your sister. I don't want you going to his apartment when no one else is there. It's like the old rule your grandma made about me."

"Oh, yeah. We couldn't be alone with you in your trailer," Emi recalled.

"Some guys think if you're willing to be alone with them, it means you're giving your consent for… you know," Ty stated.

"Aww. Ty, you're giving her the same speech you gave me a few years ago," Sophie stated. "That's sweet."

He rolled his eyes at her.

"Grandma was wrong about you, so isn't this a little extreme?" Emi asked.

"Your grandma was right to make that rule. It sounds extreme, but I knew guys who thought like that. Don't be alone with a guy in an apartment, in a bedroom, or a hotel room."

"Hotel room?" Alia asked. "You're talking about Emi, not me."

"Like on an overnight field trip or something," Ty clarified.

"Before you go for rides with Joel, we should meet him," Sophie said.

"Sheesh. Y'all are taking the parenting thing too seriously," Emi complained.

"Judge Bell-Ross said we could," Ty pointed out. "And it's because we care about you. Labor Day is next Monday." He looked over at Sophie and saw her nod almost imperceptibly before he continued with Emi. "You can invite Joel so we can meet him. We can make hamburgers outside on the grill."

"They're right about checking this guy out first, Emi," Alia said. "Just because a guy acts nice at first doesn't mean he really is nice. Trust me, I know."

Ty and Sophie both smiled at Alia for the support.

"Annie, too?" Emi asked. "She'd kill me if she thought I was trying to monopolize Joel."

"Monopolize, huh? Because she got first dibs on him?" John asked.

"He did kiss her, so she feels a connection."

"Yeah, invite Annie, too." Ty looked around at the family. "Anyone else?" Then he looked at John. "Lizzie?" He turned to Alia, "Andy?"

"I'll ask Lizzie" John stated. "But we might hang out with friends. Jaxon has a pool, so we might go to his house."

"Andy can't come. Can you believe A&M doesn't have off for Labor Day?" Alia asked.

"What about Griffin from your Bible study group?" Emi asked Alia.

"He transferred to A&M this year, so he can't come either."

Ty looked at Sophie again. "Do you want to invite anyone from Prairie View?"

She scrunched up her face and shook her head. "I don't expect high school freshmen and college juniors to mix very well."

"It worked for that karaoke party last year," Ty recalled.

"Don't you remember? One of the guys called it calamity karaoke because three people got hurt. Besides, I think they already have their own activities planned."

"Hey, only two got hurt," Ty corrected. "Lizzie just had ripped shorts. Why didn't your college friends invite you to their stuff? I'm offended on your behalf."

"They've invited me to things. I just don't always tell you about them because sometimes I'd rather be here than go to some drunken college party."

"What if *I* want to go to a drunken college party?"

Sophie frowned, tilted her head slightly, and stared at Ty. He leaned over and kissed her forehead. After a moment, he wiped his hand across his lips and held up a curly hair.

"Hair stuff," Sophie suddenly announced, to puzzled looks. "Since we're going to Bullseye after dinner, I need to get jojoba oil for my hair."

"Will that make it taste better?" Ty asked.

"You can come with me and taste test all the hair products," Sophie retorted.

* * *

"Who was that guy calling you in the hallway?" Joel asked Annie at lunch.

"When?"

"Just a few minutes ago. Tall Black guy. Is he another fake boyfriend?"

Annie smiled. "That's John, Emi's brother." She looked over at Emi. "I think he's being a little goofy. He practically shouts 'Hi Annie. How's it going?' louder than necessary. Then everyone looks at me. He's been doing it all week."

"Don't let him get to you. I can tell him to stop," Emi offered.

"That's okay." Annie smiled again.

"You like the attention, don't you?" Joel asked.

"I don't think you have to worry about John being a rival fake boyfriend," Emi explained. "He has a girlfriend. But Annie's had a thing for John since our Grand Canyon trip."

Annie opened her mouth to speak, but then closed it.

"A little vacation romance?" Joel asked, grinning.

"I wouldn't call it romance, exactly," Annie responded.

"It has to do with fear of heights and puking on a skyway in Albuquerque," Emi added.

"Shh," Annie scolded.

Joel whispered to Emi, "Tell me later."

"Have you seen the ads for that new movie, 'Ghost Hunters' coming out in October?" Annie said, trying to change the subject. "We should go together."

Chapter 7
~Join the family~

Previous June – vacation day two

Alia was waiting outside the airport arrival doors when the Jentler family arrived.

"I'm sorry we weren't there to meet you when you first got here," Ty told Alia as he loaded her suitcase into the Escalade.

"I'm the one who should be apologizing. I screwed up your vacation."

"No you didn't," Emi stated. "We had to go to Albuquerque anyway. I'm glad you're here."

"She's right. You didn't screw up anything," Sophie added. "You're just in time for the Sandia Peak Tramway."

"Is that the skyway ride that goes to the top of a mountain?" Alia asked.

"Yes, that's it. People say the view is fantastic," Sophie answered.

"How high is it?" Annie asked.

Sophie thought for a moment, trying to recall what she had read. "I don't know how high it is, but the website said it's the third-longest single span in the world. It takes fifteen minutes to reach the top."

"Fifteen minutes? Has it ever broken down?"

"I don't know. But the website says it's closed every Tuesday for maintenance, so I'm sure they make sure everything's working like it's supposed to."

* * *

The Jentler crew boarded the Sandia Peak tram car with about twenty other people, all taking positions around the windows. The car moved out of the building and the ground dropped away.

John stood beside Alia at one of the windows and bumped his shoulder against hers. With the height difference, it was more of a bump of John's upper arm to Alia's shoulder. "Sorry things didn't work out in Arkansas. You'll have more fun with us than water skiing with a bunch of strangers. And now I get a hiking buddy."

"Thanks," Alia responded with her own shoulder bump while smiling slightly.

"You seem to have a thing for gas stations," John said.

Alia smiled again and shrugged her shoulders. "And your family seems to have a thing for rescuing girls at gas stations."

They looked out at the rocky valley with short pine trees scattered throughout. The sun was low in the western sky, casting long shadows on the rocks and trees. Everyone but the cabin operator had their phones out, taking pictures and shifting positions to catch the view from different sides of the gondola. After a few pictures, Annie stepped away from the window and leaned against the center pole.

"What're you doing, Annie?" Emi asked. "You're missing a great view."

"I'm okay. There're too many people at the windows, anyway."

John reached out and grabbed Annie's arm and pulled her over to the window. "You can take my spot. I can see over you anyway."

"I don't need to see out," she said as she spun around to face the interior and ended up with her face in John's black T-shirt, which was showing through his unbuttoned wrinkled blue plaid button-down. Her reaction startled him, and he automatically put his hands on her arms to keep them both from losing their balance.

John stepped back and looked down at her face. It was noticeably pale.

"Are you okay, Ant Bi'…I mean Annie?"

"It's the height. I thought I would be fine with it, but I guess not."

John put his arms around her and pulled her closer.

"To tell you the truth, it bothers me a little, too," he whispered. "Just keep your eyes closed."

With her eyes closed, she didn't see the others in her party looking at her and then exchanging glances with each other.

"Did John make a new friend on the trip?" Alia asked Sophie in a whisper.

"This is new to me," Sophie admitted.

Annie focused on John's heartbeat and the light scent of vanilla and chocolate coming from his T-shirt. She wasn't sure if it was cologne or deodorant.

* * *

As soon as the tram car reached the station, John released his embrace of Annie and stepped out onto the platform. He pulled out his phone and started pecking at the virtual keys.

"Lizzie?" Alia asked.

"Yeah. I want to send these photos to her before I forget."

"Send her one of me, too," Alia said, posing by the railing overlooking the valley.

Photo session complete, Sophie commented, "I didn't expect it to be cold up here," as she led the way to the gift shop. An hour later, the family sat at the dinner table in the mountaintop café, wearing matching blue Sandia Peak sweatshirts.

Ty said, "Annie, if we knew you had an issue with heights, we could have done a different activity."

"I thought I could handle it. I have trouble with ski lifts and skyways, especially ski lifts. But this was an enclosed car, so I thought I would be fine. And then we started moving, and my mind started going crazy."

"Will you be alright going back?" Ty asked.

"Yeah. I'm sure I'll be fine now that I've done it before."

"I'll be there if you need me," John added.

Annie smiled in response.

"Did you send Lizzie any pics of the area?" Emi asked John to direct the conversation away from Annie's phobia.

"Oh yeah, I've been texting her the whole trip, including pics. It's about three in the morning in Lebanon now, so she's probably gone to bed. But she'll see the tramway pics when she wakes up."

"Then she'll see the pic I sent her, too," Emi stated.

"What did you send?" John demanded.

"Remember just before we came into the restaurant when we were standing out by the railing overlooking the valley and I got a photo of you with Annie on one side and Alia on the other?"

"Oh yeah. That was a nice one."

"I sent it with the message, 'You've been replaced. I'm just not sure by which one'."

"What? No, you didn't! Let me see your phone." He grabbed her phone and tapped the screen to wake it up. "Unlock it so I can see."

"I was just kidding! I like Lizzie. I don't want to mess with her head like that. Only with yours."

"You can believe her about that," Alia confirmed. "She's told me before to back off, 'cause you're with Lizzie. And I wasn't even trying anything."

"Alia, how's Andy? Is that over?" Emi asked.

"I'm not sure. I like Andy. A lot. I know he wanted something more serious, but I just like him as a good friend."

"Poor Andy," Emi said. "Stuck in the friend zone. He's probably really hurt that you left."

"I texted him several apologies from the airport in Little Rock and again when I got to Albuquerque. I just couldn't stay there; that whole family is so messed up."

"Andy's family?"

"Just his cousin Brody's family. Brody was basically trying to get Andy and me to have sex so he could secretly record it for a private porno. I already felt uncomfortable around him yesterday. Did Sophie tell you he tried to take off my bikini top?"

"No!" Emi exclaimed in surprise. "Sophie didn't give us any details; just said you didn't feel safe around some of his family."

"When I found his hidden camera in our room this morning, that was it. I was done. I packed up and left while Andy was yelling at them."

"That was a good move," Ty stated.

"Andy smashed the camera against the side of the house," Alia explained, "and threw it in the pool. He sent me a picture of the camera at the bottom of the pool. But the video is already stored on some remote server. Andy said he would try to get Brody to delete that, too. At least there's no sex to see. Brody's probably really disappointed about that, but he may have recorded me changing clothes."

"I'm so sorry you had that experience," Ty said. "Most guys aren't like that, but you seem to have run into more than your share."

"I think it runs in Brody's family," Alia noted. "His father owns a chain of fast-food restaurants that makes the girls wear sexy outfits to bring in customers. And you wouldn't believe how his father ended up marrying his live-in housekeeper. Brody and his stepsister Val tell it like it's some kind of sweet love story."

"But you don't think so?" Ty asked.

"They have security cameras around the house and Brody got videos of the dad's so-called dates from those cameras. Jeez, that family likes to video things. Anyway, the woman – Claudia – looked scared when Brody's dad first came onto her. The way he touched her…. It made me cringe."

"If he's her boss, that's just wrong," Sophie interjected.

"But they're married now," Ty pointed out, "so it must have worked out."

Alia continued, "Yeah. He gave her a lot of wine to loosen her up. I can imagine the decisions she had to make: if she pushed him away, she could have ended up out of work and homeless. Maybe she loves him now, but I think it was just about survival at first. Maybe that's what an arranged marriage feels like. At least, that's how I relate to it. It's just so…." Her voice trailed off and she scrunched up her face. "Messed up," she finished.

"So, the housekeeper married a rich businessman?" John asked rhetorically. "Sounds like she came out way ahead. Is she good-looking?"

"That's not the point. But she looks like a middle-aged Hispanic mother. A very short middle-aged Hispanic mother."

"So, not a trophy wife," John stated.

"Maybe I'm being too hard on Andy's uncle, but the way he did it could have ended up very bad. Claudia couldn't have known if she would end up as a wife or a play toy to be tossed out when he got bored with her."

* * *

The light was fading in the valley, but the reds and pinks of the clouds provided enough beauty for the ride back on the tramway to make up for the shadows hiding the landscape. The wind had picked up a bit.

"You can do this," Emi told Annie as they stepped on board the tram car.

"Yeah. I know what to expect. I'll be fine this time."

After a brief look at the view from the windows, Annie stepped back to again lean against the center pole of the tram. After a few minutes, John joined her, leaning against the pole from the opposite side, his back to hers.

He turned his head to the side and asked, "How're you doing?"

"Okay. I thought I'd be better on the way back, but I just need to stay here and close my eyes."

A gust of wind made the tram car sway a bit. Passengers reached for the handrail around the windows to steady themselves.

John reached above his head and gripped the pole with one hand. Annie turned around to face the pole and held onto it with both hands.

"I don't feel good," she stated.

John turned around to face her with the pole in between them. Holding the pole with one hand, he patted Annie's shoulder with the other.

"It's going to be fine. We're halfway there."

Another gust shook the car again.

"I don't know if I can wait," Annie stated.

For what? John thought to himself. *It's not like we can get off early.* He placed his hand on her shoulder and held it there.

At another gust, Annie slid her feet back from the pole, leaned forward, and made a sound like something between a sigh and a moan. Passengers turned to look at her and saw that the color had drained from her face. The moan turned to a gagging sound. Annie had a vague awareness of the people staring at her, but couldn't control what was happening; nausea overpowered embarrassment.

Alia rushed over to grab Annie's ponytail and hold it up to prevent it from getting in the way of whatever might happen.

"Annie?" Emi and Sophie asked at the same time, just before Annie opened her mouth wide and expelled her dinner onto the rubberized floor of the tram.

John had quickly stepped back at the first sound of what was happening, a move that avoided all but a few splatters that hit his shoes.

"Mommy, that girl threw up," a young boy said, stating the obvious.

Alia rubbed Annie's back. "Is there more?"

"I think that's it," Annie replied. She looked up to see the entire carload of passengers staring at her. As Annie stood upright, Alia let go of her hair.

"Come over to this side," John said, guiding her to move to the other side of the pole, away from the mess on the floor. Then he removed the button-down shirt he had tied around his waist by the sleeves before donning the Sandia Peak sweatshirt. He put his left hand under her chin to lift her face and used the other to wipe her mouth with his shirt.

"Do you feel better now?"

Annie nodded.

"Mommy, it's stinky," said the young boy.

"Shh," the mother scolded.

John covered the mess on the floor with his shirt and looked back at the boy and his mother as if daring them to make further comments.

As another gust swayed the car again, John widened his stance and leaned into Annie, sandwiching her between himself and the pole. "I'll hold onto the pole; you hold onto me."

She wrapped her arms around his waist and closed her eyes.

Alia watched the interaction of John and Annie solemnly as the tramcar continued its journey.

"You were pretty quick to get Annie's hair out of the way," Sophie commented to Alia.

"The other wifeys got drunk a lot so I've got experience with girls puking, but it was usually over a toilet. We all helped each other."

"Wifeys?"

"That's what we called ourselves; the girls at the house."

Sophie noticed a smile form on Alia's face. "What are you smiling at?"

"John's a good guy."

"I have to admit, that's the kindest thing I've ever seen him do."

"I don't think most guys would ever do what John just did."

"What about Andy?" Sophie asked.

"I was just wondering about that. Maybe."

When the tram finally reached its destination, the passengers seemed to collectively breathe a sigh of relief; not for themselves but for Annie. As they exited the car, John hung back and looked down at his shirt on the floor.

A tramway worker entered the car with a mop and a bucket.

"Leave it; it's not worth it," the man said, upon seeing John start to reach down for his shirt.

"But I like that shirt."

"Leave it," Ty echoed.

The Lingering Scent

* * *

Alia:
I hope you're having fun. FYI,
your guy did the sweetest
thing tonight. It has to do with
vomit

Lizzie:
I don't think I've ever seen sweet
and vomit in the same sentence.
☺ Please explain

Give me a few minutes.
We're walking to the car

BTW, I thought you would be
asleep. Isn't it middle of the
night there?

I'm still messed up from jet lag.
I'll probably get over it by the
time we go home

* * *

In the girls' hotel room that night, Annie asked Emi, "Does your brother have a girlfriend?"

Emi paused before answering and smiled briefly. "Yeah. Lizzie. That's who he's been texting the whole time."

"Oh. Is Lizzie the girl that always wears the side ponytails and glasses?"

"That's her."

"I thought maybe she was just a good friend."

"Ready to turn off the lights?" Alia asked upon exiting the bathroom and seeing Emi and Annie already tucked in their bed.

"Go ahead," Emi stated.

After the lights were out Annie tapped Emi's arm. "How would you feel if John dated one of your friends? Hypothetically speaking."

"Well, hypothetically speaking, our family already has experience with that. Ty is the brother of Sophie's best friend from high school. Anna, Ty's sister, thought it was cool that her best friend became her sister-in-law."

"Anna. That's almost like Ann."

"Is this still hypothetical? Because I like Lizzie and I don't want to see her break up with John."

"But what if Lizzie wasn't his girlfriend."

"I think Alia's next in line."

"I heard that," Alia responded, from her position directly across the nightstand from Emi.

"Am I wrong?"

After several seconds of silence, Emi asked, "Alia?"

"I don't know how to respond."

"I think you just did."

Chapter 8
High school football

Continuing the conversation, Joel exclaimed, "Wow! And you said your brother has a girlfriend?"

"Yeah," Emi confirmed.

"Did she go on that trip?"

"No. She had her own family vacation."

"That was dangerous."

"What was dangerous?" Emi asked.

"A girl lets her boyfriend go on a trip with his sister's cute friend."

Annie grinned at the compliment before deciding it was time to eat. Today's school lunch entre was steak fingers. They ate a few bites of lunch in silence.

"Are you two going to the football game tomorrow night?" Joel asked, breaking the silence.

Annie looked at Emi and shrugged her shoulders. Football wasn't either girl's idea of a good time but hanging out with friends was.

"I plan to, but I haven't discussed it with Annie yet," Emi replied.

"Do you need a ride?"

"Yeah, that'd be great!" Annie answered immediately. Joel looked at Emi.

"Sophie and Ty said I couldn't ride with you until they meet you. And, they said I can invite you over for Labor Day for a cookout, so you can meet them then."

"You're inviting my fake boyfriend to your house without me?"

"You're invited, too."

"Yeah, as an afterthought," Annie grumbled.

"Can you come?" Emi directed the question to both Joel and Annie.

"I can. I'm pretty sure my sister will spend Labor Day with her boyfriend, so I'd love to come." He put his arm around Annie. "What do you think, Babe?"

Annie tapped her cheek that was closest to Joel.

"You are gonna milk this fake boyfriend thing, aren't you?" Joel commented.

Annie tapped her cheek again. Joel leaned over and kissed it.

"I'll come, too," she finally answered.

* * *

"Ryn, thanks for letting me use the car tonight," Joel told his sister Kathryn as he walked out the door of their apartment.

"I'm being a homebody tonight. If I have to leave, I can take your moped."

"Do you even know how to ride it?"

"It can't be that hard. But I was just kidding anyway. I'm glad you made friends."

As he walked to the white SUV, he watched a heavyset girl in black lipstick and wearing black slacks and a dark green sandwich shop shirt walk from the next building of the apartment complex and head to the street. He had seen her throughout the summer, always in the uniform.

"Hey, Gretchen!" he called out, giving a small wave.

"Hey."

"Not going to the game tonight?"

She pointed to her uniform shirt. "What do you think?"

"I think it's an awesome fashion choice."

"You're weird."

He got in the SUV and rolled down the window. "Do you need a ride to work?"

"It's only a block. I think I can handle it."

"Suit yourself."

He checked his phone for Annie's address and started the navigation app before finally pulling onto the street. He waved one last time to Gretchen before turning in the opposite direction.

* * *

Emi rode with Alia in her pink Ranger to the football stadium. Emi arranged to meet Joel and Annie at the southwest entrance of the stadium. John left the house earlier to pick up Lizzie and a few other friends in the Escalade. Lizzie had invited Alia to sit with them for the game. Although Alia was older than most seniors, she hadn't yet found a friend group she felt comfortable with.

"John just texted that he's already inside saving seats," Alia told Emi and her friends upon their rendezvous at the stadium entrance. "Left of fifty-yard line on the home side."

"Does that include us?"

"I don't know. Let's go in."

The stadium didn't have the metal bleacher structure like the practice field back at Cy Grove or the main football field at Alia's old school in St. Louis. It was made of concrete and rivaled many college stadiums. It was one of two stadiums in the school district that were shared among its thirteen high schools. Football was serious business in Texas, even at the high school level, and required an equally serious venue.

Upon arriving at the seating section, Emi called out, "There they are." She pointed to John and his group of friends seated in the stands. They walked down the steps to the rows with John, Lizzie, and their friends, most of whom were on the basketball team.

John and Lizzie looked up as Alia stood on the steps of their row.

"Hey!" Lizzie smiled at Alia. "I saved you a seat."

As Alia took her seat next to Lizzie, John looked beyond her to see Emi, Annie, and Joel.

"Hi, Annie! How's it going?" John shouted.

"See?" Annie said to Emi and Joel, glad that they got to witness the greeting she had been experiencing. "I'm doing great. Thank you for asking," she replied in a loud voice, but not as loud as John's.

"Is that my shirt?" John asked, pointing to the gray Cy Grove Athletic Dept. shirt Annie was wearing. It was long enough to hide her shorts.

"Yes?" Annie stated with a grimace, unsure of where the conversation was going.

"I thought you only used it for sleeping."

"It was the only shirt I had with the school's name on it."

"Why does Annie have your shirt?" Lizzie asked John.

"We talked about this. I left it in the girls' room on the trip when I used their shower."

"And his gym shorts, too," Annie added. "I washed them in the sink at the hotel."

Lizzie looked at John for a moment. "You never gave *me* your clothes to wear."

"I didn't give them to her. I just forgot them in their hotel room."

Joel listened to the conversation in amusement. "Maybe you two girls should go to the restroom and switch shirts."

Lizzie looked directly at Annie for two seconds before speaking again. "Are you trying to make a move on my boyfriend?"

Annie's eyes widened and her face turned red. "Um…."

"I'm kidding, Annie. Keep the shirt. If I ever decide to dump John, I'll let you know."

At that statement, Emi glanced over at Alia. Alia sat expressionlessly.

John finally turned his attention to Joel. "Are you the kissing stranger?"

Joel looked over at Emi, wondering what she had told John about him. He looked back at John. "I...uh... I guess so. I'm Joel."

"Come on and get a seat. We saved enough for you and a few others."

Just then, a couple of taller-than-average guys came down the aisle steps carrying popcorn and drinks and made their way into the row behind John's.

"Is that her?" One of the guys asked John, pointing to Annie.

"Yeah."

The guy nudged the other with his elbow and nodded. They both grinned.

"Hi, Annie! How's it going?" they shouted in unison.

Emi burst out laughing.

"Great. Thanks," Annie replied without enthusiasm.

* * *

From the next section, Sienna watched the interaction with interest. She couldn't hear the conversation, other than the loud greetings.

"Look at that. How did she suddenly get so popular?"

"Who?" Sienna's sidekick Bailey asked.

"Ant Bites."

"Do you mean Annie Bates?"

"Yeah. Last year, she was just a nerdy little bookworm. Now she's got a boyfriend and she's sitting with the athletes."

"Her boyfriend's kind of cute. I heard his parents are overseas or something. I'm happy for her."

"Don't talk to me about boyfriends," Sienna stated.

"Sorry. But this is high school. You get to start over, with four grades of potential new boyfriends."

"I said don't talk about boyfriends. And I don't want to start over if I have to start at the bottom. We were at the top in eighth grade."

"If you're enjoying yourself, what does it matter?"

Chapter 9
Labor Day

Labor Day

"I brought paper plates, napkins, and forks; you know, the plastic kind," Joel announced when Emi opened the door. He opened his backpack to show his supplies.

"I told you that you didn't have to bring anything."

"That's what people say to be polite. I had to bring something or it would be rude."

Annie poked her head out. "I brought drinks and they had the same conversation with me," she admitted, pulling the door open wider. She took the party supplies from him as if she was the host of the Labor Day lunch. "You need to meet the rest of the family."

"Is your family here, too?" he asked, stepping inside.

Emi rolled her eyes. "Annie thinks she's part of our family," she explained. "Sophie's in the kitchen with Aunt Ruth and Ty's out back at the grill with Uncle Ayo."

"What about your brother?"

"He's out with Lizzie. They'll be here later."

They walked through the living room on the way to the kitchen.

"Who's the teddy bear collector?" Joel asked Emi, noticing the row of bears on the mantle in the living room and several others placed on shelves next to the fireplace.

"Sort of all of us," Emi stated. "People brought us teddy bears when my parents died."

"The ones on the mantle represent their current family members," Annie added.

"There are five. Is there another family member I haven't met?"

"The middle one is for Alia," Emi explained.

"The girl who brought you to the football game?"

"Yeah. She lives with us."

"Is she Ty's sister? Because she doesn't look like you."

"She doesn't look like Ty, either." Emi clarified. "Her family's a little messed up, so she lives with us."

"And she's in the center of your bear family," Joel pointed out.

"That's to make sure she knows she's surrounded by people who love her," Emi explained.

"Sometimes Emi rearranges the bears to fit her mood. Like if she and John get in a fight, she puts his bear on the other side of the Sophie and Ty bears," Annie said. "Emi's got a giant teddy bear in her room. It's like the size of a person."

"Do you want to see it?" Emi asked.

"Sure," Joel said. "This is about as far as I got the day of your birthday party."

"Oh, yeah. I forgot you were here before. We can hang out in my room until Sophie calls us for lunch."

"Not until you introduce us," Sophie called out from the kitchen.

Joel turned around to face Sophie and Ruth through the pass-through window into the kitchen.

"I'm Joel," he announced.

"Nice to finally meet you. I'm Sophie, Emi's sister." Sophie turned to a Black woman who appeared to be in her mid-thirties, and added "He's the one who crashed Emi's birthday party."

"I'm sorry about that. I was at the wrong house," Joel said. "But your cake was good."

"Thanks. It was store-bought."

"And that's my Aunt Ruth," Emi said, referring to the woman with Sophie. "She's a doctor."

"Nice to meet you, uh, Dr. Ruth. Is that what I should call you?"

"I'm Dr. Odeku at the clinic," she answered, in her distinctive Nigerian accent. "But I've learned that kids in Texas call their friends' parents by their first name, with a Missus or Mister in front. So, you can call me Dr. Ruth. But for my husband," she pointed toward the door that led to the back patio where her husband and Ty were grilling burgers and jalapeño sausages, "he prefers to use his last name. You can call him Dr. Diya."

Joel looked out the window to see a Black man in a beige cowboy, western-style shirt, and jeans standing by a barbeque grill, talking with a slightly younger White man in a T-shirt and shorts.

"I didn't know that," Emi said. "I thought he was into everything Texas, so why not use his first name."

Aunt Ruth began to explain, "When we were in New Jersey, the name tag on his coat said, 'Dr. Ayodeji Diya'. When he treated children, he told them to call him Dr. Ayo." She paused to laugh. "Then he had some Chinese patients and found out that 'ayo' means 'ouch' in Mandarin. Not a good name for a doctor." She laughed again. "Since then, he just goes the formal way: Dr. Diya."

After further introductions to the men on the patio, Emi led her friends upstairs to hang out in her room.

On the way up the stairs, Joel commented, "Your aunt said they used to live in New Jersey. When did they move here?"

"A little over a year ago they moved to Navasota."

"Not Houston? Navasota's a small farming town on the way to A&M. Is that why your uncle wears a cowboy hat and boots? Trying to fit in?" Joel asked.

"Yes. Ty says he's undergoing a Texification process," Emi answered as she paused at her bedroom door. "His chili-making skills have improved, but he still puts beans in it."

Annie didn't wait, but opened the door and walked in as if it was her room. "Now you get to see Emi's secrets."

"Yep, that's a big teddy bear," Joel quipped as he walked in and saw the life-size toy sitting up on the bed. He scanned the room before focusing on a table with a stack of T-shirts and an iron press. "What's all that?"

"It's for my hair styling YouTube channel. I make T-shirts for Jentler Hair." Emi picked up a blue shirt that already had her logo printed on it in white. The design was a line drawing of the top of a girl's head, from the eyes up, with tight coils of hair extending upward and outward.

Annie picked up the giant teddy bear and held it as if it were standing up on the floor.

"Nice," Joel noted about the T-shirt. "Do you sell many of them?"

"Not really. It was dumb to think people would go from watching a hairstyling video to buying a shirt. It probably doesn't compare to your online business."

"I get by. It also gives me something to do."

Annie wiggled the teddy bear to make it look like it was dancing.

"Well, I'm still impressed with Emi's video channel," Annie stated as she put the bear back on the bed. "Even if it's not for my kind of hair."

By the time Ty called out that the food was ready, John had arrived with Lizzie and Alia had arrived from her morning shift at Bullseye Home Essentials.

"Annie!" John called out enthusiastically. "How's it going?"

"Fine, John," Annie said in a monotone. "Thanks for asking."

* * *

"Mom, how do I look?" Sienna asked upon emerging from her bedroom. She wore a swimsuit under her jean shorts and white tank top. The blue of the bikini top showed through the white shirt. She held up her phone with the Instagram image of a girl who looked like a model. "Does the makeup look like hers?"

"Sienna, you always look good. But why put on makeup just to go swimming at Bailey's house?"

"In case some of the guys are there." She slid several bracelets onto her left hand.

"You mean Hunter's friends who ignored you at school?"

"There could be others there," Sienna replied, adding more bracelets to her right hand.

"If you're going in the pool, you don't need all that bling," her mom mocked.

"It makes me look sophisticated."

Her mother sighed.

"You just don't understand people my age," Sienna complained.

"You're right about that."

* * *

After a few innings of kickball in the street with neighbor kids, Ty, and a few parents, Emi announced she and her friends were taking a break.

"What? You don't think you can go another inning with the Dad Squad?" Mr. Tommy Wong joked.

"Dad, y'all are losing," twelve-year-old Carolina pointed out.

"We want to quit while we're ahead, Mr. Tommy," Emi stated.

One of the other dads mouthed, "Thank you."

The only mother among the players mouthed back, "Wimp."

"We're going to Annie's house to hang out in her hot tub," Emi told Ty and Sophie.

"Remember it's a school night," Sophie warned, in her most motherly tone.

"I know."

"Ty will pick you up at eight."

"I will?" Ty asked.

Sophie glared at him.

"Oh, yeah. I'll pick you up at eight," Ty responded.

"Eight? That's too early," Emi directed at Sophie. "You're channeling Mom again."

"It still gives you three hours," Sophie said.

Joel cleared his throat. "I can bring her home."

Sophie tried to think of an excuse to say no without sounding rude.

"He did help with cleanup after lunch," Ty told Sophie.

"What does that have to do with driving Emi?"

"He's responsible," Ty explained.

"Yeah, he's responsible," Emi echoed.

"Okay. Fine."

* * *

As Sienna and her mother left Bailey's neighborhood after Sienna's swim outing, Sienna couldn't avoid the annoying questions.

"Did you have a good time?" her mother asked.

Sienna shrugged her shoulders before answering, "It was okay." It was the first social event that she went to since Hunter moved and it just didn't feel the same.

"Any guys show up to admire all that bling?"

"Mom," Sienna stated with disdain. "Just leave it alone."

"I want to know what's going on in your life."

"There were a couple of guys there, but not anyone you know." Before her mother had a chance to ask another question, she added, "And no one I'd be interested in."

It was only by chance that Sienna noticed the white SUV at the traffic light facing them. She recognized Annie Bates in the front passenger seat with her new boyfriend at the wheel. When the light turned green and the cars began to move, she turned her head for a closer look as Annie and Joel passed them.

"Do you know them?" Sienna's mother asked.

"They go to my school."

After a few minutes of silence, she mumbled, "It's not the same without Hunter."

"I'm sorry, Baby."

* * *

Joel seated himself across from the two girls in the circular hot tub built into the swimming pool. Joel stretched his arms out and rested them on the ledge, holding a can of Dr Pepper in his right hand.

"We used to have a pool," Joel said. "Ryn would have people over all the time for swimming or just hanging out. Me too, but I had to arrange my pool time around her schedule. Such are the troubles of having a popular older sister." He brought the soda to his lips and took a sip.

Annie noticed Joel's muscles, looked down at her red ruffled bikini top, then back up at Joel. "Look. Even Joel has bigger boobs than me," Annie lamented.

"These are pecs, not boobs," Joel clarified. "And I had to work out to get these muscles."

"They're still bigger than mine. What kind of workout?"

"Practicing the butterfly on the swim team worked for me, but there are other ways."

Joel slid off the underwater ledge and knelt in the water in front of Annie. He held up his left hand, palm towards her.

"Put your hand against mine."

She put her right hand up flat against his.

"Keep your elbow close to your body and push."

She pushed.

"Did you feel that muscle tightening?" he asked, patting his left pectoral muscle to indicate the muscle in question. "Push again, but this time use your other hand to feel the muscle tighten."

She placed her left hand on Joel's left pectoral muscle and pushed with her right hand. Joel smiled.

Emi laughed out loud. "I think he meant for you to put your hand on your own muscle."

"Oh!" Annie exclaimed, blushing. She immediately withdrew both hands and placed them on her lap under the water.

"What did you feel?" Joel asked, trying to continue the lesson, despite the faux pas.

"Your boob," Emi answered for her, chuckling.

"It's not a boob," Joel insisted.

"Man boob," Emi stated.

"Fine. Man boob. Whatever." Joel splashed water on Emi.

Emi and Annie both laughed at Joel's annoyance.

"Annie," Emi started, grinning. "Maybe you should let Joel feel your… uh… pec. You know, for training purposes."

Annie looked at Emi with her mouth open. She glanced at Joel, still with her mouth open, but didn't say anything. She slid her hands down to her knees and pressed them against her knees, feeling her pectoral muscles tighten.

Joel couldn't tell what her silence indicated. He stood up and took his seat back on the underwater bench across from her and took another gulp from his Dr Pepper. Looking back at Annie, he said, "I think you're fine just the way you are, but if you want to do something, you need exercises that involve pushing, like pushups."

"Thanks. Maybe I'll try it," Annie said, recovered from her embarrassment.

Chapter 10
Storm brewing

Mid-September

Joel set the temperature on the oven, then checked the recipe on his phone again to make sure he had done all the right steps. Once satisfied, he opened the oven and slid the casserole dish inside. He looked over at the table. It had four chairs, but only two were ever used. He set a plate on the table and carefully placed a fork on the left of the plate and a knife on the right. He then set a cup down, just above the knife. Next, he tore off a sheet of paper towel and neatly folded it in half across the diagonal. He set the triangular napkin next to the fork. He had learned the correct placement of dinnerware at Cotillion etiquette training two years earlier.

He sat down at the table in the chair opposite his place setting – Ryn's chair – and sighed. He looked back at the timer on the oven. It would be a while before the casserole was ready. He pulled out his phone and opened YouTube. He looked up Emi's Jentler Hair channel and found one of her early videos. He watched Ty carefully separate sections of twelve-year-old Emi's hair while they talked to each other.

From the banter, he wasn't sure Ty even knew he was being recorded. Joel stopped the video and looked for a more recent one. This time Emi was alone. He recognized the location as the bathroom sink area off Emi's bedroom. He watched as she created an updo with bobby pins, forming a couple of braids and a puff of coiled tendrils on top.

He stopped the video before it finished and looked for another that included Ty.

Why am I looking at hair videos? I should be looking for advice for reselling online.

Ignoring his inner voice, he found another Jentler Hair video that included Ty. He smiled at their playful conversation. Although hair styling was not at all similar to camping, Emi's interaction with Ty reminded him of those long-ago occasions when he and his dad set up a campsite. Tents, cots, cooking equipment, and discussions about life. He paused the video and opened the text app.

> Joel:
> I made an enchilada casserole
> for dinner

Emi:
Sounds tasty. You never told
me you could cook

> Did you think I just ate
> sandwiches every night when
> Ryn's not here?

Maybe you have a tab at the
noodle shop

                              Have you had dinner yet?

No

                              Can I bring it over and eat with
                                                    y'all?

Come on over

Emi went downstairs to see who was home. Sophie had not yet arrived from classes at Prairie View A&M, but Ty was home and about to get into the shower.

"Ty," Emi called from outside the closed door to his and Sophie's bedroom.

"What's up?"

"Joel's coming over to eat with us. He's bringing food, too."

"Okay. Does that mean his sister is out of town?"

"Yes."

"Let Alia know. She's in charge of dinner tonight."

A half-hour later, Joel rang the doorbell.

* * *

On Wednesday morning, cell phones across the Cypress Fairbanks Independent School District buzzed with a text message about the looming storm.

CFISD:
Tropical storm Ulysses is
predicted to hit our area
Friday afternoon. We are
monitoring the situation and
will decide on school closures
at noon today.

At lunch, Joel commented on the morning text. "My sister's on a business trip and she already planned to stay with her boyfriend in Dallas for the weekend. It looks like I'm on my own," Joel told Annie and Emi. "I bought a case of water on Monday and filled up the car with gas. That's what my father used to do for big storms."

"We always buy batteries," Annie proclaimed. "Then we don't use them. We've got a drawer full of batteries that have expired."

"If you already have batteries, why do you buy more?" Emi asked.

"I don't know. My mom can never remember if we have enough."

Phones buzzed across the cafeteria. The chattering among students rose noticeably. The noise quickly escalated into cheer.

CFISD:
Due to the impending landfall
of tropical storm Ulysses, all
CFISD schools will be closed
Thursday and Friday to allow

time for the families of our
students and staff to prepare
for it. Please take the
necessary precautions and
stay safe.

"I guess we get a four-day weekend," Joel noted.

* * *

When Joel pulled his sister's SUV into the Jensen driveway behind Ty's truck Thursday afternoon, he, Emi, and Annie found Ty trying to fit the patio furniture into the garage, which already had the Escalade and Sophie's car parked in it. Two of the chairs were sitting on the workbench and two more were laying on top of Sophie's Mazda.

"Should we start calling you the Three Amigos?" Ty asked Emi, Annie, and Joel, once they had climbed out of the vehicle.

"You think we spend too much time together?" Emi asked.

"I'm not saying it's too much. I'm just saying it's a lot," Ty responded.

"Why are you home this early?"

"They sent us all home to prepare for the storm. Isn't that the reason you have off today?"

"Yeah."

"And what did you do to prepare?"

The three teens looked at each other.

"We went to a movie?" Annie said, with an inflection that sounded more like a question.

Ty laughed.

"There's not much to prepare for at my place. But I can help you here," Joel offered, grasping the edge of the table. "Where do you want to put this? The garage looks full."

"Emi, open the back of the Cadillac." They turned the table upside down and set one end on the edge of the cargo area.

As Ty began to push the table into the vehicle, Joel said, "Wait!"

"What?" Ty asked.

"Annie needs to do this. She wants to do exercises that require pushing."

Annie stepped up and pushed the table into the SUV. "That wasn't exercise; it didn't take much effort."

Ty closed the door of the vehicle.

"Push against the door," Joel ordered Annie.

"It's already closed."

"Just step back and lean in and push. Standing pushups."

She moved into position and performed one pushup. "That doesn't seem like it would do much."

"Do a hundred of them. Or do ten with some weight on you."

"Weight?"

"Stand up straight," Joel stated.

He turned around and leaned against her, back-to-back. "Now lean forward with your hands against the car."

When she leaned, he went with her, using his body as the weight.

"Push."

Annie grunted at the effort to push her and Joel's combined weight away from the car.

"Yeah, now it feels like exercise."

"Now nine more."

After eight pushes, Annie asked, "Is that enough?"

"Two more. You can do it," Joel encouraged.

"Yeah, Annie, just two more," Emi interjected, "and then maybe he'll let you touch his man-boobs again."

Ty had been observing the entire effort in silence until now. "Should I be concerned about leaving you three alone together?"

"Do you really think the storm will be bad?" Joel asked, ignoring Ty's question.

"It looks like it," Ty said. "It may not be hurricane strength, but it could still toss around the outdoor furniture and knock out a window or something. Do you have flashlights or candles in case the power goes out?"

"I have flashlights. And Annie gave me extra batteries."

Ty nodded in acknowledgment. "Are y'all staying for dinner?"

"Can I?" Joel asked.

"Sure. What about you, Annie?"

"Mom wants me home for dinner and doesn't want me going out again until the storm passes."

"It doesn't hit until tomorrow afternoon."

"I know. She's just paranoid. My dad stopped arguing with her a long time ago. I'll just spend my time organizing the batteries."

* * *

Friday morning, Joel texted Emi and Annie with news of his pre-storm shopping experience.

> Joel:
> I just went to the store to get some chips and salsa. The shelves are empty. No bread. No snacks. No bottled water. No toilet paper. I've never seen that in real life

Emi:
Ty's dad made us stock up a few days ago. You shouldn't be out driving

> Joel:
> It's weird. A lot of the apartment people left. I don't know where they went. It feels like waiting for the apocalypse to happen
>
> Is surreal the right word?

Annie:
It's only Friday, but it just feels like a rainy Saturday to

me. People even went out for
walks like usual before the
rain started. Except my
parents keep the TV on for
the weather

Emi:
Joel, pack some clothes for a
couple of days. Ty and I are
coming to get you. You're
staying with us until the storm
is over

Joel:
Are you sure? I can handle it
here

Emi:
Ty says to drive your car to
the Metro Park & Ride garage
and park on floor 2 or 3. We'll
meet you there

Joel:
Why do I need to park there?

Emi:
Ty said last time we had a
bad storm the parking lot of
your apartment flooded

Annie:
I remember that. Some kids
were floating on a pool float in

the parking lot. I'm jealous of
you guys

Emi:
You can come, too. Do we
need to pick you up?

Annie:
My mom said no

* * *

The wind picked up throughout the afternoon. The teenagers watched through the windows of the upstairs den as the wind blew an unsecured plastic trash bin down the street, out of sight. Smaller tree branches had broken off and were dancing around lawns.

"At least we still have power," Emi pointed out. "We can watch more movies. Now that we've seen *Little Women*, let's watch *Pride and Prejudice*."

"Oh, come on, Emi," John complained. "Someone else pick a movie. Not a girly one."

"How about *Pride and Prejudice and Zombies*?" Joel offered.

"Is that a real movie?" John asked.

"How about a Harry Potter marathon," Alia contributed.

"Haven't you already seen those, like, twice?" Emi asked.

Alia grinned and clarified, "I only saw the first three twice."

At Ty's suggestion, they settled on the sci-fi classic *Alien*. As the namesake alien began its predatory search of the remaining survivors on the TV screen, each girl in the upstairs den had picked a guy to hide behind for the suspenseful scenes. Emi latched onto Joel and leaned behind him to hide her eyes at the designated scenes. Alia did the same with John.

"Don't forget John has Lizzie," Emi whispered to Alia.

"You tell me that every time I do something with John," Alia whispered back. "Get over it. You should know by now we're just friends."

"Yeah, Emi, get over it," John added.

"Sorry. Sometimes it's hard to tell," Emi said, just before a cat on the screen jumped out at the main character, causing the group to flinch.

"A cat in space? Seriously?" John exclaimed.

Just then, a loud boom caused everyone to jump. The TV and lights went out.

"Ty, did you do that to scare us?" Emi shouted.

"It sounded like a transformer blew out," Ty yelled back from downstairs. "The storm could have blown down a power pole or maybe a tree branch hit it."

A few minutes later, Sophie came upstairs holding a flashlight. Ty followed behind dragging a couple of twin-size air mattresses.

"Everyone alright?" Sophie asked, setting a battery-powered lamp on the coffee table.

"Yeah. How long 'til the power comes back on?" John asked.

"No telling," Ty answered. "I wouldn't expect it until at least tomorrow, though. I don't think the power company will send out work crews until the storm passes. I didn't know if you wanted to sleep in the den, like one of Sophie's study group sleepovers, or sleep in your own rooms. I went ahead and inflated two before the power went out, just in case. I'll prop them up in the corner for now."

"I'll sleep in my own comfy bed tonight," John stated, "but y'all can do whatever you want. What do we do now?"

Sophie held out a pack of playing cards. "I think we have enough light to play Uno."

* * *

Ty answered the door early Saturday morning to find his dad standing there with work gloves tucked under one arm.

"Hi, Dad. Is everything okay at your house?"

"We're fine. A few fallen branches, but nothing major. What about here?"

"John will be upset that we lost the basketball goal. The garage roof's okay, but the backboard broke off the frame."

Ty's dad asked, "Remember that generator you left in my shed? I got it out and tried to run it, but it won't start. First, do you mind if we use it? And second, can you get it running?"

"It's probably the carburetor. Those things get clogged up when they sit for a while. John's our resident expert on small engines; you know, due to his experience with lawnmowers. I'll get him up and we can take a look at it."

Ty headed upstairs to check the status of the teens. He poked his head into the den. Joel and the girls were still asleep. They had moved the coffee table out of the way and arranged the twin-sized air mattresses head-to-head, up against the sofa. Alia was asleep on the sofa with one arm hanging down, and Emi and Joel were in sleeping bags on the air mattresses. If Alia had tried to get up, she would step on one of the two sleeping below. Joel and Emi shared one pillow that straddled the two beds so that the tops of their heads touched. Ty smiled at the sight.

A little too intimate, he thought. *But cute.* He took out his phone and snapped a photo of the slumbering kids and sent it to Sophie before leaving the room and going to see John.

"Time to get up," Ty called upon entering John's room.

"What?" he grumbled. "It's too wet to mow lawns."

"Dad needs help with a generator. I told him you could check the carburetor."

"Ugh. Give me a few minutes."

Ty's phone vibrated while he was still upstairs. "Hi, Dad. John and I will be over in a few minutes."

"That can wait. Do you have a chainsaw?"

"No."

"Then, your muscles will have to do. John's, too." Ty set the phone to speaker mode so John could hear. Mr. Butler continued, "Several trees are down around the neighborhood and some are blocking streets and driveways. The neighbors are forming work crews to help out."

"Okay." Ty looked at John. "Give us a few minutes to get dressed and we'll meet you outside."

"Hey, Ty. I want to help," Joel called from the den.

"I'm sure they can use more muscles," Ty said. "Come on down and grab some breakfast."

Ty set out a carton of orange juice and a box of cereal bars. John, Joel, and Alia reported to the kitchen table within minutes and began gathering their breakfast items.

"Can they use my muscles, too?" Alia asked, holding up her arms and tightening her biceps.

John reached out to one of her arms and squeezed her biceps. "I'm sure they can use your enthusiasm," he noted with a grin.

"Hey! I can get the lawnmower into the truck. That takes muscles."

Ty cleared his throat to get their attention. "Let's take trash bags and rakes. Whoever's not moving logs can bag up debris. Let's go."

"Where are y'all going?" Emi called from the railing on the upstairs landing that overlooked the living room.

"We're going to clean up the neighborhood," Alia stated.

"Wait! I'm coming, too," Emi replied.

"Me, too!" came Sophie's voice from the master bedroom.

"Call me when you're ready and I'll let you know where we are," Ty said.

* * *

Andy normally slept late on Saturdays, but the last evening's storm watch disrupted his routine. He returned from a brief inspection of the debris-strewn neighborhood when his phone chimed with a message.

Alia:
Were you affected by the
storm?

Andy:
Very windy. I found a random
orange bucket stuck under my
car and trash cans blown around
in the streets.

Shelby:
Andy, you forgot about the
patio chairs.

We didn't put the chairs away
and now we can't find two.
They were the cheap plastic
kind

Alia:
I forgot you two share a
house in College Station

Shelby:
You need to come visit

Andy:
Alia, I'll buy you a ticket to a
football game. You'll get the true
Aggie experience

Shelby:
BTW, I saw Griffin on campus

a few days ago. Did you know
he transferred to A&M?

Alia:
He told me. He was excited
about it

Shelby:
See, all your friends in one
place. You have to come visit

Alia:
Ok

Andy:
I'll check the game schedule and
let you know when to come

Alia:
Ok. Pushy

Shelby:
He's starting to get as bossy
as Ella

Alia:
Who's that?

Andy:
Housemate. Her parents own the
house. And she's hot!

Shelby:
He's only saying that because
he saw her naked

Andy:
Are you jealous?

Shelby:
I hope that wasn't meant for
me

Andy:
LOL. For Alia

Alia:
Andy, are you getting a Brody
complex? After all, you are
related

Andy:
No no no and NO!

I didn't plan the Ella sighting. It
just happened

Alia:
What's the story?

Andy:
I'll only tell you if you come to
College Station

Alia:
Let me know when that
football game is

Chapter 11
Guests for dinner

Thursday evening, Sophie walked in the back gate with three girls following her for the almost-weekly study sleepover. Ty was at the barbeque pit on the patio, grilling hamburgers. He stepped away from it for a kiss.

"This is LaShonda," Sophie said, pointing with an empty beer bottle to a girl with hair styled in Bantu knots. "And you already know Toni and Alayna."

"Welcome," Ty said.

Joel stepped out of the house with a plate of cheese slices as Sophie was making introductions.

Ty finally noticed the bottle Sophie was holding. "Babe, what's with the Shiner bottle?"

"We went out for lunch today and I got a beer," Sophie answered.

"I thought you didn't like beer."

"I don't."

"Then why'd you get it?"

"Because she could," Toni answered for her. "The waiter wouldn't let her buy any for us, though."

"Oh, that's right!" Ty stated, finally realizing the significance. "We just celebrated your twenty-first birthday; old enough to buy alcohol on your own."

"Yep. I don't need you to buy it for me anymore. I still don't like beer, but I'm keeping this bottle as a memento."

"Well, we don't have any beer, but we have hamburgers. I hope you like 'em, 'cause that's all we got tonight."

Joel finally spoke up, "Emi told me to take this to you." He handed the plate of cheese to Ty.

Joel looked at the girls. "Not just hamburgers, we also have lasagna."

Sophie looked from Joel to Ty with raised her eyebrows.

"I made it," Joel explained.

Toni looked at Sophie. "Did y'all pick up another kid at a gas station?"

"That's Joel," Ty explained. "He's Emi's friend."

Toni went to the open door and looked around until she spotted Emi in the kitchen. "Emi, you got a boyfriend? He's a cute one."

Emi responded with a wave and a grin.

Alayna looked Joel up and down before turning her attention to Ty. "Ty, you better keep an eye on them."

Joel turned red as he tried to think of a comeback to Toni's warning. All he could get out was "Um…"

"He doesn't live here," Sophie explained. "But he does hang around here a lot."

"As I said, you better keep an eye on them." Alayna looked at Joel again and winked.

Emi finally emerged from the house and whispered to Joel, "Now you get to be *my* fake boyfriend."

She looked at the college girls and explained, "He was a birthday present."

"From Boys 'R' Us," Ty added.

Joel's fading blush reddened again. "Uh…I should go warm up the lasagna."

* * *

Saturday morning, Joel waited for Alia outside his apartment when she pulled into the driveway of the complex. Her pink "art" truck was an unmistakable sign that it was her, so he walked out to meet her before she tried to park. Joel glanced at the pressure washer in the back of the truck before opening the passenger door.

"Do Ty and John need a pressure washer or was that already in the truck?" Joel asked as he settled into the seat.

"Ty asked me to bring it," she answered. "I'd loaded a lawnmower before he called. His team was supposed to clean the lady's driveway, but no one brought a pressure washer." She put the truck in gear and drove down the driveway to the street.

"Thanks for picking me up."

"My pleasure." Alia handed him her phone. "You're in charge of directions. I already put the address into the map."

Joel looked at the map displayed on the phone. "Go past the freeway. It's a couple of miles before we have to turn."

Alia turned right onto the street and headed toward the freeway.

"I saw you wave to Gretchen when you pulled into the parking lot," Joel noted. "How do you know her?"

"She's in my shop class."

"You take shop? Which one?"

"Welding."

"I don't picture you as a welder."

"What do you picture me doing?"

"Um…. Art? Just look at what you drive. Did you know Gretchen works at the sub shop across the street from my apartment?"

"No, I didn't. It never came up in class."

"I met her there in the summer," Joel continued. "I bought a lot of sandwiches from her over the last few months. That's before I found out she lives in my apartment complex." Joel looked down at the map displayed on Alia's phone. "Turn right at the next light. Then right again at the first stop sign. It should be just a few houses up from the corner."

"Judging from all the trucks parked on the street, this must be the right place," Alia told Joel as she navigated between vehicles parked on both sides of the residential street. "But which house is it?"

"The one on the right, past that red pickup," Joel responded. "I see Ty and John in the driveway."

"I'll back into the driveway to unload the equipment, then I'll find a place to park on the street."

The group of men and boys on the driveway in matching blue T-shirts couldn't help but notice the pink pickup truck even before it pulled into the driveway. They gathered around to see what it was about. John walked up and opened the tailgate before Alia and Joel even closed their doors upon getting out.

"Thanks, John," Alia said. "I guess you won't need the ramps to get the pressure washer out."

When John pulled the machine to the edge of the lowered tailgate, Joel grabbed one side while John grabbed the other. Together they lowered it onto the driveway.

"Thanks for bringing the extra help and equipment, Alia," Ty said. "And I'm sorry about interrupting your Saturday morning lawn work, but the guy who was supposed to bring his pressure washer got reassigned to another team."

"No problem."

Ty turned to Joel. "Joel, I'm glad you were available. The church got a lot more requests for help after last week's storm and we're shorthanded."

"I'm glad I can help," Joel responded. "When Emi told me you needed help I dropped everything, which was easy because I didn't have anything else to do this morning."

"And my lawns can wait," Alia said. "I can still get one or two lawns done this afternoon and do the rest tomorrow."

Ty looked momentarily puzzled. "Oh, you don't have to stay. I'll bring your stuff back."

"I bring the equipment, I use the equipment," Alia stated, putting her hands on her hips. She looked around at the men in their matching shirts that said, "Father and Son Task Force".

A middle-aged Black man behind Ty called out, "Hey Romero, we need two more Task Force shirts!"

A man, presumably Romero, jogged to the red Dodge Ram and retrieved two new T-shirts.

A boy who appeared to be in middle school stated to a boy next to him, "I thought this was only for guys. She's not a father or a son."

"If she's a son, then I might be gay," his companion responded.

Ty stepped forward to introduce the new arrivals to the team. "This is Alia and Joel. And I'm their father for the day."

Ty leaned to Alia and whispered in her ear, "Go to the bathroom to change into the new shirt."

"Do you think I'd change out here in front of everyone?" Alia asked indignantly.

"I remember you changing in the Buc-ee's parking lot last year."

"Don't worry. I've gotten better at being 'normal'. I'll change inside."

"Ty, where do you need us to help?" Joel asked, interrupting the whispered conversation.

"I guess Alia will clean the driveway. You can help me fix the fence that blew down last week."

"I'll move the truck and be right back," Alia added.

When she returned from parking the truck down the street, she was wearing the Task Force shirt. *I said I would change inside. But I didn't say it would be inside the house.*

* * *

"Did you notice those boys were staring at you all morning?" Joel asked Alia on the way to Whataburger to join the rest of the work crew after the completion of the volunteer assignment.

"Yeah. I couldn't tell if they were annoyed that I intruded on their men's club, or if they'd never seen a girl clean a driveway or what. Remember when one of them was on the ladder to trim that tall bush by the garage? I winked at him, and he almost fell off."

"I saw that!" Joel laughed. "I didn't realize you caused it."

"I wasn't trying to cause an accident. They just kept looking at me. It was either ignore them completely or show them that I knew they were staring."

"Did you enjoy it?"

"Getting ogled by middle school boys?"

"No. I mean, did you enjoy the whole thing? You know, helping that grandma get her house fixed up."

"Yeah. I felt like I accomplished something and made someone happy. What about you?" Alia asked.

"I just liked being part of something. I was on a swim team until high school. That felt like being part of something. But the last year or so has been crazy. You know, new school and all. I don't know many people, and at home, it's just me and my sister. Sometimes, just me."

"Is that why you've been coming to our house for dinner? To be part of something?"

"I don't mind doing things on my own, but sometimes I feel like I need to be around other people," Joel admitted.

"Then I hope John and Ty saved us a seat at Whataburger."

"You mean you don't want to sit with those boys? I bet it would make their day," Joel teased.

"I'm eighteen. I'd better not get stuck at the kiddie table."

Upon entering the restaurant, Alia and Joel noticed that most of the work crew were already in line to order.

"Alia!" a youthful voice called out.

Alia turned towards the dining area where the call had originated. The boys were already seated at a table.

"We saved you a seat!" one of the boys called.

Chapter 12
Stuff that drives me crazy

On the ride back to his apartment, Joel perked up when he recognized the ukulele melody that came on the radio. The music was from the classic Francesca Battistelli song, "This Is The Stuff". Joel sang along energetically with the first line, "I lost my keys, to the great unknown!"

Alia laughed at the sudden outburst. "I've never heard that song before. Is it new?"

"No. It's pretty old. But my mom likes it. My dad was always misplacing his keys and when he did, she would start singing that line." He smiled at the memory. "You heard the next line about losing her phone. My dad's revenge was to sing that line when my mom lost her phone."

Alia chuckled at the image of a couple singing a silly song to each other while trying to find lost articles. It sounded like something Ty and Sophie would do.

By the end of the song, she'd learned enough of the chorus to sing along with Joel and the radio for the line, "This is the stuff that drives me crazy!"

When the song ended, Joel decided to broach a sensitive topic. "Alia, are we friends?"

Alia knitted her brows and glanced at Joel as she drove, wondering where he was going with that question.

"Yeah," she finally answered, but with a slight questioning tone.

"I mean, we've known each other for a few weeks, but weren't really friends, just acquaintances."

"We're friends now."

"Then can I ask you a personal question?"

She glanced at him again. "Okay." Again, she used a questioning tone.

"Emi told me that your father's in prison."

Alia nodded, still wondering where this was going.

"Have you ever tried to visit him?"

"No. Why would I do that?"

"Because he's your father."

"Did Emi tell you why he's in jail?"

"She said it was for kidnapping and attempted murder. But still, he's your father."

"Did she tell you who he tried to kidnap and kill?"

"No. She was kind of vague on details. I just figured it was a gang thing."

"It was me. I'm the one he tried to kidnap and kill."

"Oh, crap! I'm sorry. I didn't know."

"He's dead to me. So, no I've never tried to visit him in prison, and I never will."

Joel didn't know how to respond to that and just remained silent. After a couple of awkward minutes, he finally spoke up. "I'm sorry. I didn't...."

Alia cut him off before he could finish. "It's okay. We're friends, remember. My parents weren't the kind of people who sang to each other."

Joel pointed to the radio and asked, "Can I turn up the music?"

"Yes, but don't mess with my station."

* * *

"Ty!" Sophie called from the hallway bathroom that evening. "I got a text from Kumiko."

Ty went over and stood next to the closed door. "Oh yeah? Is she inviting us to Vegas? I've never been to Vegas."

"No, she's coming to Houston. Business trip with her husband. She said her husband wants to meet me."

"Only you? John and I put in a lot more effort carrying her up the Canyon than you did."

"Well, I drove her around more. I'll ask her about you."

A minute later, Sophie called out, "She wants to see our whole family again. Her husband's company is expanding a factory in Sealy and is meeting with the plant manager. Sealy's only an hour from here. Wait. She's typing again."

After a pause, Sophie continued, "There may be an internship opportunity for me."

"Wow! That's great! Is it engineering?"

"I don't know," she said as she flushed the toilet.

Ty heard the water running in the sink.

"Dang. No one replaced the hand towel after doing the laundry. This kind of stuff drives me crazy," Sophie stated before continuing the previous conversation.

"When I was driving Kumiko's family around, we talked about college. I told her I was hoping for an engineering internship."

"Are you lucky or blessed?" Ty asked.

"Both. And it's 'we', not just me," Sophie said as she shook her wet hands over the sink.

"How so?" Ty asked as Sophie opened the bathroom door.

"You're lucky and blessed you have me." She wiped her wet hands on Ty's shirt.

"Hey!"

"I was wet," she stated simply. She lowered her voice to a whisper, unnecessary since her siblings were out with friends and Alia was working. "Good news gets me excited."

"Then I guess we'd better do something about it," Ty responded. He put both hands on her waist and kissed her before pushing her backward down the short hallway and into the bedroom.

"Mid-October," she said.

"Sweetie, this can't wait 'til October."

"No. That's when Kumiko's coming. Mid-October."

Chapter 13

~Grand Canyon~

Previous June – vacation day three

The family arrived at Grand Canyon Village in the early afternoon, giving them plenty of time to check into their rooms at the lodge and take a short hike along the canyon rim.

"Wow!" John exclaimed, looking across the canyon. "You just can't appreciate how big this is from the videos.

"The whole thing is striped," Annie added. John looked at her, waiting for further explanation. "Just look. I'm talking about the layers. Beige, pink, yellow, green."

"Can we hike down to the bottom?" Emi asked.

"No, that takes all day," Ty responded

"But it's only about a mile deep. Why would it take all day?"

"The trail doesn't go straight down. Look down there," Ty pointed. "It zig-zags."

Their whole party took notice of the multiple switchbacks on the otherwise steep, rocky terrain dotted with small scrubby trees, bushes, and prickly pear cacti.

Ty continued, "I looked it up. The trail's almost ten miles to the river. The people who go to the bottom usually stay overnight."

Emi looked excited. "Cool! Can we do that?"

"I don't think any of us are in shape for that kind of hike, even if overnight," Sophie observed.

"Hey!" John exclaimed. "Speak for yourself. I'm in great shape."

"Maybe for basketball, but not for hiking up and down a canyon," Sophie said.

"Put it on your bucket list," Ty added. "Then train for it. And then you can come back and hike down to the bottom."

The group watched as hikers came up the trail.

"Okay," Ty said after a few minutes. "Let's hike down for an hour or so. I bet there are some good photo spots further down. And I want to get a better look at those goats."

"What goats?" Sophie asked.

"I see them. They're cute," Annie exclaimed. "Let's go!"

"I can barely see them," Ty stated. "How can you tell they're cute?"

"Because the goats at the petting zoo are cute."

As they descended into the canyon, a line of mules carrying tourists passed them on its way up to the rim.

"Where did y'all come from?" Emi asked one of the mule riders.

"From Phantom Ranch at the river. We stayed there overnight."

"Ty, can we do that?"

"You have to make reservations a year in advance," the mule rider pointed out.

"I think we can find enough to keep ourselves busy without spending hours riding a mule," Ty stated.

"That's crap," Emi muttered.

As if to emphasize her point, one of the mules decided to empty its bowels on the trail as it passed the Jensen/Butler party.

* * *

About an hour into the hike, Sophie noted, "Ty, those boys are waving at us." She pointed to two young boys further down the trail who were waving their hands over their heads. Sophie waved back. One of the boys began flapping his hand, fingers down as if waving flies away. The other boy said something to him. The hand motion boy nodded and turned his hand palm-side up and made the "come here" motion.

"Our mother is hurt," the older boy called out in an unfamiliar accent, pointing to an Asian woman sitting on the ground. "She fell off mountain." He paused. "She fell off *the* mountain," he corrected. There was no mountain, but from the perspective of someone on the trail, the walls of the canyon looked mountainous.

"Ah. Sorry," the woman said, as the group arrived at the Asian family. "My foot turn." She made a twisting motion with her hands. "I cannot walk."

Ty pulled out his phone and looked at the screen. No signal. No ability to call for help.

"Can you stand?" He extended his hands towards her.

"Only one foot." She took his hands and he helped her to stand up. She leaned on her left leg, keeping the weight off her right. As she tried to put weight on her right foot, she closed her eyes tightly and grimaced. She steadied herself with Ty's arm and lifted her right foot off the ground.

Ty surveyed the situation. She was barely five feet tall, if that, and looked to weigh less than ninety pounds. "If I put my arm around you to hold you up, do you think you can walk?" As Ty asked, he put an arm around her back, and under one arm.

"Maybe I hop like rabbit," she said, keeping her right foot off the ground and hopping with her left.

"What if we have someone on each side? John, come to her other side."

"Ty, some parts of the trail aren't wide enough for two, definitely not three," John pointed out.

"Yeah, that's not gonna work," Ty agreed.

"You know what we have to do?" Sophie stated rhetorically. "Piggyback ride."

"What is 'piggyback ride'?" the woman asked.

"*Okaasan, mite,*" the older boy called out to get his mother's attention. He said something to his younger brother and turned his back to the sibling and squatted slightly. The younger boy held on to his older brother's neck as the older brother stood up. The younger boy lifted his legs to each side of his brother and the older boy grabbed ahold of them to keep the weight off his neck. He took a few steps to demonstrate the piggyback ride.

"*Hontōni?*" the mother responded.

She turned to Ty and said, "*Onegaishimasu.* Can you do it?"

Ty removed his backpack and handed it to John. The mother pointed to her backpack and indicated for her older son to carry it.

"Let's do it," Ty replied, turning his back to her and squatting slightly.

"*Arigatō gozaimasu.* Thank you so much." She put her hands on Ty's shoulders and jumped with her left leg onto Ty's back.

"What's your name?" Ty asked as he bounced slightly to lift her higher onto his back and repositioned his hands on her legs for a better grip.

"I am Kumiko Moriguchi."

"Nice to meet you, Kumiko. I'm Tyler Butler. Call me Ty."

Kumiko smiled to hide her embarrassment. *Americans talk to strangers as if they are close friends,* Kumiko mused. *A Japanese man would call me Moriguchi-san. But now this man is carrying me like a child, so he calls me Kumiko.*

As the combined families made their way back up, they introduced themselves. The older boy introduced himself as Kenji.

"I am nine years old," he said proudly. He pointed at his brother. "His name is Jun. He is six years old."

Kumiko explained that they were from Japan but now live in Las Vegas for her husband's job with the American branch of a Japanese company. They planned the trip to the Grand Canyon for the whole family, including Kumiko's mother, but Kumiko's husband had to drop out to host senior executives visiting from Japan.

"Where is your mother now?" Ty asked as he carried Kumiko up the trail.

"She wait at top. Takes photos with camera."

"Does she have a big umbrella with a flower print?" Emi asked.

"Yes. Umbrella for sun."

"I saw her before we came down. She was sitting on a bench, reading a book backward."

"Backward?" Kumiko asked, puzzled by Emi's comment.

"Oh, yeah. It's a Japanese book," Kenji explained. "They start from the opposite side as English books."

After fifteen minutes, John took over from Ty in carrying the injured hiker. After another twenty minutes, Sophie insisted she has a turn, trying to prove her capabilities. After ten minutes, she gladly switched with Ty. With the slower pace, the upward incline, multiple stops for rest, and a change of carrier, the journey up took considerably more time than the trip down. As they neared the rim, John took over once again. He had proved that he had the most stamina of the family. With the rim of the canyon in sight, Kumiko sent her sons up to alert their grandmother to their mother's injury.

The group could hear calls of *"Obaachan!"* as the boys reached the top.

As John caught up to the boys, an older Asian woman yelled, *"Hanashinasai!,"* as she swung her closed umbrella at him, striking him on his side. Annie ran up and slapped her arm, then quickly retreated before the woman swung at her.

Kumiko yelled, *"Okaasan, yamete!"* as John stumbled, dropped to one knee, and banged his chin on the railing, also causing Kumiko to slide off his back and land on her rump on the ground.

"What was that for?!" John shouted angrily.

Kumiko pulled herself up by holding onto a guardrail, as she had a heated discussion with her mother with voices raised and words expelled in rapid-fire. When Kumiko was fully standing and leaning against the handrail, she included her hands in the conversation, waving them to punctuate points. Presently, she lowered her hands, turned back to John, and hung her head down.

"I am sorry. My mother not understand you help me. She think you hurt me."

A circle of onlookers had formed around the two families. Everyone stared at John.

"Oh my god, John," Sophie exclaimed when her attention moved from Kumiko to John.

He reflexively put his hand to his sore chin. When he pulled it away, it was covered in blood. Annie opened her backpack, pulled out a clean pink bandana, and held it to his chin.

"Hold it tight to stop the bleeding," she commanded.

"Thanks," he said, reaching up and putting his hand over hers to hold the bandana in place.

Annie looked into his eyes and smiled as she slid her hand out from under his.

"You girls go to the lodge and get cleaned up," Ty ordered. "I'm taking John to that clinic we passed on the way in."

"I'm coming with you," Sophie stated. She saw Ty about to say something, but before he could object, she added, "He's my brother. I'm coming."

"Fine."

Kumiko leaned on her mother as they hop-walked along the Rim Trail to the parking area near the lodge. "I am sorry," she called out again.

Ty navigated the Cadillac Escalade through the aisle of the parking lot towards the exit. He stopped at a minivan that was seemingly stalled in the middle of the aisle. The driver's side passenger door slid open and Kenji hopped out.

"What now?" Sophie asked, more to herself than to Ty or John.

Ty lowered his window as Kenji approached the SUV.

"My mother can't drive because her foot is hurt."

"I'll go check," Sophie said, opening her door.

Minutes later, Ty and John watched as she helped Kumiko out of the driver's seat and into the passenger seat behind it. They saw Kenji's face through the back window of the van. He had moved to the third row.

After ensuring Kumiko was settled into her new seat, Sophie called back, "I'm driving their van to the clinic. We'll meet up there." Sophie took the lead as they pulled onto the Village Loop Drive and headed toward Center Road, which cut through the pinyon pine woodland.

* * *

In the waiting area of the clinic, Kumiko's mother got John's attention and put her hands together as if in prayer.

"*Mōshiwakearimasen.*"

"She say she sorry," Kumiko translated, before scolding her boys to behave.

While waiting in the clinic queue behind victims of squirrel bites, dehydration, and scraped knees, the boys had become increasingly active, running between imaginary points in the waiting area.

"You were parked in front of the Bright Angel Lodge," Sophie stated to Kumiko. "Is that where you're staying?"

"Yes. *Blite Anjeru Raj.*" Sophie couldn't help smiling at Kumiko's pronunciation.

"Us, too. I can take the boys back to the lodge," Sophie offered. "Emi's good with kids; she does a lot of babysitting."

"You don't mind?"

"I think we're all getting in the way here. That includes me."

After a brief conversation with her mother, Kumiko agreed. "My mother go, too. I'm sorry. She still not trust strangers. I tell her you not strangers. But she want to go to hotel with you." Kumiko held out her van keys.

"I'll call Emi to meet us in the lobby," Sophie said, taking the keys. Sophie kissed Ty, patted John's shoulder, and looked at the boys. "What's your grandmother's name?"

"Yunohara-*san*," Kenju answered.

"Okay. Yunohara-san, Kenji, Jun, let's go."

* * *

Emi, Annie, and Alia arrived in the lobby, freshly showered. When Kenji announced his grandmother would buy ice cream for the entire group at the soda fountain in the lodge, Sophie decided that was her opportunity to shower and change clothes before the guys returned.

"Wait, I'll go up with you," Alia said.

"No ice cream?" Sophie asked.

"Maybe later. I feel bad."

"Oh, are you sick? Maybe you're dehydrated."

"No, not like that. I feel bad about Andy's family. I've been texting Andy. I ruined their vacation. The whole family is mad at each other."

"What do you mean?"

"Andy and Shelby didn't go to the lake house. Shelby's mother is mad at Brody's father. She wanted to back out, too, but they already paid for the house rental and Shelby's father said they had to go. 'They' as in Shelby's mother and father. Shelby refused to go. That's another thing: on the ride to the airport, Shelby said Brody groped her when she was ten and

124

Brody was fourteen and he was babysitting her. She told her mom and her mom talked to Brody at the time and then her mom told her it was just a misunderstanding. Andy said Shelby brought it up again with her mom yesterday in front of everyone, and her dad agreed it wasn't just a misunderstanding, that no normal fourteen-year-old boy would think it was reasonable to do what he did to a ten-year-old girl. That's when her mom exploded on Brody. Then Brody's dad tried to defend him and.... Andy said it got messy. And now everyone's mad at everyone else."

"That's not your fault. You didn't ruin their family vacation, that cousin did."

"Yeah, well...."

"Alia. Stop. There is no excuse for what that guy did. You were right to get out of there as soon as possible. And I'm glad you're here with us."

As they entered Sophie's lodge room, Sophie asked, "Is Andy upset with you?"

"He said he's not. He apologized over and over. Shelby did, too."

"Are you mad at Andy?"

"No. But I feel bad for him."

"Because he missed the lakehouse trip?"

"No. Because I can tell he likes me, but I don't know if I feel the same way. And then I abandoned him."

"You can't force a relationship. You do things on your own time and if it's not meant to be, it's not meant to be. You have a lot of time to figure that out. High school relationships rarely last anyway."

"It did for you."

"Um… Ty wasn't in high school. And we didn't start dating until the summer after graduation, so I don't think it counts as a high school romance."

"And 'rarely' does not mean never," Alia pointed out.

"Go back and have some ice cream. I'll come down after I shower."

* * *

Sophie was toweling off after the shower when she heard Emi in the hallway calling for her. She quickly wrapped the towel around her body and went to the door. She looked through the peephole but didn't see anything. She was about to return to the bathroom when she heard her name again. She opened the door to the hallway. She still didn't see Emi but saw a group of people loitering in the hallway a few doors down.

Thinking Emi may have been on the other side of the group and had forgotten which room was hers, Sophie stepped into the hall and called Emi's name. The people in the hall looked over, but Emi was not in or beyond the group. As the group turned back to their own business, Sophie heard one of the group members call another 'Sophie'. The presence of another Sophie was the source of Sophie Butler's confusion. Unfortunately, Sophie let the door close behind her when she stepped out and it locked automatically. She was stuck in the hallway, wearing only a towel.

She walked across to the girls' room, hoping at least one of them had returned from the ice cream outing, but not surprised when no one answered her knock. She went back to her door and leaned against it, waiting for Ty and John to return. She nodded as other guests passed by.

* * *

Ty, John, and Kumiko greeted the ice cream group upon returning from the clinic. Kumiko sported a new crutch and a medical boot on her ankle. While she explained her condition in Japanese to her family, the English speakers gathered around John.

"Did you get stitches?" Emi asked.

"No, they glued it shut."

"Cool."

"We're gonna go get cleaned up, then we'll meet you down here for dinner," Ty stated.

* * *

Upon reaching their hallway, Ty and John saw Sophie sitting on the floor by the door.

"Babe, why are you in the hallway in a towel?" Ty asked as he walked up.

"I locked myself out when I thought I heard Emi calling me from the hallway."

Sophie extended her hands and Ty reached down and pulled her up.

"Why didn't you call anyone?"

"I'm wearing a towel. Where do you think I'd put a phone?"

Ty inserted a finger in the front of the towel wrap, pulling it away from Sophie's chest, and looked down.

"Did you see a phone down there, Tiger?" Sophie asked.

"No, but I saw something worth investigating."

John made a face. "Come on, guys. I'm standing right here," he complained, annoyed at their public flirtation.

Ty pulled out his keycard and unlocked the door. He opened the door and held it open for Sophie, then quickly went in, closing the door before John could enter. He heard a feminine squeal followed by giggles coming from beyond the door.

"Y'all are disgusting! That's my room too!"

"Use the girl's bathroom!" Ty called out.

"I need my clothes. And besides, I don't have a keycard for their room."

Shortly, the door opened and John's suitcase slid out into the hallway.

"Call Emi to let you in."

* * *

"We just needed a little private time," Sophie told the family at dinner.

"It's been over a year and you two still act like newlyweds," Emi pointed out.

Alia smiled broadly at Emi's statement. "I think it's sweet."

"It's not sweet when I get kicked out of my own room," John grumbled.

"It's a sign of a strong marriage, as long as they both enjoy it," Alia stated.

"Did you enjoy it?" Ty asked Sophie.

"I can't talk about that in front of my brother and sister," Sophie exclaimed with a pained expression on her face. She leaned over to Ty, put her mouth close to Ty's ear, and whispered, "Yes." John and Emi both rolled their eyes.

"We can still hear you," John stated.

Annie giggled. "Are they like this all the time?" she asked.

"Pretty much since I've been with them," Alia answered.

"Are you gonna let me back in the room tonight?"

"I guess we have to," Sophie responded.

"Now to more serious business," Ty stated. "Kumiko won't be able to drive for another couple of days. And yet she's here with her kids and mother on vacation."

"That stinks," Emi said. "What're they going to do?"

"They're going with us for the next two days. By then her ankle should be good enough for driving again."

"The Escalade's big, but not big enough for four more people," Emi pointed out.

"Wait 'til he tells you the next part," John said.

"John, Sophie, and I will take turns driving them in their van. Kumiko changed their hotel reservations to stay at the same hotel as us for the next two nights in Sedona." Ty paused and looked around the table. "Comments?"

"Did you take that woman's umbrella away?" Annie asked.

"She promised not to hit anyone."

Emi shrugged. "I guess it's fine as long as we still get to do the stuff we wanted."

"We'll still drive along the rim tomorrow for sightseeing, and we'll still spend the next day in Sedona at the park with the natural water slide. Just as planned."

"Slide Rock State Park," Sophie clarified.

Chapter 14
Dinner at Joel's

Late September

Wednesday evening, Alia pulled into the parking lot of Joel's apartment complex and stopped behind a gray Lexus RX350 parked in a parking space.

"That's Emi," Annie told her mom when the pink pickup stopped behind the car. Annie opened her car door, carrying a bag of groceries she had been holding in her lap.

Emi stepped out of the truck, also carrying a shopping bag of supplies for dinner. She waved to Alia as the pink truck drove away, then waved to Mrs. Bates.

"I'll be back at nine to pick you up," Annie's mom told her. "Call or text if you want me to come earlier."

"Okay, mom," she said before turning her attention to Emi.

"My mom wouldn't let me go in until you came because Joel's sister's not home," Annie confessed to Emi. "But we didn't have to wait long."

Emi smiled at the recognition of the alone-with-a-boy rule. "Ty and Sophie gave me that speech a few days ago. Do you think there's a parent handbook they all read?"

Inside the apartment, Emi, Annie, and Joel spread their dinner supplies out on the dining table.

"I thought you were bringing meatballs," Annie said to Emi.

"I did. Sort of. I brought the stuff to *make* meatballs," Emi replied, referring to the ground beef, eggs, garlic powder, and other ingredients she brought. She looked at Joel. "You said you wanted to make dinner together, right?"

He looked at the dry spaghetti and Italian sausages he had contributed. "Yeah. I have to boil the spaghetti and heat the sausage."

"But Emi brought stuff for real cooking," Annie whined. "I just brought salad and dinner rolls."

"Then we'd better get started," Joel stated. "Emi, show us what to do."

Annie pulled a mixing bowl and a baking sheet from her shopping bag and added them to the supplies on the table.

* * *

Emi slid the baking sheet of meatballs into the oven. "This will take twenty minutes," she announced. She also took note of Joel's pan of tomato sauce simmering on the stove. *It's probably too early to start the sauce*, she thought, *but the setting is on low heat, so it should be okay.*

"We can start eating the salad while the meatballs are cooking," Joel said. "It's an appetizer."

"They're meat shapes, not meatballs," Annie corrected, as she set bowls of salad on the table. "You know, 'cause the ones I made are not balls. I made cubes and pyramids."

"Right," Joel stated, chuckling. "Meat shapes. You've got a real talent for food sculpting. When they're done, we'll see if you can make a career out of it."

"Hey, don't pick on my friend," Emi joked. She seated herself at the table between the two other place settings, strategically positioned to have a friend on each side.

"Annie has another food talent," Emi stated, once the others had joined her at the table.

"I do?" Annie asked, puzzled.

Emi picked up a cherry tomato from her salad and leaned back to put more space between her and Annie. Then she made a motion with her wrist to act as if she would throw the tomato. Annie's face brightened in recognition. She leaned back, too, increasing the space between them. Then Emi tossed the tomato at Annie's face.

Annie caught the tomato in her mouth and held up both fists in triumph.

"I'm impressed," Joel admitted. "Does it only work with tiny tomatoes?"

"M&Ms, popcorn, whatever," Annie stated.

Joel picked up a dinner roll and threw it at her. It bounced off her forehead and onto the table.

"Hey!" Annie kicked Joel under the table. "It has to be small enough to fit in my mouth. And you have to warn me first."

Joel pinched off a small piece of the dinner roll and tossed it into the air towards himself. He tried to catch it in his mouth and failed. It bounced off his nose and into his water glass. All three burst out laughing as he fished the piece of soggy bread from the glass.

"Let's try again," Joel stated. "He pulled another piece off the dinner roll and pointed at Annie.

"Oh, me again?"

"You have to prove the first time wasn't just lucky."

Joel leaned back and tossed the piece to Annie. She once again caught the item in her mouth.

"Okay, I'm convinced," Joel admitted again. "Catching things in your mouth is your superpower. Maybe after dinner, we can go outside and see if you can catch a frisbee."

Annie kicked him under the table again. "I'm not a dog. I don't do frisbees."

Emi started laughing. "I just got this image of Annie holding a frisbee in her mouth and running through the park."

Joel started laughing too.

"Y'all are so mean!" Annie replied, also laughing.

She picked up a tomato and threw it at Emi. Emi caught it with her hand and popped it into her mouth.

"That doesn't count," Annie said.

"It counts as salad," Emi answered.

The oven timer beeped to signal that the meatballs — meat shapes — were done. All three rose from the table to prepare the main course of the meal.

* * *

After dinner, they cleared the table and stacked up the dishes in the kitchen sink. Emi started to rinse off the plates, but Joel stopped her. "Let's hang out on the sofa before y'all have to go. The dishes can wait."

Joel walked to the sofa, kicked off his shoes, sat down in the middle of the sofa, and propped his feet up on the coffee table. The girls came and sat down, Annie on his left and Emi on his right. He closed his eyes and smiled.

"When I moved here, I thought my life would suck." He opened his eyes. "I didn't know anyone, and I figured everyone else would already have their friend groups set."

Annie put her feet up on the coffee table and slid her bare right foot over to rest against Joel's left sock foot. "That sounds pitiful. Do you think life sucks now?" She tapped her foot against his.

"Only occasionally," he answered, smiling.

"Friends," Emi stated. The others turned to look at her, awaiting an explanation.

Emi pointed to an iPad laying on the coffee table. "Is that your iPad or your sister's?"

"It's mine."

Emi picked it up and handed it to Joel. "There's an old TV show called 'Friends'. We should watch it in celebration of being friends. Let's see if we can find it."

Failing to find a free version of the episodes, they settled for a video of 'Friends' funniest moments. Joel, as the center person on the sofa, held the iPad. Emi pulled her legs up onto the sofa, her knees touching his thigh, and rested her left arm on his shoulder as she leaned in to see the iPad screen. Annie crossed her right foot over Joel's left and also leaned in. They laughed as they watched, sometimes at the exploits of the characters in the show, sometimes at their own reactions.

Before the highlight video ended, the phone in Annie's lap buzzed with a text. She knew what it would say before she even looked at it. She held up the phone for confirmation. "My mom's here." She looked at the kitchen. They had cleared the table, but the kitchen still had dirty dishes. "I'm sorry. We didn't finish cleaning up."

"Don't worry about it," Joel replied. "I'm just glad y'all could come."

"Emi, do you need a ride?" Annie asked.

"No. Alia will get me on her way home from church. But thanks."

"What about that parent handbook rule?" Annie whispered.

"It's just a few minutes. I'll see you at school tomorrow."

When Emi left, Joel asked, "What parent handbook rule?"

Emi paused, thinking of what to tell him. If she mentioned the rule about not being alone with a boy in his home, she feared he would send her off with Annie. Or wait with her outside. The evening was fun, and she didn't want to waste the remaining minutes.

"It's just a joke about parents making silly rules that don't make sense. Such as curfews that are unnecessarily early." She walked back to the kitchen. "I'll wash and you dry."

They stood side-by-side at the sink. Emi rinsed the cups and plates, and Joel loaded them into the dishwasher. The mixing bowl and baking sheet took more effort.

Emi used a paper towel with dish soap to scrub the meatball residue from the baking sheet. Upon adequate washing, she handed it to Joel to dry and picked up the mixing bowl. Emi removed the sprayer from the faucet and sprayed warm water into the mixing bowl. Unfortunately, she didn't adjust for the water pressure of the sprayer against the concave surface of the bowl. The water ricocheted out of the bowl and onto Joel's shirt.

"Hey!" he yelped, jumping back. His shirt was streaked with lines of water.

"Sorry!" Emi said immediately. She watched him look down and his drenched shirt. She tried to suppress a giggle, but that turned into a snort, which triggered a laugh from Joel, which triggered more laughter from Emi.

"I'm sorry," she said between laughs. "I can't help it."

"Next time, I'll wash, and you dry," Joel replied.

* * *

"You're late," Emi said, smiling, as she got into Alia's truck. The clock showed nine twenty-five.

"Sorry. I didn't know Bible study would get out so late," Alia explained.

"When did you start going to Bible study on Wednesdays, anyway?" Emi asked as they pulled out onto the road in front of Joel's apartment complex.

"Today. Amina asked me to go with her. She thinks she's ready to move beyond the Sunday night pizza thing."

"Who's Amina?"

"Shakir's sister."

"Shakir's the math teacher from your Sunday night Bible group, right?"

"Yeah," Alia confirmed, stepping on the clutch and shifting to neutral as she stopped at an intersection with a red light. "His sister started coming in the summer, but she said Shakir already told her everything we talked about at our Sunday pizza meetings, so she thinks she knows more than a typical newbie. She wanted to see what a traditional 'Sunday school' was like, but most of the young singles at our church don't do Bible study on Sunday. They do it on Wednesday. So, I met her for a quick dinner, and then we went to church."

"How was it?"

"It's more structured than the meetings at Paolo's Pizza and had more people. At Paolo's, it just feels like a conversation. This was more of a class. The teacher had a lesson plan."

"Who else was there?"

The light changed to green, and Alia shifted into first to pull through the intersection. "There were nine others, including the teacher, but I didn't know anyone. A couple of them are college students at Lone Star. One goes to college somewhere else, but I didn't catch where. The others have jobs, like real full-time jobs. But they're all in their twenties, except maybe the college students. I think I was the youngest one."

"Did you tell them you're in high school?"

"No. I told them I worked at Bullseye."

"How did Amina like it?" Emi asked.

"She was really into it. I was a little surprised since she hadn't been going to the pizza group very long."

"Your pizza group is for people who aren't Christians, but are thinking about it, right?"

"Yeah. And for new Christians who want to know basic concepts. People like me," Alia stated.

"So, if Amina wants to go to a regular Bible study, does that mean she's a Christian?"

"I didn't ask," Alia said as they pulled into the driveway of their house. "Can you become a Christian if you don't say out loud that you became a Christian? Like if you just think it in your head, but never tell anyone?"

"I guess so," Emi replied. "It's what you believe. It's not like a relationship between people, where both sides have to decide it and want it."

Alia turned off the ignition and opened her door, but Emi hesitated.

"Alia. Can you be in love with someone if they don't know it?"

"You're not talking about God anymore, are you?"

"No."

Alia thought for a moment. "I think being in love with someone is up to you, not the other person." She recalled the story in the Bible of the toxic relationship between the prophet Hosea and his cheating wife. "But if the other person doesn't feel the same way, it will hurt a lot."

Emi nodded and opened her door. "Like Andy?"

"Andy and I are just friends."

Emi stared at Alia without speaking.

"Okay," Alia finally said after several awkward seconds. "I know Andy likes me more than I like him. I mean, he likes me in a different way than I like him."

Emi continued staring.

"I mean, I like doing things with Andy; he's...," she paused, searching for the right word. "Comfortable. I just don't feel that spark that means he's the one."

Emi goaded her, "Have you felt that spark before?"

"Well, I thought I felt it with...." She started to mention the guy who gained her trust and then pushed her into prostitution. Then she thought of the guy who dumped her after finding out about her sordid past. "I don't know."

"So, you thought you felt it before, but the only other guys you ever mentioned didn't care about you," Emi summarized.

Alia heard her statement but didn't respond.

Emi continued, "What if the spark is just a myth and love is a gradual process?"

"I guess that can happen. My sister had an arranged marriage. She barely knew the guy before she married him, but later she said they love each other. Maybe they do. Or maybe they're just trying to convince themselves of it."

"If the gradual process is a possibility, how do you know when 'like' turns into 'love'?

"You ask too many hard questions. We're in high school. What do we know about love?" Alia got out of the truck and closed the door.

Emi did the same.

As they walked to the gate of the backyard, Alia added, "If you're talking about Joel, you've only known him a few weeks."

Chapter 15
The scheme

Early October

Joel entered the sandwich shop and headed for the counter. The only other customers in the shop, two girls in a booth, looked up as he passed by.

"Hey," he stated, acknowledging their presence since they had looked up. He recognized them from school but hadn't met them.

"Is that Annie's boyfriend?" Bailey asked quietly of Sienna.

"Yes, that's the bookworm's boyfriend," Sienna confirmed.

"He doesn't look like a bookworm himself."

Joel picked up a bag of Nacho Cheese Doritos from a stand next to the cash register and placed it on the counter.

"Hey, Moped Guy," the girl behind the counter greeted.

"Hey, Sandwich Girl," Joel replied.

"One or two this time?"

"Just one. Ryn has her own dinner plans tonight."

"Gotcha. Wheat bread and ham, right?"

"Am I that predictable, Gretch?"

"You are with sandwiches."

"Okay, then add jalapeños."

"Wow, you're living dangerously," Gretchen replied sarcastically.

Sienna heard the banter and frowned.

"He called her Gretch," Sienna whispered to Bailey. "It sounds like retch."

"Is that retch, as in vomit?" Bailey whispered back. "Or wretch with a 'w', as in a miserable person?"

"Don't they both fit?" Sienna replied.

"That's a little judgmental, don't you think?"

Sienna looked over at Gretchen for a moment. "Look at her. Purple lipstick, black fingernails, the whole emo thing. I don't think anyone does that to themselves unless they're already miserable."

Bailey twisted her body around to glance at Gretchen. She turned back to Sienna to respond to the comment when she noticed Sienna tap her phone to see the time. "What time is your dad picking you up?" Bailey asked.

"In about fifteen minutes. It sucks that he doesn't even like to come to the house. But do you know what the worst thing is?"

"What?"

"Every other weekend I have to miss my friends and the football games and all that stuff, just so I can hang out with dad and his trophy wife."

"Trophy wives are usually a lot younger and have fake boobs. Your stepmother just looks like a normal mom."

"And they drag me to watch whatever sport my stepbrother is doing that weekend. I don't care about eight-year-olds playing soccer. And sometimes they make me babysit him so they can go out and have fun."

"If I remember correctly, they've done a few fun things with you too. Ice skating, zoo, Kemah Boardwalk."

"The zoo's for toddlers."

"Remember last spring there was that girl in the news because her father tried to kill her. You know she transferred to our school this year, right?" It was a rhetorical question. She didn't wait for a reply. "But, yeah, your life sucks."

"As my friend, you're supposed to commiserate with me even if I don't make sense."

Joel picked up the bag with his sandwich and chips and said, "See you around, Gretch." Gretchen smiled and gave a small wave as he left the counter. Her smile disappeared as she heard Sienna make a quiet gagging sound. Maybe it was just a cough.

Joel passed by their table on his way out.

"Ladies," he stated. "See you at school Monday."

The girls nodded.

"I just thought of a plan on putting Annie in her place," Sienna announced to Bailey.

"What is Annie's place?" Bailey asked.

"You know she's just in a popularity bubble, right?"

"I have no idea what that means."

The girls looked up as Gretchen came out from behind the counter and began wiping down tables.

Sienna lowered her voice. "Annie got too popular too fast. It's like a bubble that'll eventually pop and leave her disappointed. And miserable like her," she explained, nodding towards Gretchen. "It's an unhealthy situation. So, the sooner the bubble bursts, the easier it is to recover."

"I think you made that up. Besides, how can having new friends be unhealthy?"

"Do you want to hear my plan?"

"Fine. Whatever."

"I'll get Joel and Annie to break up."

"And that's supposed to be healthy?" Bailey asked sarcastically. "How will you do that?"

"Maybe I can get him to like me instead."

"What if he really likes Annie and is not interested in you?"

"I don't have the exact plan yet. I'll just look for an opportunity."

Sienna's phone chimed with a message.

"My dad's here. I gotta go."

Gretchen watched the girls leave without taking their trash to the bin by the door. As soon as their backs were turned, Gretchen gave them the one-fingered salute.

* * *

Sunday evening, Joel perused the clearance section at Bullseye Home Essentials for items to resell online. He examined a nail polish dryer before tucking it under his arm and pulling out his phone. He was looking up the selling price online when he heard his name.

"Joel, right?"

"Huh?"

"Your name is Joel, right?"

"Yeah."

"I'm Sienna. I've seen you around. You don't look like the kind of guy to wear nail polish."

"I'm glad you think so. Not that it's bad for some other guy. It's just not my style. This is for business."

"You do manicures?"

Joel smiled at the image of that. When he was in kindergarten, he got into his mother's red nail polish and tried to paint his nails. He ended up with red fingers. His mother took pictures and posted them on Facebook.

"I sell stuff online."

"Nail polish dryers?"

"Whatever I can get that sells for a significantly better price. Nail polish dryers, Nike shoes, college shirts, saw blades, whatever."

"So, what's the current hot item for online sales?"

"A jewelry cleaning machine. But not just any jewelry cleaning machine. It's got to be the Davco brand. I've stocked up on several, just waiting for the orders to come in."

"I could use one of those. My jewelry needs cleaning."

Joel smiled and pulled two more nail polish dryers off the shelf before announcing that he was going to the checkout. Sienna followed him.

"You didn't buy anything?" Joel asked Sienna when he noticed she wasn't carrying any products, only a slightly worn backpack that was slung over one shoulder.

"No. I was just looking around. My dad dropped me off. It was his weekend. My mom's supposed to pick me up, but dad was a little early, and mom always runs late."

Joel didn't mind the attention and he couldn't help but notice that the girl was attractive. *A little more made up than the typical teenaged Bullseye shopper,* he noted. *And lots of jangling things.* She wore long dangling earrings, several bracelets, and a necklace. *High maintenance*, he concluded. *But she* is *attractive.*

"Hey, do you want a smoothie?" he asked, pointing with his thumb to the coffee shop across from the checkout.

"Are you buying?" she asked sweetly. She tilted her head and bit her lower lip while awaiting his answer.

Girls look so hot when they do that, Joel thought. *Even if you know why they're doing it. Definitely high maintenance.* "Sure. I'll buy." *Just like I bought into that look.*

"I want to hear more about your business," Sienna said, as they carried their smoothies to an empty table.

Once seated at a table in the store's cafe, Sienna pulled out her phone, pouted her lips, and snapped a selfie with the drink. "I'm just capturing the moment. I might post that later."

"It's just a smoothie at Bullseye. I don't think it would impress anyone," Joel commented.

"Oh. I need to get one with both of us." She got up and pulled her chair next to Joel, sat down again, and leaned towards him. She held up her phone, careful to ensure both of their faces were on the screen. "Smile." She snapped the photo, again with her pouting lips.

Joel chuckled. "I don't get why girls like to post pictures so much."

"So, people are willing to pay big bucks online for stuff you can get on clearance at a store?" Sienna asked incredulously, ignoring his comment about female social media habits, and continuing the earlier conversation. "Why?"

"Maybe they're too busy to go to the store, or the stores in their area don't have what they want. I don't know. I just know I can make money at it."

"More than working at a real job?"

"Yeah. It depends on how much time I want to spend driving around looking for stuff. And it depends on my ability to borrow my sister's car."

"She gets a car, but you don't? She must be the favorite child."

"My grandma gave her that car when she was in college."

"Can't you borrow your parents' cars?"

Joel paused while he sucked the thick smoothie through the straw. He paused further, closing his eyes tightly and shaking his head. "Brain freeze," he stated. When he opened his eyes again, he resumed the conversation. "You know, if you put your thumb against the roof of your mouth, it helps the brain freeze," he commented. "But it looks pretty stupid in public," he added as an explanation for why he did not use the technique. "But in answer to your question, no. My parents recently moved away because of work. I live with my sister now."

"Is that why you transferred to Cy Grove, to live with your sister because your parents moved away?" Sienna asked.

"Yeah. My sister already lived around here, so this was just easier. And when my sister's out of town, which is often, I get the apartment to myself. Like this weekend she was gone. She spends a lot of time in Dallas with her boyfriend. She's coming back tonight, probably after ten."

Sienna suddenly removed the smoothie straw from her mouth and popped her thumb in.

"Now you've got a brain freeze?" Joel asked.

She nodded, thumb still in her mouth. She stared at Joel and closed her lips around her thumb. After a few seconds, she slowly pulled her thumb out.

Joel blinked. He couldn't explain why, but she suddenly looked hotter than when she bit her lower lip. He self-consciously looked away and adjusted the napkin in his lap.

"Can you give me a ride home?" Sienna asked.

"Sure," he responded. "But what about your mom?"

"I'll let her know I've got a ride." She held up her phone and made a few taps on the screen. "There. I'm good."

* * *

Joel clicked the remote key fob when they approached the Volkswagen Atlas. Partly to unlock the doors and partly to indicate to Sienna where the SUV was parked.

"This looks like a mom's car, not a single girl's car."

"Well, it's good for hauling around stuff for my business, so I can't complain. But my sister didn't choose it exactly. My grandmother and mom decided on the car. My mom used it for a couple of years before handing it off to my sister."

Joel checked the mirrors and backup camera before backing out of the space. "What direction are we going?" he finally asked as he shifted gears into Drive.

"Head towards the school and I'll tell you where to turn."

"Got it."

When they approached the exit from the parking lot, Sienna noted, "Hey, you mentioned you had a jewelry cleaner to resell. Can I buy it?"

"Sure, I have four. I can bring one to school tomorrow."

"How about now? Can we stop at your place and get it before going home?"

"Uh, sure."

* * *

Joel pulled into the parking lot of his apartment complex and parked in front of his building. Gretchen saw him pull up as she walked home after her shift at the sub shop. She raised her hand to wave and almost called out his name until she saw his passenger.

Sienna got out of the SUV when he did.

"You can wait in the car," Joel said. "I'll just run in and get it."

"I want to see your place."

He hesitated, wishing she hadn't said that. "It's super messy right now. I wasn't expecting company."

"I don't mind. My room's messy, too."

I doubt it's as messy as this, Joel thought, wishing he had cleaned it up before going to the store.

Gretchen watched the two go into Joel's apartment and twisted her mouth at the sight of him with Sienna.

He unlocked the front door and pushed it open. Sienna walked in and stood in the middle of the living room, looking around.

"Wow! When you said messy, you really meant it."

Boxes of merchandise were scattered on the coffee table, sofa, and dining table.

Someone might think a hoarder lives here, he thought, seeing it from the perspective of a visitor. There was a box of cereal on the dining table that he hadn't put away after breakfast and dishes in the sink from breakfast and lunch. *A lazy hoarder.*

"I need to get all this stuff put away in my room before Ryn gets home. She hates when I leave my business stuff all over the living room." *And clean up the kitchen*, he mentally added but didn't want to point that out in case Sienna hadn't noticed. He set the bag of nail polish dryers on top of the pile on the coffee table.

Joel left the front door open as he searched among the stacks of merchandise for a Davco jewelry cleaner; the open door being a sign that they wouldn't stay long.

"Teddy bears?" Sienna questioned, staring at two teddy bears propped up on the low cabinet under the television. "Those must be your sister's," she noted.

"Uh... actually, I bought them as decorations. One for me and one for Ryn. I was inspired by a friend's house."

"Well, your decorating skills leave something to be desired," she teased.

Sienna walked further into the apartment to an open doorway off the dining room. "This must be your room. More boxes."

"I found it," he announced, holding out a boxed jewelry cleaner to Sienna.

Gretchen stood close enough to Joel's apartment that she could see him through the open doorway, but far enough that she couldn't hear the conversation. He appeared to be talking to the girl who was out of sight.

Sienna ignored the box and walked into his bedroom. "Yep, you're definitely not much for decorating." The walls were bare. No pictures, posters, or art of any kind.

"I just hadn't gotten around to it. Here's the jewelry cleaner," he said, once again holding out the box. This time she took it.

Sienna sat down on the foot of the bed; the bed that Joel now realized was not made, a task he often skipped when Ryn wasn't home to nag him about it. He kicked the pile of yesterday's clothes under the bed in case Sienna hadn't yet noticed.

"Are you sure you don't want to hang out longer?" she asked, leaning back on the bed, propped up on her elbows.

For a moment, the idea that a hot girl wanted to hang out with him pulled him towards agreement. But the image of the mess – both business and personal – and knowledge of Ryn's reaction when she came home to the mess, and the fact that it was a school night, overtook his willingness to hang out with Sienna. He pictured her angry mother complaining about his bad influence. "Come on. Your mom will be worried if we take too long. And I've still got to put all my stuff away before Ryn sees it."

"I just wanted to see your bedroom," she said as if that made the intrusion acceptable. She stood up and looked around as if studying the details. Flattened cardboard boxes leaning against a wall, rolls of packing tape on the dresser, and a box of office supplies on the desk next to a printer.

"Maybe you can come back another time when everything is straightened up," Joel offered.

Sienna finally directed her attention to the jewelry cleaner. She held it up and turned the box to see the product photo and description printed on it. "You know, I think my mom has one of these jewelry cleaners in her room. I just never knew what that thing was until seeing the picture on this box. I should pass on this until I confirm it with my mom."

Gretchen watched as they finally emerged from the apartment. When Joel locked the door, she broke from her surveillance and resumed the walk to her apartment.

Chapter 16
Stranded

Ty listened to music while cleaning the kitchen Wednesday night. Sophie walked in to return a cup that had somehow made its way to the living room.

"I don't know why Emi and John can't remember to take their cups to the sink when they're done."

Ty walked up behind her put his arms around her waist and started swaying to the music. Sophie smiled and let out a soft hum that signaled her enjoyment. Ty turned her around to face him and held her again, once more swaying to the music.

"Saturday night. You. Me. Dancing," he said.

Sophie leaned her face against his shoulder. "Sounds nice. Are Anna and her boyfriend in town?"

"No. We don't need them to go dancing. This will be a date night with just you and me."

"I like that. Are we going back to the Empire Ballroom?"

"Yes. With that, we'll be caught up with Emi's dances."

"What do you mean?" Sophie asked.

"I've been to four father-daughter dances with Emi. And I've only gone dancing with you three times. I should be dancing more with my wife than my sister-in-law."

"Definitely. Can we have dinner out beforehand?"

"Sure. And I know the place that will make you happy."

Sophie gave him a puzzled look.

"Naija Love Kitchen," he announced.

Sophie gave a little squeal, followed by a big smile, followed by a squeeze. "Nigerian food and country dancing. You know how to please a girl." She paused before adding, "Do you know who else likes Nigerian food and dancing?"

"Who?"

"Aunt Ruth and Ayo. We should invite them."

"Uh, okay. But isn't Ruth seven months pregnant?"

"She can still eat. And she can decide for herself if she wants to dance or not. And it gives Ayo an excuse to wear his cowboy hat."

Ty chuckled at the last remark. "Okay, call your aunt. But tell her that if she has that baby on the dance floor, she has to name him after something related to the song that's playing."

"Hm. 'Whiskey Diya' has a nice ring to it," she laughed.

* * *

Late Saturday morning, Emi saw a message flash on the screen of her phone. It was from Joel to both her and Annie. A minute later, Emi called out from her upstairs bedroom to Sophie, who was cleaning the downstairs hallway bathroom.

"Joel asked me to go with him to get his sister from the Dallas airport."

"Airport?" Sophie shouted back.

"Yeah."

"Where is she coming from?"

"Dallas."

"Okay," Sophie acknowledged, brushing the toilet bowl with chemicals.

"It'll take a while," Emi warned.

"So, I guess you'll be eating lunch out?"

"Yes."

"Okay. Keep me posted if things change," Sophie said while spraying the outside of the toilet bowl with disinfectant.

"Okay," Emi finished the shouted conversation.

Within minutes, Joel pulled up in his sister's Volkswagen Atlas and Emi was out the door.

"Nice Halloween decorations," Joel commented. "I like the witch that crashed into the tree. I sold a few of those online a few weeks ago."

"We've had that one for years. I call her Rosemary."

As he pulled the vehicle away from the curb, Emi stated, "What about Annie?"

"She called to say her parents wouldn't let her come."

"Sorry. I know you're disappointed," Emi teased.

"I didn't think either of you would be able to come, so I'm just happy you said 'yes' and can keep me company. And awake."

"That almost sounds believable."

"What do you mean 'believable'? Do you still think Annie and I have a thing?"

"Well, there's the kissing."

"You're still bringing that up? It's just on the cheek. And it's to keep the illusion going. I don't think it should count as anything serious."

"Everyone else thinks it's serious."

"I spent the night at your house. A sleepover. Wouldn't that make things even? And I've already told you that I like hanging out with both of you."

"Sleeping in the same house isn't the same as a kiss," she continued teasing.

At the traffic light, Joel leaned over towards Emi with pursed lips, but couldn't quite reach her.

Emi leaned away. "What are you doing?"

"Trying to make it even between you and Annie."

"Just watch the road. The light's green."

As Joel pulled forward through the intersection on the way out of the neighborhood, he reached out with his right hand and patted Emi's left breast.

Emi opened her mouth in momentary shock and uttered a gasp as she turned to look at Joel, trying to process what just happened. Then, without warning, she backhanded him hard across his face. He involuntarily jerked the steering wheel and swerved a bit before the car behind honked its horn and changed lanes to pass.

"Don't touch me like that again," Emi said sternly.

"I'm sorry. It was a joke."

"Touching my boob is not a joke."

"Since I couldn't give you a kiss on your cheek, I was trying to be funny," he defended. "I'm sorry," he repeated before pulling into a crossover in the median and making a U-turn.

"What are you doing?" Emi asked.

"Taking you back home."

"Why?"

"Because you're mad. I don't think you'd want to go with me now."

"No more boob grabbing, understand?"

"Yes." He touched his mouth where his upper lip was starting to swell. "You made your point."

"Good. Let's go get Ryn."

He looked at her in disbelief.

"Pay attention to the road," Emi warned.

Joel made another U-turn to head back to the highway.

* * *

As they passed Navasota, Emi lowered her window, put her arm out, and waved. Joel was about to ask what that was about when Emi explained, "My aunt and uncle live near here."

"Near the highway?"

"No, but it's our tradition to wave when we go through Navasota." This was only the second time a Jensen family member had waved while passing Navasota. If doing something twice made it a tradition, Emi's current action effectively made it so. "They're having a baby, so I'll be an aunt soon."

"If she's *your* aunt, you can't be the baby's aunt. You'll be a cousin."

"Oh. But I'll be fifteen years older than the baby. That's more like an aunt."

"It's still a cousin."

Emi looked disappointed. "Can we stop for lunch soon? I skipped breakfast today."

"We're almost to College Station. We can stop there. My favorite food place in College Station is Firepit Fajitas. Ryn and I go there when passing through."

* * *

As they sat in the booth waiting for their food order to be called, Emi noted, "Your lip's swollen."

Joel reflexively touched the injured lip.

"I'm sorry I hit you so hard," she added

"It was a pec peck."

"What?"

I used to have a girlfriend. Kayleigh. We broke up last year. Sometimes she...uh...." His voice trailed off.

"She what?"

"Never mind."

"No. You started it. What were you about to say?"

"Sometimes when we sat next to each other and I had my arm around her shoulders, like at a movie...." He lifted his arm to mimic having it around his girlfriend. Then he lowered his arm and looked at the receipt that had the order number printed on it.

"And?" Emi questioned, prompting him to continue.

"Sometimes, she would grab my hand that was on her shoulder, and she would push it down onto her boob. She called it a pec peck. The first 'pec' is p-e-c, for pectoral. The second 'peck' is p-e-c-k, as in a quick kiss. So, I didn't think what I did would be so...." He paused, searching for the right word; "...that it would make you mad." He quickly added, "But I get it now."

"Did y'all do that in front of her parents?"

"No."

"In front of *your* parents?"

"No."

"Why not?"

"Um... I get it."

"And I'm not your girlfriend unless you forgot to tell me something."

"How many times do I have to say I'm sorry?"

"Once is enough if you're sincere. And you're the one who started talking about it again."

Joel was relieved that their order was called at that moment. He quickly rose to get their food from the counter.

He waited for Emi to take a bite from her taco before asking, "Have you ever had a boyfriend?" The corners of his mouth turned up in the slightest of smiles as he knew she had to finish chewing before she could answer.

Emi raised her eyebrows and pointed to her mouth. Eventually, she responded, "Does a crush count?"

"Did the guy know you had a crush on him?"

"No."

"You don't seem shy; why didn't you do something about it?"

"He was too old for me. It wouldn't have worked out."

* * *

Once they were seated in the SUV with refilled drinks safely stowed in the cupholders of the center console, Joel asked, "Do you have a playlist you want to listen to on the way?" After asking, he shifted into reverse and began to back out of the parking space.

"Sure." Emi rummaged through her sling-style backpack. "I can't find my phone," she said, sounding alarmed. She began looking on the floor by her feet and then in the crevice between the seat and the center console.

"Can you call it?" she asked.

Joel's response was not what Emi was expecting. He began singing, "Call me please; I can't find my phone." It was the second line of the Francesca Battistelli song.

Emi looked at him with her mouth open, unsure of his mental state.

"Sorry. It's a family thing," Joel said as if that explained his sudden musical outburst. He pulled the car back into the parking space. "I don't think I've seen you use it today," he said before pulling up her number on his phone. "Did you have it in the restaurant?"

"No. At least, I don't remember looking at it." She thought for a moment. "The last time I used it was back home, texting you."

"It's ringing," Joel said, holding up his phone. "But I don't hear your phone making any sound. I don't think it's here."

After checking inside the restaurant, they returned to the car.

As they pulled back onto the road, Joel asked, "How did you bring a bag, but not your phone?"

"I was texting you, and I must have set it down on my bed. When I'm home I don't keep it in my bag."

"At least you're not one of those girls who stare at her phone when she's with other people."

When riding with Ty and Sophie, Emi would be on her phone nearly the entire time. But on the ride with Joel, she hadn't even tried to pull out her phone; they just talked the whole time or sang along with the radio.

"What'll I do without my phone?" Emi asked, unable to imagine being disconnected for a day.

"We can't go back for it. That'll delay us two and a half hours. Didn't you tell your sister where we're going?"

"Yes."

"And that it'll take a while?"

"Yes. I told her we were going to pick up your sister at the Dallas airport. She should know how long that takes since we drive to Dallas every year at Christmas to visit my grandparents."

"You can handle being without a phone for a few hours," Joel said encouragingly. "Did you bring an empty backpack?"

"No. It's got my wallet, some girl stuff, and a couple of books."

"Books? Were you planning to make me drive in silence while you read a book?"

"No. If we ran out of things to talk about, I was going to read to you."

"Read to me? What books did you bring?"

"*Smart Girls Get What They Want*. It's about a smart nerdy high school girl trying to get a boyfriend."

"Uh. That does not sound like my kind of story."

"Annie would've appreciated it. I didn't think you'd like it, so I also grabbed one of Sophie's books."

"And what's that one about, a college girl trying to find a boyfriend?"

"No. This one's called *Hidden Threat*. It's about an environmental investigator falling in love with the son of a Florida rancher she's investigating."

"So, the choices are a crime story romance or a high school romance."

"Sorry, I didn't have much time to look around. I'll go with the crime story because the woman is Black and the guy is White."

"Are you hinting at something with the Black/White thing?"

"Noooo." She drew out the word. "But it's a theme that runs in my family."

Their journey would take them up Highway 6 to Waco and, from there, switching to I-35 for the final leg into the Dallas-Fort Worth area. When they crossed the city line between College Station and Bryan, Joel lowered his window. At Martin Luther King Street, he put his arm out of the window and waved.

"What's that about?"

"Just waving to someone I know who lives over there," Joel explained

"A relative?"

"Distant relative."

Before she had a chance to ask further about his relative, he asked, "Do you want to start reading or do you want to just listen to music for a while?"

* * *

Sophie walked into the house carrying several bags of groceries. "Guess who I ran into at the grocery store," she said to Ty.

"Who?"

"Mrs. Bates."

"The geometry teacher?"

"No, that's Mrs. Barnes. I'm talking about Annie's mother."

"Oh. How is she doing?"

"She asked if I let Emi go to Dallas today with Joel. Apparently, he asked both Annie and Emi to go to Dallas with him, and Annie's mother wouldn't let her go."

"Is Emi with Joel now? Did you let her go?"

"She asked if she could go with Joel to pick up his sister from the airport," Sophie explained. "I didn't know she meant the airport in Dallas."

"Why didn't his sister fly to Houston?" Ty asked.

"Mrs. Bates said his sister lost her purse, including her driver's license, and couldn't get on the flight back to Houston. "Then she practically scolded me for letting Emi go, said she thought it was irresponsible. She blamed me for Annie getting into an argument with her. She said she had to take Annie's phone away as punishment. 'Had to', like she had no choice."

"Forget about Annie's mother. Think back. Did Emi tell you she was going to Dallas?"

"She said the word 'Dallas', but I wasn't paying close attention. I thought she meant Bush airport and that the sister was coming from Dallas. But maybe I heard wrong. Anyway, I called Emi's phone and it just went to voice mail."

Ty pulled out his phone and opened the app that tracked the movements of all the family members. "This shows she's at home."

He headed upstairs to Emi's room with Sophie following behind. Once in her room, he called her phone. A muffled buzzing came from the direction of her bed.

"There," Sophie pointed. Emi's phone was laying on the tummy of the life-size teddy bear that was on the bed.

"Do you have Joel's number?" Ty asked.

"No." Sophie picked up Emi's phone and touched the screen to wake it up and display the login screen. She tried several combinations of numbers.

"I don't know her password."

She held the phone up to her face and clicked the link to see if she could fool the phone into interpreting her face as Emi's.

"It's not working."

"Wait here," Ty said. He left and returned a moment later with a photo of Emi that had been hanging on the stairway wall. He held it up.

"Hold the phone up to the picture and see if it will think it's Emi."

Sophie tried the phone's face ID feature again, this time with the photo. She shook her head. "It's too smart for us."

"Okay. When did they leave?"

"Around eleven."

"It takes around four hours to get to Dallas," Ty estimated. "That's eight hours round trip. Add a couple of hours for meals and we're looking at ten hours. So, she should be back about nine."

"She's gonna be in so much trouble when she gets back."

"For what? She thinks you gave her permission."

"I didn't know she was going to Dallas," Sophie defended.

"But you said you weren't paying attention and she might have said Dallas."

"Well, she'll be in trouble for forgetting her phone while going to Dallas."

Ty shook his head in disagreement. "I'm sure she didn't forget it on purpose. Should we cancel our date night to wait for her?"

"No. She'll still be awake when we get back. We can deal with her then."

"I think most kids would think being without a phone is enough punishment. At least, Mrs. Bates thinks so. And don't take your anger out on Emi because you're mad at Annie's mom."

* * *

On the interstate between Waco and Dallas, just past Hillsboro, construction debris fell from a truck ahead of them. Joel swerved into the right lane to avoid the debris, but it bounced into his lane as if determined to interrupt the drive. Joel couldn't help but run over it and as soon as he did, they heard a loud bang. Emi let out a scream and the car began shaking. Joel pulled onto the right shoulder of the road and shut off the engine.

"Are you okay?" Joel asked.

"I should be asking you that. I'm fine. It just scared me."

They both got out to look at the damage. Both tires on the right side had blown out.

"What do we do now?" Emi asked.

They looked around at the landscape and, except for a lone gas station about a half-mile behind them, saw only farmland that continued for miles.

"What about that gas station?" Emi asked.

"It's just gas pumps and a store. I don't see a repair shop. We passed a Walmart a little way back. We can take one of the wheels there to get a new tire and use the spare tire for the other one."

They removed the spare tire from under the vehicle and used it to replace the rear wheel.

"It looks a little squishy," Emi stated.

"We can put more air in at a gas station. Alright, now for the front tire."

It took almost an hour to roll the tire to Walmart. By the time they got there, it was almost four o'clock. The staff let them jump the queue since they had only a wheel without the car. Joel called his sister to explain the delay. At four twenty, they were rolling the new tire back up the interstate to the Atlas.

By five-thirty, they had replaced the wheel.

"The back tire looks more deflated than before," Emi observed, pointing to the spare they had put on before the trip to Walmart.

Joel sighed. "I'll drive slow to the gas station."

They took the next exit and doubled back to the gas station they saw earlier. Joel added air to the spare tire, then went into the convenience store of the gas station for a restroom break and to buy drinks for the road. Upon returning to the car, Emi pointed to the tire they had just inflated.

"It looks like it lost air again."

"That's not gonna last," Joel stated. "We'll have to get another tire."

They reinflated the spare and drove slowly to the Walmart that had replaced the other tire.

By the time they got to Walmart, it was six o'clock. The tire center closed at five. Joel tried the door to the automotive area, but it was locked. He peered through the window of the door but didn't see anyone. The automotive center was deserted.

Joel walked back to the SUV and reached in to get the drink he had purchased at the gas station. He took a sip and just stared at the three overhead garage doors of the closed automotive center.

"Joel?" Emi called softly.

Joel took another sip, then suddenly threw his drink at the middle garage door, where the Styrofoam cup burst open and spilled its contents on the pavement. Then he let loose a flurry of expletives.

Emi froze at the sudden outburst, waiting to see if there would be more to Joel's tantrum. When it was clear he was done, she reached into the vehicle for her own soft drink. She stepped a few paces towards the building and hurled her cup at the garage door, yelling, "Yeah! What he said!" The cup fell short of the door and some of her beverage splattered onto Joel's shoes.

It took a second for Joel to realize Emi was mocking him. "I'm sorry Emi. It's Saturday evening. There's nowhere else open to get a new tire, and I don't think we can keep stopping at every gas station to add air. From here to the Dallas airport and back to Cypress is a long drive. We're stuck here."

"Attacking the building felt good for about two seconds," Emi responded, "but now we're stuck here without drinks."

Joel moved the Volkswagen away from the garage and parked it at the edge of the parking lot, adjacent to a field of wheat. Then he called Ryn to let her know about the tire situation. "It's not my fault. I didn't dump the junk on the road," Emi heard Joel say.

"Well, if the spare tire worked, we'd be there by now."

…

"The spare's not my fault either. It's your car. You should have a good spare." She continued to listen to Joel's side of the conversation.

…

"Okay. How are you getting back to his apartment, I thought you lost your wallet?"

…

"Well, I've never had to use the Uber app. At least you'll have a decent bed."

…

"I'm sixteen. No one's gonna rent me a car." *Especially in a small farm town.*

…

"Yeah. I'll let you know what we figure out."

After Joel ended his call with his sister, he handed the phone to Emi. "You should call your parents; I mean, your sister or Ty."

Emi took the phone. She put in the area code and stopped.

"I don't remember their numbers."

"Are you kidding? I had to memorize my parents' numbers when I was in kindergarten."

"I still know my parents' numbers and they died four years ago. I just don't know Sophie's or Ty's. No one remembers phone numbers after they get their own phones."

"Do you know anyone else's numbers?" he asked.

She used Joel's phone to access her Snapchat account and sent Sophie a snap, providing Joel's phone number. She knew that Sophie didn't have her notifications turned on and knew from experience that Sophie didn't check Snapchat very often. It might be a while before Sophie saw the message.

Joel called Annie but ended up leaving a message. He texted as well, asking her to relay a message to Emi's sister. No response.

Emi decided to use Joel's phone to create a YouTube video and posted it to her Jentler Hair channel. It was an explanation of the situation and appeal to any fans who knew where she lived to go to her house and tell the family what was going on.

"Tell them to check Snapchat," she appealed to her fans, "because I put Joel's phone number in a chat."

* * *

A silver sedan pulled up to the Jensen residence and a preteen girl with box braids hopped out of the passenger side. She ran up to the door and rang the doorbell. Even before ringing, she could tell no one was home. Several notes were attached to the door, either by their own adhesive or were wedged into the crack between the door and the door jam. The girl walked back to the car.

"No one's home," she told her mother.

"Do you want to leave a note? There's some paper in the glove compartment."

"No. Several people already left notes on the door."

"Why don't you leave Emi a comment on the video so she knows you tried."

Sophie was out shopping, Ty was at his parents' house down the street, John was with friends, and Alia was working. The family generally used the back door, so the notes on the front door went unnoticed.

* * *

"We'll probably be back after eleven," Sophie told John as she and Ty were getting ready to leave for their date night. "When Emi gets in, tell her she's in trouble for not letting us know where she is. She could have at least called us on Joel's phone to let us know her status."

"Just let her know we were concerned," Ty added, getting a scowl from Sophie.

In response to the scowl, Ty ran his hand lightly up Sophie's back, then slid it over to her armpit, where he gave her a little tickle.

She jumped and yelled, "Hey!" with a laugh, but trying to sound serious at the same time. "Emi's situation is…"

Ty tickled her again.

"Stop!" she said with a giggle that she tried desperately to control. "I'm serious."

"We can talk to Emi about it tonight or we can skip our date and just sit around here looking grumpy," Ty admonished.

"Fine. Let's go," Sophie stated without cheer.

"It sounds like you're still grumpy." Ty pulled her in for a hug with both arms, but instead of the comforting embrace, he tickled her under both arms.

John watched Sophie's contortions with amusement. "Y'all are not normal. Mom and Dad never acted like that."

"Not around you, they didn't," Ty pointed out, after releasing Sophie.

"I know where your tickle spots are, too, you know," Sophie told Ty, ignoring John.

"The proper response is to give me a kiss and promise that you won't complain about Emi's lack of phone responsibility until we get home tonight."

Sophie kissed Ty and stated, "I promise." She paused before adding, "At least until we're on the way home."

"Close enough," Ty stated, winking at John.

John uttered, "Ugh," while shaking his head.

* * *

"Anything?" Joel asked before taking another bite of his sandwich.

"No. If Sophie got the message, she'd call your phone." She said that as she held up his phone.

"Then what are you checking?"

"YouTube comments. A couple of people said they went to my house and left notes on the door. Others just commented about being sorry for the situation. One said she lives in Hillsboro, and she asked her parents to let us stay with them, but her dad said no. That would be kind of awkward, anyway."

"More awkward than sleeping in the car in the Walmart parking lot?" Joel asked.

"Do you think that's what we'll have to do?"

"It's nighttime, your sister hasn't called, and it's about a three-hour drive from your house. I think we'll have to."

Emi pressed her lips together and nodded as if accepting their fate. Finally, she asked, "Are you done eating?"

"Yeah, I'm done." Joel gathered up the empty sandwich wrappers and chip bags and stood up. "Let's go buy pillows at Walmart."

* * *

"Put the Walmart stuff on the front seat for now," Joel directed. "We need to fold down the back seats for sleeping."

After folding down the seats, they sat on opposite sides of the cargo area, leaning against the opposite walls, legs extended towards each other.

"I don't know why you just had to buy a blanket. It's still hot outside," Joel pointed out.

"I checked the weather app earlier. It'll cool down. Later you'll thank me for getting the blanket."

* * *

When Alia got home from work in the evening, she noticed a dark square on the window of the front door. She opened the door to investigate, and several pieces of paper fell to the floor. She pulled the sticky note from the window, gathered up the papers on the floor, and closed the door.

After reading the messages, she sent a text to Sophie.

> Alia:
> Hi Sophie. Hope u r enjoying your date. People left notes for u on the front door. One has a phone number on it and says 'Call' and the others say to check your Snapchat

* * *

"Any messages?" Emi asked again.

"Still nothing. I can't believe Annie hasn't called or texted," Joel stated. "Did she lose her phone, too?"

"Or she broke it. Again. When it comes to phones, she's a bit clumsy."

Joel put his phone down again, careful not to tangle the charging cable.

"Homecoming is in a few weeks," Emi pointed out.

"Yeah. Are you going?"

"You need to ask Annie."

"Do we have to have dates, or can we just go as a group?"

"You need to ask Annie."

"What if I want to ask someone else?"

"I'll help you make a poster for your proposal. To Annie. We need to think of a clever line."

"How about, 'Annie, will you go to homecoming with me?' Short and simple."

"And boring."

"You know we're not really dating, right? It's just a long-running joke among us three. But, if I'm going with Annie, who will you go with?"

"I'll find a friend later."

"So, you're gonna ask a guy?"

"Sure. Why not?"

"I haven't heard you talk about any guys."

"I'll figure it out. By the way, you can dance, can't you?"

"My parents made me go to Cotillion, so, yeah, I can dance."

"Sophie did that, but John and I didn't. My parents died before it was our turn to go, and we didn't bring it up."

Joel pulled up music on his phone and climbed out of the SUV. He held out his hand to Emi.

"Seriously? In the parking lot?"

"This one's a waltz. Come on. This may be the last time your sister lets me do anything with you," he lamented. "At least give me one dance."

She gave him several.

* * *

Ty watched his wife doing the Texas Two-Step with Ayo on the crowded dance floor. At the sight of Ayo twirling Sophie, Ty turned to his own dance partner and asked, "Have you and Ayo been practicing at home?"

"Of course. It's part of that — what's that word you used? — 'Texification' process," she replied. She lifted her left hand, the hand holding Ty's. "Twirl me."

He twirled her.

"Are you sure you should be doing this in your condition, eight months pregnant?" Ty asked.

"That's the third time tonight you pointed that out," Ruth said. "When will you and Sophie start having babies?"

"We have plenty of time. We're waiting until she finishes school and gets in a couple of years with a job."

"Don't wait until you're as old as us."

"I don't think that'll be a problem for Sophie, and she'll keep me young."

At 10:30 the foursome left the ballroom for the parking lot, early by dance club standards. Sophie finally looked at her phone and saw Alia's message. She called Alia.

"Is Emi home?" Sophie asked Alia.

"She's not here."

"Do you have Joel's number?"

"No, but the notes say you need to check your Snapchat. I'll send you a pic of the note with the phone number."

* * *

Emi and Joel lay down in the back of the SUV with their feet towards the open cargo door, shoes off. Emi covered herself with the blanket and rolled onto her right side to look at Joel. "Tell me about your parents."

Joel looked at Emi briefly then looked out across the parking lot to a family loading bags from a shopping cart into the back seat of a pickup.

"Do you think it's strange that a family with little kids would be out this late shopping?" Joel asked. "I mean, if they need groceries for tomorrow, why not just have one of the parents do the shopping? The other parent could watch the kids at home and put them to bed."

"Maybe they don't get out much and this is their entertainment."

He watched the family until they got into the truck and closed the doors. "Hypocrites."

"What?"

"My parents are hypocrites. Dad was a deacon at church. Mom taught Sunday school. Now they're both in jail for lying about company finances."

"Everyone at church is a hypocrite," Emi stated.

"That's kind of a cynical view. I thought you liked church."

"I do. We have these high standards, but no one can meet them all the time. At some point, no matter how good you try to be, you're going to screw up. It doesn't mean you shouldn't have the standards."

"You didn't seem surprised when I told you my parents were in jail."

"Annie's dad recognized your last name from the news. Vaclavik's not that common. Something about a company that went bankrupt because the people cheated or something. And you were kind of secretive about your family."

"Ryn told me one of the business classes at Baylor talked about the case. Her friends in that class asked her about it. 'Moral failings.' That's what they called it in class. My parents' moral failings are part of a college class. It's embarrassing."

Emi extended her left arm out from under the blanket and touched his arm. "It's their moral failing, not yours."

"I feel like my mom got pulled into the whole scheme because of my dad; that she wouldn't have covered up for him if he hadn't pushed her. He got them both in trouble. Family friends stopped talking to us. My friends stopped inviting me to things. By the end of last school year, I was ready to move to a school where people didn't know me. I used to want to be like my dad. Now I don't want anything to do with him."

They heard voices in the distance of a couple talking as they left the store and walked to their car. Too far to hear the conversation, but close enough to hear the woman laugh.

"I would give anything to have my parents back," Emi said.

A light breeze blew a plastic shopping bag across their view through the open cargo door. Joel reached over to the edge of Emi's blanket and pulled it over to cover himself as well as her. She pulled her arm back under the blanket.

"Aren't you glad I made you get this?" she asked, referring to the blanket.

Joel rolled onto his side and looked at her for several seconds before nodding. The distant parking lot lamps provided a dim light, but not enough to see the details of Emi's face. Still, he stared, remembering what she looked like in the light.

"What?" Emi asked, unable to stand the silence.

"What if I want to take you?" Joel asked in a whisper.

"Take me where?" she whispered back.

Joel reached over to touch her face, the left side at the hairline above her ear. Her hair was pulled back into a puff behind her head, but he imagined he was pushing a lock of hair out of her face.

"To homecoming," he answered in a barely audible reply.

Emi put her hand over his and pressed it to her cheek.

He leaned his face closer until their foreheads touched. She closed her eyes, not that she could see much with them open.

"I don't want to hurt Annie," Emi whispered back. She shifted her head and felt her nose slide by his. It was a slight movement, but just enough to bring their lips together. She kissed him. Or did he kiss her? It was hard to tell. The warm feeling that spread from her lips, across her face, and throughout her body didn't care who initiated it. She moved her hand – the one holding his to her face – over to his neck. She could feel his pulse; his heart was beating fast. So was hers.

They were both startled when Joel's phone chimed. Joel pulled the phone out from under the blanket and looked at the number displayed on the screen. He didn't recognize it. He handed the phone to Emi.

"Hi," Emi said, rolling onto her back.

The phone was not set to speaker mode, but Joel could still hear the agitation in the caller's voice.

"Sophie, you don't have to yell. I can hear you just fine. We're at a Walmart in Hillsboro."

....

"I didn't leave my phone on purpose."

....

"I don't have your phone number memorized."

....

"Yeah?" Now Emi sounded irritated. "What's my number?"

....

"See? Don't lecture me about not knowing your number."

....

"Past Waco on the way to Dallas."

....

"It's not my fault the tires blew out."

....

"It's not Joel's fault either. Some stuff fell off a truck right in front of us on the highway and we ran over it. He couldn't help it."

....

"So, what do you want me to do, walk home?"

....

"Hi, Ty. Joel's fine."

....

"No! I didn't run away with Joel!"

....

"Oh, sorry. After Sophie's attitude, I couldn't tell you were joking. We were supposed to go get his sister and come back by nine or so."

....

"Remind Sophie about Sedona; that we had to call the police to find y'all. And at least we smell better."

....

"Okay. See you in a few hours. Bye."

Emi laid the phone on the blanket covering Joel's chest and pulled her arm back under the blanket.

"Does that mean they're coming to get us?" Joel asked.

"Yeah. Sophie's booking a hotel room around here. They'll stay with us until we get a new tire."

"I'm sorry I dragged you into this mess. I ruined everyone's weekend. Annie's probably glad she couldn't come."

"I know this will sound weird, but I'm glad I came. I had a good time with you." Under the blanket, Emi slid her right hand down her thigh until it rested on the cargo floor between her and Joel, palm against her thigh.

She spoke again. "That was my first."

"First what?"

"My first kiss."

"Thank you for not hitting me."

She flicked her index finger against his leg in response.

Joel slid his left hand down so the backs of their hands touched. He extended his pinky finger and hooked it around Emi's pinky. She curled hers around his to lock them together and turned her face to look at him. The warm feeling returned.

"What was that about Sedona?" he asked.

Chapter 17
~Stumbling in the dark~

Previous June – vacation day five, evening

"What's this place called? Castle Rock?" John asked as they pulled into the parking area at the base of the trail.

"Cathedral Rock," Alia corrected.

"I don't care what it's called, as long as we get there for sunset," Sophie commented. "I want pics that will make the girls jealous."

"What girls?" John asked.

"She's talking about her college mates. No one who'd be interested in you," Emi commented.

Alia smiled and stifled a chuckle.

"Hey, you don't have to be rude. I don't need to look for girls. I've got Lizzie."

Alia and Annie looked at each other and smiled.

"There is much climbing here," Kumiko observed.

Ty looked down at Kumiko's bandaged ankle. At Slide Rock earlier in the day, Kumiko took the bandage off to get her feet wet in the water. Her ankle was still swollen and purple.

"I don't think we can do the piggyback rides on the rocks."

"No problem. I will walk on flat trail with this." She wiggled her crutch. "When you climb on rocks, I go back to car."

"What about Kenji and Jun?"

"Is okay they go with you?"

Ty looked towards the head of the trail where the family members were gathering. "Yes. I think they'll be fine since their bodyguard will be with them."

"Bodyguard? You are bodyguard?"

Ty pointed to Kumiko's mother.

"Ah. *Wakarimashita.* My mother is bodyguard."

Ty smiled. "She can bring her umbrella."

The climb was not difficult for able-bodied persons, but Kumiko was smart to turn back when the group began scrambling up the rocks. The others continued their trek to the line where the sloping base of the butte met with its vertical walls. Dozens of hikers gathered on the western side of the "cathedral" to get photos of the sunset, forming an unruly line at the most scenic spots, as they waited for their turns to pose. The pink clouds and lavender sky provided a photogenic backdrop to the valley of rocks, cacti and scrub brushes; a scene that all the hikers wanted to capture for their vacation memories.

Immediately after sunset, all of the Jentler/Moriguchi crew but Sophie and Ty headed back down. Sophie had picked a particular outcropping of rock for a couple's selfie, but they had to wait for other hikers to vacate the spot as the lavender sky darkened to purple. Looking at the photo on her phone, she smiled.

"Look at this," she told Ty, holding up her phone for him to see. "The view is gorgeous. It was worth it."

"It's only gorgeous because of the woman in the picture." That earned him a kiss.

"Okay. I'm satisfied now," she said. "Let's hurry back before it gets too dark."

They made it off the rocks in the dim light, but at the base, they had to use the light from their phones to see the trail. The howls of distant coyotes greeted the night. Eventually, Ty and Sophie came to an intersection in the trail where they had to turn either right or left.

"It's this way," Ty pointed to the right.

"This doesn't look right. I think it's the other way."

"No," he corrected. "We turn right here and a little further down, we'll make a left."

"I think what you're thinking of is a place we already passed," she said. "This is where we turn left."

She couldn't see his exasperated expression when he asked, "Can you just trust me in this?"

Sophie started walking down the left-hand trail. "You'd better keep up or you'll get lost."

Ty ran up in front of her, picked her up and threw her over his shoulder. Then he turned around and walked the opposite way.

"You're going the wrong way," Sophie insisted. "Put me down!"

After about two minutes of walking, and several brushes of thorny bushes against his bare legs, Ty put her down.

"I can't do this. You keep wiggling and throwing me off balance. You'll have to walk."

"You've carried me lots of times. Are you saying I've gained weight?"

"No, I'm saying you wiggle too much, it's been a long day, and I'm just too tired."

"If I have to walk, then I'm going to walk in the *right* direction."

"It's the wrong direction," he insisted.

"We'll come find you later," she said.

Ty gave up arguing. "Fine, I'll go with you, and we can get lost together."

* * *

"Where are they?" Emi complained. She looked at her phone for the millionth time and the screen still showed no signal. "I'm hungry."

"Sophie's probably making Ty take nighttime pictures with cactuses," John said.

"Cacti," Emi corrected.

"Huh?"

"The plural of cactus is cacti," Emi explained.

"What's the plural of hungry?" John asked.

"Hungi?" Alia offered. "We have snacks in the car."

"Wait. Where are Kenji and Jun?" Emi asked.

"They left twenty minutes ago," Annie said.

"I thought Ms. Kumiko couldn't drive," Emi said.

"She said her foot was good enough to drive now," John pointed out. "Kenji and Jun were acting up and she said she needed to go back to the hotel for dinner and to put them to bed. She said she'll see us tomorrow before we leave."

The calls of the coyotes rang out in the darkness.

"Should we go look for Sophie and Ty?" Alia said. "It's getting late."

* * *

The flashlight on Ty's phone shut off abruptly. He tapped the screen to wake it up. Nothing. "My phone just died. How much power do you have?"

"Three percent," Sophie responded. "And still no cell service."

"Do you hear something? Like people shouting?"

"I hear something, too. But it's very far away. I think it came from that direction," she pointed, not that Ty could see her gesture.

"Your phone light still works, so lead the way," Ty directed.

* * *

"Are you sure this is the way back to the Cathedral Rock?" Annie asked.

The four teenagers had been searching for thirty minutes, calling out Sophie's and Ty's names as they walked. They were at the fifth stop to reassess the direction when Annie made her inquiry.

"I think so, but it's so dark, I'm not even sure," John replied. "Does anyone else know?"

The movement of something on the ground caught their attention and they shined their lights onto the path. A black and gray snake slithered across the trail in front of them.

"I'm done," Emi announced. She turned toward the direction they had come.

"Yeah, we should go back, or we'll get lost, too," Alia warned. "We need to get help."

* * *

"Now both our phones are dead and my legs are scratched up," Sophie stated. "I'm sorry. I should have taken your advice."

"Wait. I'd record that if my phone wasn't dead."

"Then you can't record this either." Sophie leaned over and kissed him.

"Was that an apology kiss? At least, if I'm going to be lost, I've got the company of a hot babe. If I wasn't so exhausted, I'd take you right now." He removed his backpack and dropped it on the ground. "As it is, I'm gonna sit down," he said as he lowered himself to the ground and leaned against a boulder. Sophie sat beside him. Ty took a water bottle out of his backpack and handed it to Sophie. He pulled out another for himself and guzzled half.

"Are you too exhausted to cuddle?" Sophie asked.

"Come on." He put his arm around her and pulled her close.

Ty chuckled.

"What's so funny?"

"We're both dirty and sweaty but your hair still smells good."

* * *

John left the others in the parking area while he drove out to find cell phone service. Halfway to Sedona, he got a signal, pulled over, and called 9-1-1. After explaining the situation to the emergency dispatcher, he drove back to the parking area. A few minutes later a park ranger and a sheriff's car pulled up.

The kids' relief at the arrival of the ranger and deputy ended with a demonic scream.

"Crap!" John cried out involuntarily and he and the girls ran to the SUV.

"Mountain lion," the park ranged stated. "She'll stay away from the parking area if she knows we're here. Just make your presence known."

John honked the Escalade's horn.

"I guess that'll work," the sheriff's deputy said, smiling.

* * *

"The stars are so bright," Sophie observed. "We can't see a sky like this from home. Nature can be so beautiful."

"Shh. I heard something," Ty said.

Sophie strained to hear it. "I hear shouting again way off. Still can't make out what it is."

A rustling sound came from nearby.

"No. Something's here. An animal," Ty stated.

"It could be a mountain lion. What do we do?" Sophie grabbed Ty's arm.

"Let's not panic. It's probably just a raccoon."

"I'm still scared."

Ty stood up and Sophie followed suit.

"I'll try to scare it away," he explained. He stepped towards the sound of the rustling and did his best to imitate a lion's roar.

Suddenly, they both felt a wet spray cover their arms, legs, and clothes. The wetness only registered to their senses after the strong pungent smell hit them. Sophie let out a scream.

Chapter 18
~The smell~

Hillsboro, early October

Despite Emi's interesting tale of Ty and Sophie getting lost in the wilderness, Joel couldn't hide his weariness. He yawned.

"Skunk?" he asked.

"Yeah. The smell was awful," Emi noted.

"That explains your comment to Ty about us smelling better. Then what happened?"

Sedona, Previous June

"Did you hear that?" the sheriff's deputy asked, upon hearing Sophie's scream.

"Yeah, it's west. They got way off course," the park ranger stated. "Now that we know a direction, let's pick up the pace."

"How well do you know these trails?"

"Like the back of my hand," the ranger responded.

"Maybe we should've let the kids come with us. We could spread out and cover more ground."

"Nah, we'd just end up having to search for two groups of lost people."

* * *

"Did it get in your face?" Ty asked.

"No, but it's everywhere else," Sophie whined.

"The shouting is getting louder."

"Hey! Over here!" Sophie called out.

Ty yelled, "Marco!"

"Marco? Really? You think we're in a swimming pool?"

"Polo!" came a distant shout in return.

It was too dark to see Sophie roll her eyes or Ty smile smugly.

* * *

"We're getting close," the ranger observed. "And their calls don't sound like they're in distress."

"What about that scream we heard?"

"That sounded more like a surprised scream than a hurt scream."

"If you say so," the deputy said. "I got the first aid kit, just in case. I just hope they can walk out."

* * *

At the last return of "Polo", Ty and Sophie could see the lights of the rescuers.

"We're over here!" Ty shouted, rather than the calls of "Marco" he and Sophie had been making.

"You don't need to shout anymore," the deputy called out. "We can smell you."

"Now we know why she screamed," the ranger noted.

The stranded couple was finally in sight of the rescuers.

"Oh, man, that's nasty!" the deputy stated. "That skunk got you good."

"At least the smell kept the mountain lions away," the ranger added.

* * *

When the rescued and the rescuers finally made it back to the parking area, the relief of those waiting quickly turned to disgust as the smell hit them.

"I'm glad you're not hurt or anything, but do we have to ride back with that smell?" John asked.

"Can they ride in the back of your truck?" Alia asked the park ranger.

"Can't do that," he replied. Looking at Ty and Sophie, he added, "I can give you a trash bag for your clothes."

Sophie started undressing in the parking lot.

"What are you doing?" Ty asked.

"I am not staying in these clothes, and I don't care who sees me."

Ty started stripping down, too.

"As entertaining as this is, I have other business," the deputy commented before turning towards his car.

"No more night hikes," the park ranger said as he opened the door to his truck. "And you may want to use baking soda and hydrogen peroxide to get rid of the smell, then wash it off with dish detergent," he added before closing the door and starting the engine.

"Thank you," Ty and Sophie said at the same time as they continued to remove their outer clothes. They stood in their underwear as the deputy and ranger drove away.

After removing everything from the pockets of their skunked clothes, Ty shoved the clothes into the trash bag and headed for the Escalade.

"Give me that," Sophie commanded, grabbing the bag before Ty could protest.

She hobbled barefoot across the gravel parking lot to a trash can and shoved the bag in.

They stopped at a 24-hour convenience store on the way back to the hotel for the non-stinky people to buy snacks to eat as dinner and buy dish soap, baking soda, and hydrogen peroxide for the smell.

* * *

Despite having discarded their clothes, the skunk smell permeated the room that John shared with Ty and Sophie. John propped the door open before climbing into his usual spot in the bed closest to the door and window. He lamented that the window did not open and hoped that by the time Ty and Sophie finished their deodorizing baths, the smell would dissipate.

Unfortunately, it didn't. It was weaker but still strong.

When Emi answered the insistent knocking on her door, she found John standing there, holding a pillow and bed covers.

"I can't stay there," he stated in explanation of his presence.

"Still stinks?"

"Oh yeah. I'm sleeping here."

"Shouldn't you ask us first?"

"I'm desperate. You can say 'no', but I'm still sleeping here."

He walked in and dumped his bedding on the floor between the two queen-size beds, then looked around. The room was a duplicate of the room he shared with Ty and Sophie. Alia was in the bed closest to the window and Emi shared the bed closest to the bathroom with Annie. Annie was sitting up in bed when John entered.

"Is that my shirt?" John asked Annie, noticing her gray Cy Grove Athletic Dept. shirt.

"Yeah, you left it in our room at the Canyon when you took a shower there. I washed it in the sink. The shorts, too." She got out of bed and lifted the shirt to show the basketball shorts that John has also left behind.

"Aren't they too big for you?

"They're comfy, but I have to hold up the shorts when I walk. They're just good for sleeping."

John stared, not sure how to respond. "Uh, okay." After an awkward silence, he lay down on the bed covers he had arranged on the floor between the beds and fluffed the pillows.

Emi and Annie returned to their bed and, after brief exchanges of "good night", Alia reached over to turn off the lamp on the nightstand between the two beds.

Hillsboro, early October

By the time Emi finished recounting the smelly adventure, Joel's interlocked pinky finger had relaxed and slipped off of Emi's finger. His slow breathing provided further indication that he was asleep. Emi wasn't sure how much he'd heard. She softly ran her finger over the back of his hand, testing his awareness. He pulled his hand up and put it under his pillow, shifting his head slightly.

Emi stared at him in the dim light, resisting sleep for a few more moments. Working up courage, she lifted herself slightly and leaned into Joel.

"Goodnight," she whispered as she kissed his forehead.

"Goodnight, Mom," he responded sleepily.

Chapter 19
Leaving Hillsboro

Early October

After breakfast at the restaurant next to the hotel in Hillsboro, Sophie and Emi dropped Ty and Joel off at Walmart's Auto Center to get the Atlas' tire replaced. Sophie navigated her Mazda through the parking lot towards the interstate, then suddenly pulled over into a parking space far from the store. She looked at Emi, quietly thinking.

"What?" Emi asked after a moment of silence.

"Do we need to go to a clinic and get you the morning after pill?"

"The morning after…? No! So, you think we were having sex in the Walmart parking lot?"

"Well, uh, things happen that, um, that you don't plan for."

Emi sighed through her nose in a sign of distaste.

"You know," Sophie started. "It's dark, you're laying close together, sharing a blanket, your inhibitions are down because you're tired and maybe emotionally drained…."

"I'm not you."

Sophie gripped the steering wheel tightly and took a deep breath. "I can't believe you said that."

"Sorry," Emi stated. "I shouldn't have said it that way. One benefit of having you as an older sister is learning from your mistakes. Joel and I did not have sex. As a matter of fact, I encouraged him to ask Annie to Homecoming. You need to trust me."

"Okay. I'm sorry I brought it up. Let's just go home."

* * *

"Did you let your sister know we're on the way?" Ty asked Joel.

"Yeah. I told her."

"That looks like a bruise on your lip," Ty pointed out to Joel, who was driving. "What happened?"

Joel took his time answering. "Emi hit me."

"By accident?"

"No."

After a brief silence, Ty finally spoke. "I'm waiting for the story."

"On the way here, I was joking with her and I... uh... I said something inappropriate."

"She hit you for saying something she didn't like?" Ty questioned with a skeptical tone.

"Well, not really what I said. I touched her as a joke, and she didn't like it."

"Like, touched her arm? Or touched her shoulder? Her knee?"

The map application on Joel's phone announced an upcoming split in the interstate and directed him to take the right lane towards Dallas.

"Her boob. I touched her boob." He quickly added, "Over her shirt."

"Yeah, that's pretty inappropriate. You deserved to get hit and I'm proud of Emi for enforcing boundaries."

"Yes, sir. I deserved it."

Ty tried to suppress the urge to smile. He wasn't used to anyone calling him sir. He may have recently turned thirty, but he still felt he was too young to be a sir.

"Was there any other inappropriate touching last night?"

"This is gonna be a long ride," Joel mumbled under his breath.

"What's that?" Ty asked.

"Nothing."

* * *

Twenty minutes into the drive back home Emi broke the silence. "Thank you for bringing it up."

Sophie smiled in response.

Once past Waco, Emi asked, "Sophie?"

"Mm-hm," Sophie acknowledged.

"Have you ever liked someone, but were afraid that if you pushed the relationship, it would mess up what you already have?"

"Yes, I have."

"With whom?"

"Ty."

* * *

As the girls passed through College Station, Emi's phone rang. She was glad Sophie brought it. She looked at the screen before answering.

"Hello, Ty." She set the phone to speaker mode.

"Tell Sophie to let you drive home. You need the practice."

"I heard that," Sophie said. "Driving practice is your job."

"Yeah, I'd rather practice with you anyway," Emi told Ty. "Sophie complains too much."

"Okay. That's not why I called, though. Guess who I met?"

"Joel's sister."

"More than that. Do you remember when we left on the Grand Canyon trip and we stopped at the gas station? And there was a flirty girl who started talking to me? Y'all gave me a hard time about it."

Emi could hear a voice in the background say, "I wasn't flirting. I was just being friendly."

"Yeah, I sort of remember her," Emi replied. "We followed her for a while."

"It was Kathryn, Joel's sister."

"Remind her that you're married," Sophie interjected.

"I wasn't flirting," Ryn insisted loudly. "I was just being friendly. And call me Ryn."

Chapter 20
Date night

Tuesday morning, Emi arranged to meet Joel at the entrance to the school before Annie arrived. She handed over the poster she prepared for him.

"Did you bring the sugar packets?" Emi asked.

"Yeah, I got 'em in my backpack."

"Well, get 'em out. We need to hurry before she comes." She reached into her own pack and pulled out a tape dispenser. She tore off a short strip of tape and held it out to Joel.

"Do I just put them anywhere?"

"Don't cover the words."

A few minutes later, Joel was holding the poster face down, waiting for Annie to arrive.

"There she is," Emi said, pointing to a gray Lexus pulling up to the curb. "Get ready."

When Annie turned around from closing the car door, Joel held up the poster. It took a moment for Annie to read it and realize it was for her. "Annie, It would sure be sweet if you went to Homecoming with me." She finally broke into a wide grin, but it took another moment to realize that the things taped to the poster were sugar packets.

She raised both hands high in the air, fingers outstretched, and shouted "Yes!" She bounced on the balls of her feet as she said it.

A car horn sounded behind her. Students on their way into the school turned to see Annie's mother waving and giving a thumbs-up signal. She got out of the Lexus and snapped a photo just as Annie hugged Joel, who was still holding the poster above his head.

* * *

"Are you sure you can't go with us?" Annie asked Emi regarding her plans to see a movie with Joel. They were on the floor of Annie's bedroom, Emi leaning against her bed and Annie laying on her stomach with her chin resting on her folded arms.

"You know I can't. The whole family is going to dinner with the Moriguchis," Emi replied.

"I should have been included," Annie complained. "I was on the trip, too."

"Sophie thinks they'll pay for dinner and thought it would be rude to add more people. Alia's not going either. She's working tonight."

"I guess I shouldn't gripe about it since she's not going either. And I've been wanting to see the movie." Annie shifted her position and put her hands, palms down, on the floor near her shoulders. She pushed, completing one push-up.

"I'd rather go with you and Joel," Emi said. "I've been looking forward to seeing 'Ghost Hunters' with you since they first started advertising for it. It looks so funny. And now…." Emi shrugged her shoulders. This was the first outing between Annie and Joel that didn't include Emi. "Do you think it'll be like a real date?" Emi asked.

"What do you mean?" Annie lowered herself and repeated the push-up.

"You know, holding hands, kissing good night, all that. And I mean a real kiss, not on the cheek."

"I don't know," Annie responded after another push-up. "That might be kind of weird. I mean, I like him and all, but we – I mean me and you and Joel – are like a team. I don't want to break up the team."

"So, you wouldn't want to kiss him?" Emi asked.

"Well, I wouldn't stop him."

"He did invite you to Homecoming."

"He told me you made him do it." Annie rolled over onto her back.

"I can't believe he told you that! Some things are meant to be secret. Besides, I know he likes you and I just had to give him a little push."

"A *little* push? Like making the poster for him?" Annie sat up. "But I'm not complaining! I do like him. And it keeps the whole boyfriend thing alive."

"Good." Emi reflected on the situation. *Am I bad for hoping their date isn't too good?* she thought.

* * *

Friday evening, Ty pulled the Escalade into the parking lot of the strip center that included Young's Barbeque and was fortunate enough to find a parking space right in front of the restaurant. Sophie looked at the byline under the name of the restaurant and then at Ty. He started laughing, which made Sophie laugh.

"When you said Mr. Moriguchi wanted to eat barbeque, I assumed he meant *barbeque*," Ty stated, emphasizing the last word.

John leaned forward to look through the windshield from his seat in the second row. "Well, it *is* barbeque," he stated. "'*And other Korean cuisine*', according to the sign."

"If you visit Texas, you should have *Texas* barbeque, not Korean barbeque," Ty said. "I was all set for brisket; now I have to adjust my mindset."

* * *

The movie theater was dotted with students from Cy Grove and other Cypress high schools. Joel, with the large popcorn, and Annie, with the large Coke, walked up to the station with their tickets extended. The usher scanned the tickets and stated, "House five on your left." Then, "Wait." He pointed to the red plastic Solo cup Annie held in the crook of her left arm, the same arm that held the Coke. "You can't take outside food or drinks into the movie."

"I'm not," Annie stated, taking the red cup and holding it out, then turning it upside down. "It's empty."

"Okay. House five." The ticket taker nodded in the direction of the auditorium.

"You're a genius," Joel said as he and Annie made their way to house five.

"I told you we could do it," she smiled.

The couple made their way up the aisle to their designated row. Most of the seats were already filled.

A sophomore basketball player called out his usual greeting from across the auditorium, the greeting borrowed from John Jensen. "Hey, Annie! How's it going?"

Annie held up the red Solo cup in salute. "I'm good, Jalen. How're you?"

Jalen Adams nudged the guy sitting next to him. "She remembered my name."

"Bro, she's got a boyfriend." A couple of guys next to them snickered.

Annie and Joel did not escape notice from Sienna and Bailey, either. After the greeting from the tall teen – Jalen, according to Annie – the whole auditorium noticed them. They took their seats and Annie opened the lid of the movie theater cup. She filled the red Solo cup from it.

Joel looked at Annie and repeated, "Genius," as he took the Solo cup she offered him.

Bailey looked over at Sienna and ordered, "Don't start. We're here to enjoy the movie, like everyone else."

"You're right. I need to enjoy tonight since the rest of the weekend's gonna suck."

Bailey rolled her eyes. "You have a dad who wants to spend time with you. Be happy about that."

"But...."

Bailey cut her off. "You think everyone else is out having fun all the time, but they're not. I'm doing chores in the morning, going to Walmart with my mom in the afternoon – the last time, my mom made me go get maxi-pads, deodorant, and mouthwash and I had to carry them through the store to meet her in the grocery section – and then I'll be watching TV with my family at night. Most stuff is not Instagram worthy."

"But...."

"Ask your stepmom to take you shopping for a dress for homecoming. She'd probably be thrilled that you asked for her help."

"I already have a dress."

"Then shoe shopping. Whatever. Your life is not as sucky as you think it is."

The lights dimmed as the screen lit up with an advertisement.

Thank goodness, Bailey thought.

* * *

"It is good to finally meet the family that helped my family," Hiroshi Moriguchi announced as they exchanged greetings with the Butler/Jensen family in the foyer of the restaurant.

"No problem, Moriguchi-san," Ty replied. "Your family made the trip more interesting."

"Please call me Hiroshi. Or just Hiro."

"Is your mother watching the boys for the weekend?" Sophie asked Kumiko once they were seated at a large round table with a grill in the center.

"No. She go back to Japan. Hiro's mother came and live with us now."

"Does she beat up bad guys, too?" Ty asked with a chuckle.

"My mother doesn't beat up anyone," Hiro noted. "What do you mean 'too'?"

"Kumiko didn't tell you that her mother's a badass grandma?" John asked.

"John! You should use a more polite term," Sophie scolded. "He meant she's fearless," she explained to Hiro.

Emi added, "Yeah, she singlehandedly beat up a family of potential kidnappers."

"She did," Ty confirmed, grinning at Hiro's disbelief.

Hiro looked at Kumiko. "You did not tell me this." He looked at Ty and asked, "What happened?"

Chapter 21
~Slide Rock~

Previous June — vacation day four, night

Alia:
I wish you could be here

Andy:
Me, too. Shelby's friends are
chill, but they can't beat
seeing the Grand Canyon
with you. Those images were
awesome

I don't think you can truly get it
unless you see it in person.
Maybe someday we can come
back

You're already planning a trip
for us together. I take that as
a good sign

☺

How's the Japanese family?
Did the grandma beat up any
other innocent tourists?

Not yet. Ty's got a new best
friend

Not the grandma, right?

No. Jun

The mother?

No. Jun is the 6yo boy. He won't
leave Ty's side. Ty started
carrying him on his shoulders

Awe. How cute

That's what Sophie said.
Adorable. She took way too
many pictures of Ty and Jun. I
think she is imagining Ty as a
dad

But you should've seen the
grandma's face when Ty first
picked up Jun and put him on his
shoulders. She yelled something
to Kumiko and Kumiko just
waved her hand at grandma. It
was funny to watch

Maybe she thinks Ty is hentai

The Lingering Scent

What does that mean?

Pervert.

You know Japanese?

I know a few words from
manga

Ty's not a pervert. That's more
for your family

Ouch!

Not you. Just Brody's family

Thanks for clarifying

* * *

"Do you want to make a baby?" Sophie whispered to Ty as they snuggled together in bed, her lips nearly brushing against his ear.

"Right now?"

"At least we can practice."

"Is John asleep?"

"No, I'm not," John said from his position on the far side of the other bed. It was his standard sleeping position for the trip: the bed closest to the window and the position furthest from Ty and Sophie. "And y'all better not start doing anything, because I don't need to hear my sister making 'ooh, ahh' moaning sounds six feet away. That'd be messed up."

"It's more like giggles and farts," Ty stated.

John heard a slap from the next bed.

"Hey!" Ty exclaimed.

"Ugh! Y'all go to sleep," John complained. "You can giggle and fart all you want at home, where I can't hear you."

* * *

Vacation day five, morning

"You're putting on makeup?" Emi asked Annie as they got ready for the day.

"Yeah."

"Why? We're gonna be in the water. And you didn't wear makeup the last few days."

"I need to look my best in case we meet boys."

Emi tilted her head to the side and looked at her. "Do you mean, like, a particular boy who came with us?"

Annie shrugged. "It doesn't hurt to look good."

* * *

"How was your room?" Ty asked Kumiko as he drove her family in their van to Slide Rock State Park, with Sophie and the rest of the Jentler clan following behind in the Escalade.

"My mother say hotel look like love hotel," Kumiko answered.

Mrs. Yunohara nodded and repeated the comment, *"Hai. Rabu hoteru mitai."*

After spending the previous day with the Moriguchi family, Ty had begun to understand the Japanese accent of certain English words and phrases. At least enough to realize *rabu hoteru* was the Japanese pronunciation of 'love hotel'.

"What's a love hotel," Ty asked, thinking he might already know the answer, but being uncertain of Japanese nuance.

"It is hotel where man and his... *eto, nan desu ka...* mistress — where man and his mistress go for sex."

"If it's a love hotel, it's not working for me."

"What do you....? Oh!" Kumiko laughed. "I'm sorry."

"Japanese men probably don't take their brother-in-law with them to a love hotel."

"Kare ga nani o itta no?" Kumiko's mother interjected.

Kumiko looked back at her sons before responding to her mother. *"Atode iu yo."* I'll tell you later.

* * *

"Will you be okay in the water?" Alia asked John, as they dropped off their towels and snacks on the flat slab of red rock that was the bank of Oak Creek in Slide Rock State Park. "I thought you weren't supposed to get your chin wet."

"They painted a protective seal over the wound at the clinic and said I could shower by the second day. I don't think sliding down a water chute will get it any wetter than a shower. I'm just not supposed to rub it dry."

"Seriously?" Emi asked.

"I promise to keep my head out of the water as much as possible."

Emi walked to the edge of the water and crouched down. "Cold! Cold! Cold! Cold!" she yelled as she eased herself into the water. "It's freezing!"

"Don't be such a wimp," John called as he jumped in. He let out a string of "Oh, oh, oh, oh" as the shock of the forty-two-degree water registered in his brain.

"See?" Emi stated. "Now who's the wimp?"

The others had similar reactions as they initiated themselves in the frigid waters of Oak Creek. Only Kumiko and her mother remained in folding chairs on the bank. No one stayed in the water for long.

"Towel!" Annie called as she climbed out after John.

"No. Don't dry off yet," Ty noted. "If you dry off every time you get out, your towel will be soaked."

"But I'm cold!" She moved into position behind John so he could block the light breeze that made her wet skin feel colder than it otherwise would in the morning air. When John stepped away, she followed, maintaining her leeward position with his movements.

"What're you doing?" John asked with mild annoyance.

"Using you to block the wind."

John pulled Annie into a hug and rubbed her back with hard quick strokes to warm her up with friction from his hands. She pressed her cheek against his bare chest and smiled.

"Warmer now?

Annie nodded.

Emi watched and rolled her eyes. Looking at John she mouthed the words, "What are you doing?"

"I guess if I told him I was cold, too, you'd get mad at me," Alia quietly told Emi.

"You should know better. He has a girlfriend. And…."

"… you like her," Alia finished. "I get it. You don't have to keep reminding me."

"I don't know what she sees in him, but he's not as annoying when she's around."

"Now, if you want to keep following me," John said to Annie, "you'll have to get wet again because I'm about to slide down the water chute." He stepped over to the slab of rock that had the chute carved by millennia of fast-moving current, sat down in the water, and launched himself into the flow. He soon joined Ty and Sophie in the deeper water at the end of the natural water slide.

Kenji and Jun followed John, with Alia, Annie, and Emi trailing. Kumiko waved from the bank of the creek while Mrs. Yunohara took photos with a real camera rather than a smartphone.

* * *

"Kenji and Jun want to jump off rock over there," Kumiko said, pointing to a low cliff where several youngsters were taking turns jumping into the deeper water.

"How well can they swim?" Ty asked. He had already seen them swim in the shallow water near the chute, but the boys could stand on the bottom if needed. He wasn't sure how they would handle water over their heads.

"They are good swimmers. We go to pool many times."

"I'll take them to jump if it's okay with you."

"*Ii desu.* Okay. Jun likes you. When you carry him on arms…," Kumiko patted her shoulders.

"Shoulders," Ty corrected.

"Yes, shoulders. When you carry him on shoulders yesterday, he became your good friend. Jun's father carry him on shoulders, too. He's happy."

"I like him, too. And he's easier to carry than you."

"He like your singing in car," Kumiko added.

"You're kidding. He'll be the first person to like my singing."

"He say it make him laugh."

"Yeah, that makes more sense."

Ty looked around for his wife and spotted her on the chute. "Hey, Sophie! We're gonna jump off the rocks! Come with us."

"Y'all go ahead. I'll just watch from here and keep Kumiko company."

"Suit yourself. Kenji! Jun! Let's go."

The trio walked down the smooth red rock bank of the creek and clambered up on the rocky cliff above the swimming hole. Mrs. Yunohara followed behind to take photos of her grandsons, keeping to the lower ledge of rock where she would be better positioned for an action shot of the jump.

Ty and the boys waited behind a group of teenagers as they each jumped. When it was their turn, nine-year-old Kenji launched himself off the rock without hesitation. After snapping several photos, his grandmother clapped and yelled, "*Ara, sugoiwane!*" Oh, wonderful!

"Ready?" Ty asked Jun.

Jun stood at the edge and looked down at the water.

"I wait."

"You got this. You can do anything Kenji can do."

Jun looked at Ty, then at the water, then at Ty again.

An older boy waiting behind them shouted, "You can do it, little man!"

That prompted support from others. "Go for it!", "Don't think, just jump!", and "It's fun!"

After looking at the crowd, Jun looked back at Ty. "You go first. Then I go."

"Okay. I'll go, then I'll wait in the water for you. I'll get you when you hit the water."

Jun nodded in agreement and Ty jumped.

Upon resurfacing, Ty looked up to see Jun looking down. "Your turn! I'll get you."

Jun continued to look down, indecisive.

A voice behind Jun said, "Go on! We're all waiting."

As Ty watched, Jun stepped back and disappeared from view. Ty swam to the bank and climbed out.

"Did Jun come down?" Ty asked Kenji.

"No."

Jun was not on the rock ledge when Ty got there. He heard a small voice call, "*Okaasan!*" from further down the creek, in the opposite direction from his *okaasan* and the Jentler party. Ty headed for the sound of his voice. Presently, he found Jun surrounded by people who appeared to be an extended family.

"*Okaasan!*" he called out again, in a somewhat panicked voice.

"Hey, Jun! I've been looking for you," Ty called as he approached. "I guess cliff jumping is not your thing."

As Jun started to go to Ty, a woman grabbed his arm and held him back.

"You don't look related," the woman said to Ty. She turned to Jun and asked, "Do you know this man?"

Jun stood frozen by fear and remained silent.

"Our families came together," Ty explained. "We were jumping off the rocks and I guess he decided not to do it. By the time I got out of the water, he was gone. But, thanks for finding him."

A man with the family – father? – folded his arms and stood straighter as he admonished, "It's irresponsible to leave a little kid his age by himself in a place like this."

"I don't think he wants to go with you," said the woman holding Jun's arm.

"I think he does, but you're not letting him. Why don't you let him go and see."

"Hey! You don't talk to my wife in that tone of voice," the man growled.

"There was no tone. Now, why don't you let the boy go so I can get him back to his mother." Ty looked at Jun and said, "Do you want to go with me back to your mother?"

Jun nodded and said, "*Hai.*" He pulled against the grip of the woman holding his arm.

"See, he wants to go with me," Ty pointed out.

"You could be some kind of predator and he's just saying that to keep you from getting angry and hitting him."

How do you argue with stupid? Ty thought to himself, trying to keep his cool.

Just then, Jun looked past Ty and called out, "*Obaachan!*" with a look of relief on his face.

The entire group turned to look at the subject of his greeting.

"Yunohara-san," Ty said. "Do you still have that umbrella?"

Mrs. Yunohara didn't understand what Ty said, but she did see that an overweight middle-aged woman was holding Jun against his will.

Mrs. Yunohara let loose a string of words in Japanese with such speed and force, that it sounded like a verbal machine gun. She looked around the area until her eyes locked on a folding camp chair. She grabbed the chair, flipped it upside down, and collapsed it into its compact form. It became a club, which she held with both hands and swung at the woman, who moved to the side to avoid contact.

"Let the kid go, Edna," the confrontational man said. "It ain't worth it."

Edna released Jun and he ran behind his grandmother. Mrs. Yunohara waved her chair-turned-club menacingly at Edna and her husband and backed away. Ty, Jun, and Mrs. Yunohara continued walking backward until they were satisfied the group was not following them.

"Hey! Gimme back my chair!" another man in the group yelled.

Whether she understood the demand or just felt it was safe to do so, Jun's grandmother dropped the chair. She, Ty, and Jun turned around and fast-walked along the creek until they were out of sight of the "kidnappers". Only then did they slow down to a safer pace to reach the area where Kumiko, Kenji, and the Jentler party waited.

Back at the site, Ty saw Mrs. Yunohara's folded umbrella lying on the straw mat she had been sitting on earlier. He picked it up and handed it to her. "You should keep this with you at all times. Just don't use it on us."

* * *

Alia:
The Japanese grandma tried to
beat up someone again

Andy:
Seriously? I was joking last
night

Some weird woman thought Ty
was kidnapping Jun and the
grandma thought the woman

was trying to kidnap Jun.
Grandma hit her with a chair

Did you get pictures?

No. We weren't there. Ty told us
about it and Kumiko told us what
the grandma was thinking.

I would love to see pics of
that

Alia clicked the back arrow to get out of the text conversation with Andy and back to the home screen of her phone's Messages app. She scrolled down to find the last conversation she had with Lizzie.

Alia:
Hi Lizzie. I think you have a new
rival

Lizzie:
What do you mean?

Annie has taken a liking to John

And how is John acting?

True gentleman. I don't think you
need to worry about Annie. It's
just a schoolgirl crush

We're all schoolgirls

Todd H. Davis

Oh, yeah

Chapter 22
Hoco Prep

The dress shop was crowded with girls trying to find the best homecoming dress. A sign on the entrance said, "All sales are final. No refunds." Such was homecoming season.

"Do you know how hard it is to find a dress that looks good when you have no boobs?" Annie asked rhetorically. She found two dresses worthy enough to try on.

Annie emerged from the dressing room with a short halter-style cocktail dress that covered her chest up to her neck but had exposed shoulders and sides. She stood in the alcove that had mirrors on three sides and asked, "What do you think?"

"I like this," Emi stated. "Elegant. It suits you. Did you try the other one?"

"Yeah. It's a no-go. It just doesn't fit in the right places. What do you think, Mom?"

"It's a little open on the sides. Turn to the side," Mrs. Bates commanded.

Annie turned.

"Now lean over a bit."

Annie leaned.

"Good. I wanted to make sure you don't show any side boob. You want to leave the boys something for their imagination. This one's a keeper."

"Mom, I have the body of a ten-year-old. The boys will need a big imagination."

"You do not have the body of a ten-year-old and, anyway, this," she waved her hand at Annie, "will all change soon. It's good that the boys have to get to know your other wonderful characteristics for now."

"I don't think that's how boys' brains work, Mom, but thanks. Can you hold onto it while I help Emi find something?"

Away from her mother, Annie muttered, "She's worried about side boob. There's not much boob to show the side of."

"Are you still doing that secret Instagram thing?" Emi asked.

"And pushups. Every week I post a new photo. I'm still waiting for the Instagram police to decide if I have what it takes to be a girl. So far, I'm still a boy."

* * *

The conversation after basketball practice turned to plans for homecoming.

"Colin's group is getting a limo."

"A limo's for prom, not Homecoming," Des pointed out.

"No, they did it last year, too. Four couples split the cost."

"Couples, huh?" Jalen Adams noted.

"Problem, Jalen?"

"I haven't asked anyone yet," Jalen replied. "I don't know who to ask."

"You're always eyeing that skinny girl that hangs with John's sister. What about her?"

"Yeah," Destrehan interjected. "You're the one who keeps pushing that 'Hey, Annie' joke."

Jalen shrugged his shoulders. "That new guy that's with 'em all the time asked her. I was hoping he was gay or friend-zoned or something."

John walked in to hear the last part of the conversation among the younger team members. "Y'all talking about Annie?"

"Yeah. Jalen wanted to ask her to Homecoming, but some other guy beat him to it."

"You mean Joel? I'll let you in on a secret." John put his arm around Jalen's shoulders. "Emi pushed him to ask Annie. She even made the poster."

"Seriously? Why?"

"The guy's over at our house all the time. Emi and Annie can't figure out the whole relationship. I think Emi's got a thing for him but doesn't want to hurt Annie's feelings. I've got a solution for you."

"How? She already said yes to the guy."

"Ask Emi to Homecoming," John advised.

"You're sister? You're telling me to date your sister?"

"No. I'm telling you to go to the dance with my sister so you can be close to Annie. They're all just friends. You start with Emi, you end with Annie."

Jalen nodded in consideration of the idea.

"But Jalen," John added, "if you do anything to my sister, I'll have to hurt you."

* * *

After the last bell rang on Thursday, Emi made her way as usual to the exit nearest the senior parking lot to meet up with Alia for the ride home. That's where the ambush happened. In the hallway, two of the younger members of the basketball team blocked her path and, oddly, one was holding a flashlight. When she moved to go around them, they parted to reveal a young Black teammate holding a poster.

The guy with the flashlight shined it onto the poster that said, "Emi, it would be a BRIGHT idea to go to HoCo with me."

Emi looked around to see if there was another Emi in the hallway.

The young man wiggled the poster and smiled. "What do you say, Emi?"

"Uh... yes?"

"Great! She said yes!"

Alia missed the proposal but arrived in time to snap a few pics of the group. "Congratulations, Emi!"

Emi looked around at the small crowd gathered in the hallway and dutifully stood next to the proposer for more photos. She grabbed his arm and pulled it to get him to lean down to her level.

"What's your name?" she whispered. "Something like Jason, right?"

"Jalen. My name's Jalen," he whispered back.

"Is this a real proposal or a prank?"

"It's real. Didn't your brother tell you it was coming?"

Emi looked back at the onlookers and tried to appear more aware than she was. "Thanks, guys! Jalen totally surprised me; I didn't see it coming."

Turning back to Jalen, she whispered, "So, John knew about this?"

"It was his idea."

* * *

The Homecoming fervor was not lost on Alia. She had gotten a small taste of it in her freshman year at her school in St. Louis. But Texas schools took it to a whole other level. There was a booth set up in the cafeteria to take orders for mums, the gargantuan chrysanthemum flower arrangements that girls expected to receive from their dates before the Homecoming game and were obligated to wear from a strap around their necks at the Friday night game and Saturday night dance.

Alia didn't care much about the mums but was interested in other aspects of Homecoming. She liked the idea of a boy asking her to the dance, as well as dressing up. The HoCo proposals had gone on for the past couple of weeks, with a notable increase in the past week. And Emi had been looking at pictures of dresses for days, long before Jalen asked her. Nevertheless, Alia had already committed to going to an A&M football game with Andy on the day of the dance.

It was Emi's dress that finally got to her. Emi came home Saturday afternoon with her pale pink, off-the-shoulder mini dress, eager to show it off to all the household members present. A homecoming dress, combined with the proper hairstyle and makeup, could transform an average teenage school girl into a princess. Not the fictional Disney kind, but the glamorous, still fictional kind featured in fashion magazines. It did that for Emi. When Emi returned to her bedroom after modeling the dress for family members downstairs, Alia followed her up the stairs. However, she paused to look at the photos on the stairway wall of Sophie and John at past Homecomings. One of the photos included Lizzie. Alia noted the dresses, the makeup, the hairstyles, and the manicures. She looked up at Emi in her new dress and recalled the discussions of manicure, pedicure, hair, and makeup that would come later.

Sunday, at the family's post-church lunch at Chili's, Alia announced she was going shopping that afternoon for a homecoming dress.

"You're not going to the A&M game anymore?" Ty questioned. "Did something happen with Andy?"

"I'm still going to A&M. I just want to dress up."

"Yeah, Ty," Lizzie agreed. "Girls don't need an excuse to dress up." Lizzie looked at Alia and added, "I'll drive."

"Hey, I thought we were gonna hang out," John complained to Lizzie.

"This is more important."

John looked at Ty with raised eyebrows and shrugged with upturned palms. Ty shook his head and shrugged in response.

"I can take my truck," Alia stated.

"Your truck is at your house," Lizzie pointed out. "I can take you now."

"Are you sure?"

"This is exciting! I'd love to help you find the perfect dress. Besides, I still need to find new heels."

* * *

Another call of "Hey, Annie" in the hallway on Monday morning irritated Sienna more than usual. Homecoming was only days away and no one had asked her to the dance. Getting a Homecoming mum was like a rite of passage, and it would be another year before the opportunity would come again. She turned around and went into the girls' restroom, entered a stall, and closed the door. She listened for the current occupants to leave and others to enter. She didn't want anyone to know she was in there. That is, she wanted them to know someone was in there, just not her.

"Rape," she said, using a word that she expected would draw attention. Sienna heard the voices of the other restroom inhabitants quieten.

"He started flirting with me at the store," Sienna continued from behind the stall door.

She paused as if listening to a response on the phone.

"Yeah. Joel. The guy dating Annie."

...

"I know, right? Then he offered to buy me a smoothie, so I thought they must have broken up."

...

"We were drinking our smoothies and just talking. Things were going well. And my mom was late, so he said he could give me a ride home."

...

"Come on, he wasn't a complete stranger. We've seen him at school. And he seemed cool."

...

"Yeah. You're right. I should have been more cautious. Especially when he said he had to stop at his place on the way to get something. We were already driving, what could I have done? Besides, I assumed his parents would be home."

...

"Well, it was white, but it was an SUV, not a windowless van."

...

"So, I go up to his apartment with him, expecting his parents to be home. And guess what?"

...

"No. He doesn't live with his parents. He lives with his sister, and she wasn't home. So, we went in, and he just suddenly gets all grabby. First, he kissed me, then he tried to pull me into his bedroom."

...

"Then he put his hands under my shirt. I was already trying to get away, but I was still trying to be sort of polite. But when he did that, I just knocked his hands away and ran."

...

"I was so scared. I thought he was gonna...."

...

"Yeah, that's what I was thinking. After that, I ran out to the parking lot, but I didn't know what to do. I was in the middle of texting my mom to come to get me when he came up to me and grabbed my phone. He said he'd been joking. 'Everything's okay,' he said. He deleted the text before I could send it."

...

"He did."

...

"I know. I was stupid. But he didn't try anything else, and he just drove me straight home."

...

"Yeah. Poor Annie. When I heard he was still taking her to Homecoming, I couldn't believe it."

...

"But it would just be my word against Joel's."

When the performance was over, Sienna waited for the other restroom users to leave before coming out from the stall. In the hallway, she smiled to herself. Only the glances from a couple of goth emo girls momentarily interrupted her thoughts. She scowled at them before heading to class, the smile returning to her face as she walked. So what if she was late; her mission was accomplished. Even if nothing became of the restroom event, it brought a bit of relief to her dark mood.

Chapter 23
Aggieland

Alia pulled onto Andy's street in College Station and immediately noticed that all the houses in the small neighborhood were identical. It reminded her of the scene in "A Wrinkle in Time" when Meg found herself in a suburban neighborhood in a parallel world where all the houses looked alike. Alia almost expected to see identical boys dribbling basketballs in the driveways. In this case, all the houses were a contemporary style painted white with a black double garage door.

Andy had explained that they were pretty much built for students. The front door was the only thing a homeowner was allowed to change according to the neighborhood's rigid rules around a house's external appearance. Andy's door was yellow.

"Wow!" Shelby exclaimed when she answered the door. She was in maroon jogging shorts and a grey sweatshirt emblazoned with A&M in maroon lettering. After a quick hug, she stated, "Alia, you are way overdressed for the game. Come in."

Alia twirled around to show off the dress, a burgundy satin A-line that fell just above her knees. The shallow V-neckline showed just enough to pique interest, but not enough to cause alarm. After all, it was a dress that a high school student would wear, not an Oscar nominee. "Tonight's the homecoming dance at Grove," Alia explained. "Everyone was dressing up."

"And you're missing it for us. On behalf of the A&M student body, we are honored." Shelby turned her head and called out, "Andy, Alia's here!"

Turning back to Alia, she asked, "Did you bring a jacket? It might get a little cool tonight."

Alia reached into her overnight bag and pulled out a white woolen bundle and shook it out. "It's a shawl. I thought it would go with the dress better than a jacket. And it keeps with Aggie colors."

Once inside, Alia set her bag on the sofa and looked around the large open room, which included the kitchen, dining, and living areas. "This is nice. I was expecting old, mismatched furniture from garage sales with empty beer bottles and pizza boxes scattered around."

Shelby chuckled at the stereotype. "All the furniture's from Ikea. We spent the week before classes putting everything together. That's when you would've seen pizza boxes. Ella and David's parents bought the house during the summer, and they bought everything new," she explained. "Ella treats us like she's the owner and will yell if we leave trash laying around."

"Did you meet Ella at school last year?"

"No. Andy's parents already knew their parents. Ella's a junior and David's a freshman. Andy and I were sort of guilted into living with them."

Andy finally made his way downstairs and stopped upon seeing Alia.

"Dang, Alia! You look amazing! I mean, you always look great, but I never get to see you this dressed up. I heard you two talking. I didn't mean for you to miss homecoming. You should have told me, and I could've picked a different game."

"It's okay. No one asked me to homecoming anyway. Did you notice the dress is maroon? You told me to try to wear A&M colors. The label said burgundy, but I think it's the same thing."

"It's perfect," Andy replied. "And you look great."

"I'm sure she'll allow you to come closer," Shelby said to Andy, who was still standing at the foot of the stairs. "Now don't you regret committing to playing makeup with your buddies?"

"I don't think I can get out of it," Andy replied. "They won't have a second 'G'."

Alia's puzzled look prompted another statement from Shelby. As Andy hugged Alia in greeting, Shelby said, "You'll see what I mean later."

Andy continued the conversation he had heard before seeing Alia. "The house isn't bad. It's nicer than the dorms – cheaper too – but we have to cook our own food, which sucks."

"Hey, it's your cooking that sucks," Shelby retorted. "My food's great."

"Are Ella and David here? Can I meet them?" Alia asked.

"They're not here now. Ella's with her boyfriend and she's spending the night at his place. You might meet David tonight after the game. We all have such different schedules, sometimes we go days without seeing one of our housemates."

"Okay. Well, show me the rest of the house," Alia requested.

"I'm still trying to finish up my part of a group research paper," Shelby stated, pointing to her open laptop on the coffee table. "So, I'll leave the tour to Andy."

Andy picked up Alia's bag from the sofa and headed to the stairway. "And we're walking. And we're walking."

"What's he doing?" Alia whispered to Shelby.

Shelby clicked her tongue and groaned. "Acting like the tour guide we had on a family trip to Washington, D.C. a few years ago."

Alia followed Andy upstairs as Shelby sat down on the sofa and inserted her earbuds for a little study music.

"Let's start with the biggest and best room," Andy stated, leading her to the right, down a short hallway.

"Yours?"

"No. Ella's. She gets the master bedroom, which has the biggest bathroom. You know, because she's the oldest and she's the owner's daughter. And she reminds us of that constantly."

"Which one's yours?"

"We'll get that later. It's two doors back. Shelby's in between."

Andy opened the door and led the way inside. He set Alia's duffle bag on the dresser.

"Nice, huh? Neat and tidy."

"Yeah, this is a nice room," Alia agreed.

"Ella's letting you use it tonight since she's staying with her boyfriend," Andy stated. "This morning it was a pigsty. I straightened it up before you came. Ella's pretty bossy about us keeping the house clean, but the rules don't seem to apply to her."

"Thank you. You didn't have to go out of your way to clean it up."

"Believe me, yes I did. I also washed the sheets. Her boyfriend's over a lot and there's no telling when was the last time Ella washed them. I don't know what kind of stains were on 'em, but, I'm just saying it was safer to wash them."

"Thank you. I prefer a stain-free bed." Alia looked around the room again as a sign of appreciation for Andy's cleaning effort. Her gaze stopped at the headboard of the bed. It was a wrought iron design of winding vines and leaves, somewhat reminiscent of the pattern on Alia's truck. The headboard vines were painted a pale yellow rather than the black designs on the truck. Alia's gaze was fixed on a particular point on the headboard.

"There are handcuffs attached to the bed," Alia stated.

"Two pairs." Andy pointed.

Each pair of handcuffs were attached to the bed by one cuff, the other dangling down, as if ready for a wrist.

"Why?"

"They're Ella's. I don't have a key to take them off."

"But why does she have them?" Alia asked again.

Andy suddenly pushed Alia backward onto the bed, grabbed her wrists, and lifted them up and over her head. He pressed her wrists down on the bed, with one next to one of the dangling handcuffs. She lay on the bed somewhat diagonally, so the other hand was nowhere near the other set of cuffs. But the point was made.

Alia's eyes grew big at the sudden aggression and her mind raced with the memory of an event she wanted to forget.

"No!" she called out before squeezing her eyes shut. More softly, "No."

In the confines of his bedroom, Doug pulled Alia's shirt up to her armpits and she obediently lifted her arms for him to finish the task, the alcohol helping her overcome her concern about his friends being in the next room. Once the shirt was over her head and off, she saw that the housemates were now in the room.

"Hey!" Alia called out before Doug — or Bulldog as his friends called him — dropped her shirt on the floor and put his hand lightly over her mouth.

"We're all family here," he said as he moved his hands to her shoulders and shoved her backward onto the king-sized bed.

Blade stood on the opposite side of the bed and reached across to grab a wrist in each hand. He pulled her arms up and over her head. Pulled until she was stretched out horizontally across the bed. He then held her wrists down against the mattress in a position of surrender. Shorty leaned over her and pressed his forearms onto her thighs, holding her lower body against the bed.

Shocked at the aggression, Alia wasn't sure if the action was a terrible prank or a cause for alarm. Shorty slid his forearms up her thighs, keeping his weight on them. When he began caressing her skin at the waistline of her jeans with his fingertips Alia screamed, "No!"

She struggled to sit up, to roll over, to do anything. But the weight of the men — the "friends" — on her arms and legs kept her pinned to the bed.

"I'm going to the store," Bulldog announced. "I'll be back in about an hour."

"No!" she shouted again, terrified.

Bulldog leaned down and kissed her lips. "Be nice to these guys. I'll bring back dinner. You like fajitas, right?"

Alia closed her eyes tightly. All she could think of was "No". She wasn't even sure if the word came out of her mouth or merely stayed in her head. Just, "No."

Shorty unfastened her jeans. "Just relax, Sweetie. Relax and enjoy it."

No!

Andy didn't anticipate Alia's reaction. At the second "no" he released her wrists and stepped back.

"Alia? I'm sorry. Are you okay?"

Alia stopped protesting and let her tense body go limp. Tears rolled from her closed eyes down the sides of her face onto her hair and the bed.

It's just Andy. He's not going to hurt me. Andy wouldn't hurt a fly.

Andy sat down on the edge of the bed next to Alia.

"I was just making a stupid joke to show Ella's fetish. I shouldn't have done that."

With her eyes still closed, Alia took a deep breath and slid her hand across the bed until it touched Andy's leg.

"I'm sorry," she said. "I don't know what happened."

Andy slid his arm under her back and gently lifted her to a sitting position. Alia dabbed the tears from her eyes with a tissue from a box on the nightstand, trying not to smear the mascara.

"Is my makeup still okay?"

"It's beautiful. But you may have to touch it up a little."

Shelby bounded up the stairs to retrieve the power cable for her laptop and saw Andy and Alia sitting on Ella's bed.

"Hey," she called. "How's the tour?"

"We didn't make it far," Andy answered. "I broke Alia."

Chapter 24
Homecoming

"Guys, remember what we practiced," Ty reminded as he pulled the black Cadillac Escalade up to the front entrance of the high school. A banner over the entrance announced the Homecoming dance and a column of green and white balloons framed each side of the row of doors. They could already hear music emanating from the building.

Jalen jumped out of the SUV, pulled the seat handle to tilt his seat up, then ran around to the passenger side to open the door for Emi. Sophie stepped out to take more photos and Ty got out to observe the results of their rehearsal earlier in the driveway before letting Emi out of the house and leaving to pick up Annie. Joel climbed out behind Jalen and closed the door, then he also ran to the other side. After Jalen helped Emi out, Joel tilted the seat up for Annie. He reached in to help her climb out.

"Good job, guys," Ty called out.

Joel and Jalen each responded with a thumbs-up of their free hands; the hand not holding onto their dates.

"We'll be back to pick you up in three hours," Ty reminded them,

"What'll you do while we're gone?" Emi asked.

"This will be the first time in ages that Sophie and I will have the house to ourselves for several hours. We plan to cuddle up under a blanket and watch a movie on the big TV upstairs," he explained.

Sophie watched the teens walk away, then looked at Ty and asked, "*Only* cuddle?"

"We can eat popcorn, too."

"That's not what I meant."

* * *

Alia looked around at the students filling A&M's Kyle Field, all of whom were standing. "Andy didn't tell me we had to stand the whole time," she commented to Shelby.

"It's an Aggie thing. The fans are like the twelfth player, so we're in the game."

Andy turned around and shouted, "Welcome to the team!" The excitement of the evening emboldened him to slap her on her rump, easier to reach than her back, as she and Shelby were standing on the row behind him. She wobbled a bit on her high heels. All the fans were noisy, but Andy and his cohorts seemed to be trying to outdo the others.

"Can I sit at halftime?"

"Yeah, it's safe to sit then," Shelby answered.

Andy interjected a caveat. "Until the band comes out. We stand for the band." He added a "Gig 'em!" to echo that of others around him.

The temperature had dropped a few degrees, but Andy and his friends were shirtless. Each one had painted their chests with a single large letter in white and outlined in maroon. When lined up properly their chests spelled "GIGEM", a mysterious term that Alia thought must be unique to Texas. Andy was the second "G".

"What does that mean?" Alia asked Shelby.

"A gig is a spear used for frog hunting," Shelby explained. "Back around 1930, the Aggies were playing Texas Christian University and their mascot was the Horned Frogs. That's when they first used the term *gig 'em*. They were essentially shouting to spear the frogs."

"Does he do this every game?" Alia had asked Shelby when he and his crew removed their shirts at the start of the second quarter.

"Not every game. I think he's trying to impress you."

Alia smiled and tried to stifle a laugh. She failed. Shelby started laughing at Alia's reaction and they both ended up clutching each other, trying to control their laughter.

Andy interpreted their laughter as enthusiasm for the game and again shouted "Gig 'em!", which was echoed by his fellow letter bearers. Several shouts of "Whoop!" were added by seniors and alumni.

At the halftime performance by the Reserve Officers' Training Corps marching band, Alia removed her shoes and stood in her bare feet.

* * *

Sienna watched Annie, Joel, and their friends laughing at some unheard joke at one of the standing tables rented for the dance and positioned around the dance floor. The usual rectangular cafeteria tables with built-in seats were set up around the perimeter of the room, with a few more in the two main hallways extending from it. The unused cafeteria tables were folded upright and positioned in tight rows to form a barrier across the hallways to keep the teens from exploring the classrooms for non-sanctioned activities.

"What does Joel see in Annie?" Sienna asked.

Does it matter what she sees in him? Bailey thought to herself. *You're going to complain anyway.*

"Does he have a thing for little girls?" Sienna asked. "Because that's what she looks like."

"And how do you explain all those basketball players who keep calling her in the hallways?" Bailey asked, sarcastically. "Do you think they have a thing for little girls, too?"

"Maybe she's giving the basketball team 'favors' if you know what I mean. How else did she get so popular so fast?"

"Oh my gosh," Bailey said with a huff. "She has a boyfriend, so I doubt she's giving any favors." Bailey wiggled the first two fingers of each hand to symbolize quotation marks as she said "favors".

"Maybe he's okay with that," Sienna countered. "There's a rumor he cheated on her."

"And where did that rumor come from?"

When Sienna didn't answer, Bailey continued, "Anyway, her boyfriend is with her tonight. I don't get why she bothers you so much."

"She doesn't bother me. It just seems strange that she shot up the social ranking the way she did."

Bailey reached out and held Sienna's face between her hands. "You need a hobby. Now, look away." Bailey turned Sienna's face away from Annie and towards the dance floor. "Look, they're starting a line dance. Let's go." She stood up and grabbed Sienna's hand, pulling her up and towards the dancers.

When most of the dancers scattered after the line dance, Bailey pointed out a boy in a lavender shirt and white necktie pouring himself some punch at the snack table. "Look at that guy."

"Yeah. What about him?" Sienna asked.

"Do you think he's cute?"

"Yeah. I guess so."

"Do you know him?" Bailey asked.

"No."

"Do you think he knows you?"

"No."

Good, Bailey thought. She left Sienna and quickly walked to the white-tie guy. After a very brief conversation, she guided him to the edge of the dance floor where a bewildered Sienna waited.

"Greg, this is Sienna. She thinks you're cute. You should dance with her."

"Hey!" Sienna protested. "You should…" Bailey put her hand over Sienna's mouth.

"You're prettier when you're not talking," she whispered.

Bailey pushed both towards the dance floor and said, "You know what to do."

She headed to the snack table, muttering to herself, "Man! I need a break." At the snack table, she saw an Asian boy by the punch bowl.

"Your name's Jeremy, right?"

He nodded.

"I'm Bailey. And I'm thirsty. Can you pour me some punch?"

"Sure. Do you want ice?"

"I don't care. You play chess, don't you?"

"Are you asking that because I'm Chinese?"

"Do you?" she asked, smiling.

"Yes."

"How accurate was 'The Queen's Gambit' TV series?"

"Well, other real women became chess champions before Beth in the show. It's fiction, you know. The movie mentions a real woman named Nona something – I forgot her last name – and said she was a world champion but had never competed against men. That's fake. Nona was a real person, and she did compete against men. She sued the movie studio for getting it wrong."

"That's impressive," Bailey observed. "By the way, I noticed you wearing a chess club shirt at school a few days ago. And I don't believe all Chinese play chess. Only the nerdy ones who wear chess club shirts."

"I'm surprised you noticed a chess player," Jeremy commented. "I thought chess made us invisible."

Bailey ignored his comment and asked, "Are you finished with your drink?"

"Yeah. Do you need a refill?"

"No. I need you to dance with me."

Jeremy looked across the room at a table where three guys watched him. When they realized he was looking at them, they all gave him a thumbs up. One even gave him two thumbs up.

Bailey caught the interaction and gave the friends an exaggerated smile and a wave. Then she grabbed Jeremy's arm and pulled him to the dance floor.

When the music changed to a slow song, Jeremy paused to see if Bailey would leave. She moved closer and put her hands on his shoulders.

"This is better than being invisible," he muttered under his breath. "I saw you hook your friend up for a dance earlier. Are you her wingman, uh, wing woman?"

"She's been having trouble making friends lately. She's going through an evil queen phase," Bailey explained.

"Evil queen? Does that make you Sleeping Beauty?"

"Wrong fairy tale. Sleeping Beauty had an evil fairy. The evil queen goes with Snow White."

"Then are you Snow White?"

"I'm more like the talking mirror. Snow White's over there," she said pointing to Annie.

"Annie Bates is Snow White? Are there dwarfs in this story?"

"They prefer to be called little people."

"Okay. Who are the little people in this story?"

"I guess it would be the guys she's with right now."

"That Black guy is definitely not a little people," Jeremy pointed out. He was taller than most of the students in the room.

"Well, maybe he can be the handsome prince. But her date is the other guy. I just hope Sienna gets over her jealous obsession before it gets to the poison apple stage."

"Well, Miss Talking Mirror, I hope you don't get shattered. All the king's rooks and all the king's knights might not be able to put you back together again."

"Now you're mixing up nursery rhymes with chess. And you forgot my name, didn't you?"

"No. Bailey. I wrote it on my hand when you were getting snacks." He showed her the palm of his left hand.

"Give me your pen," Bailey ordered.

Jeremy pulled a ballpoint pen from his pants pocket and handed it to her. She grabbed his left hand and added her phone number under her name.

* * *

"When you said a friend was meeting us, I thought it was one of your sorority friends," Andy commented quietly to Shelby as he watched Alia hug a young man at the entrance to Kyle Field. He was a bit taller than Andy and a bit broader at the shoulders.

"Alia already knows Griffin, so I thought she would be more comfortable around him than with someone she didn't know."

"You know she goes out with him every Sunday night after Bible study, right?" Andy asked.

"So? They're not together. And he's my friend, too."

"This weekend was supposed to be my time with Alia," he complained.

"Oh, yeah? Tell that to your 'Gigem' buddies," she commented. "You're still hoping she'll move you out of the friendzone, aren't you?"

Andy glared at Shelby before transitioning to a smile and extending his hand toward Griffin. "Good to see you, bro!"

* * *

"Look, there's Gretchen," Joel told his companions, indicating a group of girls with fashion taste a bit out of sync with the other guests. "I'm going over to say hello."

"Is that the Gretchen who does welding with Alia?" Emi asked.

"Yeah, that's her."

"I want to meet her."

Joel looked at Annie and said, "We'll be right back."

"Hey, Moped Guy," Gretchen greeted as Joel and Emi approached her table.

"Hi, ladies," Joel greeted. "You all look great!" He suddenly lost his smile. "Wait. Can I say that? Should I say you look wicked, instead? I'm just trying to compliment you on your unique sense of fashion. And I've just never seen Gretchen in anything but her sub shop clothes."

"This is Joel," Gretchen announced to her friends, standing up. "He lives in my apartment complex."

"Your dress is awesome," Emi commented. It was black, with long flowing sleeves. The hem and sleeves of the dress looked intentionally ragged. She noticed another wearing dark red, with black trim. "All of your dresses are awesome."

"Yeah," Joel agreed. "Spooky and sexy at the same time. Was 'wicked' the right word?"

"Sure. 'Wicked' fits," one of the three other girls said.

"That's the benefit of getting dresses at the Halloween store," another said as she stood up. "I'm Esmer. That's Sarah," she pointed to the one who just spoke, "and she's Rampage," she pointed to the other.

"That's Ramona Page," the girl said. "But 'Rampage' will do."

"Are y'all like a Homecoming coven, or what?" Joel asked jokingly.

"Be nice or we'll put a hex on you," Gretchen laughed. "Who's your date?" she asked, nodding to Emi.

"This is Emi, but she's not my date. My date's over there," he pointed. "Annie."

"I think you're in welding with my friend Alia," Emi said. "The only other girl in the class."

"Yep, just the two of us girls, with a bunch of metalheads."

"Wait. Annie and Joel?" Esmer asked.

"Uh, yeah?"

"It looks like she's going to dance with that tall guy," Rampage pointed out. Annie and Jalen were walking to the dance floor, with Jalen's hand on her back. Rampage turned back to Joel. "That's what you get for neglecting your date."

"The guy is my date. Jalen," Emi explained. "We all came together."

"Why did you say 'Annie and Joel' like that?" Joel asked Esmer.

"There's a rumor about a couple named Annie and Joel," Esmer said as if that was enough explanation.

"What rumor?" Joel and Gretchen asked at the same time.

"Ram and I overheard a girl in the restroom the other day talking about a guy named Joel cheating on his girlfriend Annie."

"She was probably talking about me," Emi said. She looked at Joel, then back at Esmer. "Cause we all do stuff together. Sometimes the three of us and sometimes just two of us."

"No. With the girl who was talking," Esmer clarified. "She said he acted rapey, and she had to struggle to get away."

"Rapey, as in attempted rape?" Emi asked. She turned back to Joel with raised eyebrows.

"The only girls I've gone out with since school started have been you and Annie," Joel defended.

Gretchen cleared her throat. "I saw you take a girl to your apartment a couple of weeks ago. It was a Sunday night. I was just coming home from my shift."

"You went out with someone else without telling us?" Emi asked, elbowing Joel in the ribs. "You should at least get our opinion. We might be able to warn you about the bad ones."

"It wasn't a date. I ran into a girl from school at Bullseye and we started talking. Her name's Sienna. I was looking at clearance stuff to resell and she thought it was funny because some of the stuff was for girls. Anyway, we talked for a while, and then she asked for a ride home because her mother was late. I was driving her home, and then she said she wanted to buy one of the jewelry cleaners I was selling. I told her I could bring it to school, but she wanted to see it right then. So, we stopped by my apartment to get it."

"And that's all?" Emi asked, staring at him. "Then you took her home?"

"Yeah, and she didn't even want the jewelry cleaner after she saw it."

"Did Ryn meet her?"

"Ryn hadn't gotten home yet."

"Joel…." Emi started but stopped. She looked back at Esmer. "Rapey?"

"That's what she said," Esmer acknowledged.

Joel stood silently, trying to process the comments.

"We just stopped by for a minute; just long enough to get the jewelry thing. I wanted her to wait in the car, but she wanted to see the apartment."

"They were only at his apartment for, like, two or three minutes," Gretchen added.

"How long does sexual assault take? Is three minutes enough time to make a move on her, get rejected, then take her home in shame?" Emi asked.

"Emi," Joel said, "you know me better than anyone at this school. Have I ever acted… uh… inappropriately with you or Annie?"

"Well, you kissed Annie out of the blue on the first day of school and you were a little grabby with me on the ride to get your sister."

"Look, we don't know this Sienna," Esmer said. "We don't know if the girl in the restroom was her. Maybe she was talking about another Joel and Annie."

Ramona stood up. "There she is," she said, pointing. "Light blue dress, strapless."

"Sienna," Emi said.

Chapter 25
Andy's surprise

By the end of the game, Andy and his Gig 'Em friends succumbed to the falling temperature and put their shirts back on and added maroon A&M hoodies as well. They were confident that their antics during the game aided the Aggie win over the New Mexico Lobos. Alia put her heels back on for the walk across campus to the cheaper parking lot that Andy had insisted on using.

Halfway through the walk, Alia stopped and sat down on a bench.

"Hold up, guys," Shelby called out.

Alia pulled off her heels and touched the sore spots on the back of each foot where the straps rubbed against the skin. They felt squishy. Blisters. Alia pulled her right foot up and Shelby shined her phone light on the area.

"I think I have some Band-Aids in my bag," Shelby offered. She dug around in her bag and handed Alia a couple of adhesive bandages. She followed that up with, "You have to be careful around here."

"Oh. Are there muggers?"

"Not that kind of danger. See that big oak tree that hangs over the walkway?"

"Yeah."

"That's the Century Tree. The legend says if lovers walk together under the Century Tree, it means they'll be together forever. So just be careful about where you walk and who you walk with."

As if demonstrating, a couple posed for selfies under the tree. The young man held his phone out as far as his arm would reach, then turned his face to his girlfriend. The flash of the camera caught them in a kiss, as intended.

"Thanks for the warning. I'll keep that in mind," Alia responded. Adhesive bandages in place, Alia began to put her shoes back on. Andy grabbed them and held them out.

"Hold these," he directed to Shelby, who accepted them with a puzzled look.

Andy turned his back to Alia and leaned down. "Climb on."

"Are you sure? It's still a long way to the car."

"If Ty and John could carry that Japanese woman for miles up the Grand Canyon, I can carry you on a flat walkway to the car."

Alia put her arms over Andy's shoulders and jumped up to position her legs on Andy's hips. Andy put a hand around each of Alia's thighs and stood upright. He wiggled a little to get Alia positioned more securely.

"Are you okay?" Alia asked.

"You have to speak to me in Japanese until we get to the car." He began walking.

"*Kon'nichi wa. Shogun.* Karate," Alia responded. "Oh, and, *aisu kuriimu.*"

"What's that?"

"Ice cream."

"Seriously? Their word for ice cream is just to say ice cream with a Japanese accent?"

"That's how the grandma said it, and she didn't speak English."

* * *

Shelby pulled into the parking lot of the Maroon 12 Bar & Grill. Her car was more comfortable for four people than Andy's or Alia's vehicles and looked nicer than Griffin's. His offer to drive to the game was overruled by the other three.

"Sorry about the limited number of restaurants in College Station that stay open late, even on a game night. This is one of the better choices," Shelby said.

"Hey, it's better than what we had in Brenham," Griffin said, referring to the home of Blinn College where he transferred from. "If you want a late-night meal in Brenham, all they have is Whataburger."

While not quite full, the restaurant already had several tables of Aggies and a couple of tables of Lobos fans, distinguished by their red shirts and loud demeanor. The chair cushions and booths were upholstered in maroon vinyl and the walls were covered with A&M football and basketball jerseys.

"Just what we need," an outspoken Lobos fan called out as the hostess led Alia's party to a table, "more Aggies."

"You better watch what you say, this is Aggie country," called an Aggie across the room.

Loud calls of "whoop!" were heard around the restaurant, followed by laughter.

"You're just mad 'cause y'all lost," another Aggie diner shouted.

Alia's party had the privilege of being seated next to the loud New Mexico fan. Apparently, the Lobos fans were of drinking age, evidenced by several beer bottles on display at their table as they waited for their food.

"This is my first time here after a game," Shelby said. "I didn't know it would be so crazy."

"Is this a typical college weekend?" Alia asked.

"On game days, yeah," Andy answered. "On non-game days, it's pretty boring. That's when we go to the creek at night and gig frogs."

Alia looked at Shelby for confirmation.

Shelby nodded. "If we catch enough we'll invite friends over for a cookout."

Andy added, "They taste like chicken. Tiny little chickens. I'm talking about the frogs, not the friends."

Griffin smiled broadly. "I must've missed this Aggie tradition, but I'm in. Next time, invite me to go with you."

Shelby burst out laughing. "We're kidding! No one goes frog hunting!"

Andy said to Alia, "The expression on your face was priceless."

Griffin looked disappointed. "I think we should start it."

The competitive banter continued throughout the meal. Additional bottles of beer seemed to increase the volume of the voices. Though they had arrived before Alia's group, they were still adding to the beer bottle collection on the table when Alia's group stood up to leave.

"Leaving so soon?" a boisterous patron with a red Lobos cap called out from the New Mexico table. "They can't stand the presence of superior intellect," he said to his companions.

"What city is the University of New Mexico in?" Alia asked her friends.

"Albuquerque," one of the New Mexico fans answered. "It's a lot prettier than College Station. You been there?"

"Yeah. My friend threw up there," Alia replied. That drew laughter from the surrounding tables.

"Girl, look at you, all dressed up. You look way too classy to be hanging around with these nutcase Aggies," the red-cap man stated. "Why don't you join our table?" He stood up as if offering her a seat.

"You're the one at an Aggie restaurant, full of Aggies, talking bad about Aggies," Andy responded. "I'd say you're the nutcase and she's with the better people."

Alia smiled in her discomfort at the unwanted attention.

Andy placed his hand on the small of Alia's back to guide her towards the door.

"Hey, little dude. You need to step back. This woman's clearly out of your league." He wasn't much taller than Andy, but more muscular. He grabbed Alia's arm.

Alia's polite smile disappeared. She tried to pull her arm away without appearing rude, so as not to antagonize the drunkard.

"Come on, join us," Red Cap reiterated.

"She doesn't want to join you," Andy said calmly. "You need to let her go."

The man released Alia's arm and turned to Andy. "You're getting annoying. Are you rich or something? Is that why she's with you? 'Cause I just don't see what you have to offer."

"I think you've had too much to drink," Andy responded. "You need to go find a bed somewhere and sleep it off."

The man poked Andy in the chest and said, "Back off." Then he turned back to Alia and grabbed her arm again. "Do you want to help me find a bed so we can sleep it off?"

Andy tapped him on his shoulder.

The man released Alia again. "I told you…" Rather than finish his sentence, he took a swing at Andy.

Andy blocked his punch and held the man's arm as he stepped behind the man, bringing the man's arm back with him. Andy twisted the man's body around, forcing him to lose his balance. With both hands now on the man's arm – one hand on his wrist and the other on his upper arm – Andy pulled the arm down, forcing the man to kneel or risk breaking his arm at the elbow.

The man stumbled to his knees, with his arm twisted behind his back in an uncomfortable position.

"You little…"

The man choked off his words with a howl as Andy pulled up on his arm.

Andy spoke softly, "You were very disrespectful to my friend. I'd ask you to apologize, but you're too drunk to say it sincerely. Go sleep it off."

The man's friends stood up and Griffin stepped forward. "I wouldn't try anything if I were you," Griffin stated. "Look around. This is Aggie territory. You're outnumbered seventy thousand to three."

Diners throughout the restaurant applauded, with a few calls of 'whoop!' for added support. Andy let go of the man's arm when several Aggies gathered around the New Mexico table. Alia stared at Andy in shock.

"Let's get out of here," Shelby stated, latching onto Alia's arm and pulling her towards the door.

At the car, Griffin clapped Andy on the back. "That was awesome!"

"He took Aikido in middle school and high school," Shelby explained. "He's a black belt. He has a certificate on the wall in his room at his parents' house."

Alia and Andy sat in the back. Before Shelby pulled out of the parking space, Alia slid to the center position next to Andy. After buckling the seat belt, she reached over and held Andy's hand. When Shelby finally exited the parking lot onto the road, Alia squeezed his hand and said, "Thank you."

* * *

Shelby drove them home, pulled up in the driveway next to Griffin's car, and clicked the remote to open the garage door. When the door was raised enough to see inside the garage, Shelby said "Oops, I forgot we put Alia's truck in there." She clicked the remote again. There wasn't enough space on the street for parking along the curb.

As the group exited Shelby's car, Griffin said his goodbyes. "I'll see y'all in the morning." He opened his car door. The remaining three walked to the front door.

"Are we meeting him for breakfast?" Alia asked Andy and Shelby.

"We're meeting him at church," Shelby answered, unlocking the door.

"All of us? Andy too?"

"Shelby makes me go," Andy said.

"I do not. The first Sunday we were back at school I enticed him by pointing out that my beautiful sorority sisters would be there," she said with a chuckle. She led the way up the stairs to the bedroom floor. "I was just inviting him out of courtesy since we live in the same house this semester. But now he's usually ready before me on Sundays. I think if anyone 'made' him go, it was you, Alia."

"Me?" Alia asked, surprised. "What do you mean?"

"When I started going to church with you in the summer, it was an excuse to spend time with you," Andy admitted. "At least at first. But I continued to go because I wanted to find what you have. Over the summer, it seemed like you relaxed more, smiled more, just seemed happier."

"Oh," Alia said. "I didn't realize that."

"Yeah. I'd like to think it was my influence, but I know it was something else. I still feel a little fake at church, but I hope it will catch on."

"Just keep going. Eventually, it will," Alia said.

Shelby headed into her bedroom and Andy followed Alia into Ella's master suite.

"While you're taking a shower, I'll try to get those handcuffs off the bed."

While Andy checked drawers for the keys, Alia dug through her overnight bag on the dresser for the tank top and shorts she planned to sleep in. She started to pull out her panties, then stopped and looked up at Andy. She dropped the panties back in the bag and put the T-shirt and shorts back in as well. She then picked up the bag and carried it into the bathroom.

Alia came back out, walked over to Andy, and turned her back to him. "Unzip me please."

Andy reached up and obediently unzipped her dress, uncertain of where this act of intimacy would lead.

Alia turned around to face him. "Andy, I just want you to know you're not out of my league."

She stood on her tiptoes and put her arms around his neck, pulling slightly to lower his face to her level. She didn't have to pull hard. She closed her eyes the moment their lips met. They continued the embrace after the kiss. Alia could feel a heart beating fast and smiled, eyes still closed. She wasn't sure if the heartbeat was hers or his.

When she felt moisture on Andy's cheek, she asked softly, "Are those tears?"

Andy shook his head, eyes still closed. "Allergies."

"You beat up that guy at the restaurant like it was nothing," she whispered. "And holding me makes you…uh…have allergies?"

"I didn't beat him up. I just disabled him," he mumbled. More clearly, he added, "I can't think of a funny comeback."

"You have all night to think of one. See you in the morning."

She didn't wait for a response before turning around and walking into the bathroom, the corners of the unzipped seam of her dress waving slightly with each step. Andy stared until she closed the door. He smiled and continued his effort to remove the handcuffs.

* * *

Upon exiting the bathroom after her shower and nighttime duties, Andy was gone. Alia turned off the overhead light and walked to the bed. After climbing in, she reached over to turn off the lamp on the nightstand and noticed the handcuffs lying next to it, next to her phone. She opened the drawer of the nightstand and looked inside to check for space for the cuffs. Along with hair ties and extra phone charging cables were several packets of condoms. *Cuffs and condoms*, Alia thought. *At least Ella's being responsible in her kinky fantasy.* She put the handcuffs in the drawer, closed it, and turned off the lamp.

* * *

Alia was panting hard as she ran through the darkness to escape Bulldog and his cohorts. She dared to glance back. They were gaining, reaching out for her. She cried out, "No!" as they grasped her arms and pulled her down. She looked up to see the drunken Lobos fan grinning down at her. Bulldog and his friends had disappeared. The grinning drunk lifted his hands to reveal a pair of handcuffs dangling from each outstretched forefinger. He laughed and soon his laughter was joined by another. Brody looked at her, then down at his phone, then back at her, laughing. He held up his phone. It displayed her terrified face on the screen.

A flash of light caused all to look up. With a swift motion, Brody lay on his back on the ground, his phone screen shattered. The drunken restaurant marauder lay face down, his hands bound in cuffs behind his back. Andy knelt beside her, then took her hand and helped her to stand. His serious expression turned into a smile as he said, "Let's go." She looked down at her soiled and torn dress and then back up at Andy.

"I'm all dirty," she lamented.

"What dirt?" Andy asked.

She looked down at herself again, wondering how he couldn't see the obvious, when he touched her forehead. He slid his hand down to cover her eyes, then quickly pulled his hand away. She saw herself from the outside, almost like looking in a mirror. But the image wasn't reversed. She was seeing herself as Andy saw her. And her dress was clean.

Alia awoke with a start, sweating and breathing hard. The dim glow of a streetlight provided enough light to see where she was. Ella's room in the house she shared with Shelby and Andy. When she finally calmed down, she leaned over to the nightstand and tapped her phone to wake it up. The screen showed the time: 3:17 am. She slid out of bed and walked through the darkened room to the door, opened it slowly, and looked into the hall. No lights on. No sounds.

She tiptoed to the second door from her room and slowly turned the knob.

Chapter 26
~Change of plans~

Previous June – vacation day two

"This morning, everything changed," Alia explained to Sophie through FaceTime about why she left Andy and his extended family and was now hiding out at a gas station.

"What happened this morning?"

"They have a teddy bear sitting on a shelf facing the bed. This morning I took it down to look at it and I found a spy camera hidden inside. It was facing the bed. That's probably why Brody wanted me to stay so badly last night. Claudia admitted the condoms were Brody's idea. She said he was being thoughtful. Andy grabbed Brody's phone while he was using it – so it was unlocked – and he checked the open apps and he found the spy camera app showing our bedroom. Brody wanted to watch me and Andy fu-… uh, I mean, have sex."

"Oh my gosh!" Sophie exclaimed.

"Andy exploded at Brody; started yelling so loud the lawn guys noticed. He yelled at his aunt, yelled at his uncle. I've never seen Andy angry like that. I just packed all my stuff and left. I snuck out. I didn't say goodbye or anything, because I didn't want them to try to get me to stay."

"Do you have a plan?"

Alia looked around. "I don't know," she said as her voice cracked. "I...I...I just want to get away from those people. I can't be with them for another five days." She sniffled. Ty and Sophie could see the tears that she was wiping with her sleeve. "As I walked, I just started praying that God would help me get back home. Maybe I can take a bus."

"Alia," Ty stated a bit loudly to get her attention. "Do you have the Uber or Lyft apps on your phone?"

"No."

"Download one of them and install it now while we're talking." Ty stopped walking. He called out to the younger travelers, "Y'all go ahead and check out the Rec Center. Meet us back here when you're done."

To Alia and Sophie, he said, "I'm looking up flights from Little Rock to Albuquerque."

"Albuquerque?" Alia asked.

"That's where we'll be tonight," Ty replied. "Is your last name still Khalifi on your driver's license?"

"Yes, I haven't applied for a new license with Jentler yet. I wanted to wait until after summer school starts."

"Okay. I'm booking a flight under 'Alia Khalifi'."

"Ty," Alia said. "The Uber app needs a credit card number."

"Hold on." He removed his wallet from his back pocket and handed it to Sophie, who pulled out a credit card and read off the number to Alia. Ty went back to completing the flight reservation.

* * *

Alia:
Shelby saw me on her way to
Brody's house. She's giving
me a ride to airport

Sophie:
Did she try to talk you out of
leaving?

I told her you already bought
the plane ticket

Is she mad?

Not at me. I told her what
happened and she's super
pissed at Brody. She said she
might skip out on the trip, too

Andy's been texting me. I
haven't answered. I don't
want him to try to get me to
go back. I'll text him from the
airport

Chapter 27
She's hot but she's psycho

October - Sunday morning

Shelby awoke first and went to Ella's room to wake up Alia. Girls needed more time to get ready for church than guys. She knew from experience that Andy only needed ten minutes if pressed. The door to Ella's room was already open, so she went in and looked around. Alia wasn't in the bed. She walked to the bathroom and stuck her head in. No Alia there, either. She walked out past her room and stopped at Andy's door. She put her ear against the door to listen for any sounds, such as talking. All she heard was silence. She knocked before trying the knob. It was unlocked.

"Hey, it's time to…. Oh." Alia was in bed with Andy. "Um…sorry."

She started to close the door when Andy responded with, "Hi. It's okay, you can leave it open."

"I, um, I just wanted to…. Are y'all still going to church?"

Andy sat up and pushed the covers down and Shelby momentarily feared she would see more skin than she anticipated. But Andy was wearing a T-shirt and Alia a tank top.

Andy gently shook Alia's shoulder until she stirred. "It's time to get up."

He got out of bed and walked to the door where Shelby still stood, frozen, mouth agape. She was relieved that his bottom half was also clothed; he had on gym shorts. "We'll be down in a few minutes."

"Okay. Just be quiet. David's still asleep."

* * *

Alia came down in jeans and a light blue, long sleeve blouse. She was smiling. "Good morning."

"Did you sleep well?" Shelby asked as she pulled boxes of cereal from a cabinet.

"Not at first, but after I went to Andy's room I did." Alia sat down on the stool at the kitchen bar that faced the island sink.

Shelby got a carton of milk from the refrigerator and set it on the counter in front of Alia.

"I had a nightmare." Alia paused, deciding whether to say more. "I've had recurring nightmares of men chasing me…. I used to have them a lot, but I hadn't had one in a while. Then it happened again last night, and I woke up and went to Andy's room. I had a good sleep after that."

"Did y'all…." Shelby started to ask before being interrupted.

Andy arrived in the kitchen and said, "Me, too. Surprisingly," having heard the statement about 'good sleep' as he descended the stairs. "Do you think the handcuffs triggered the nightmare?"

"I don't know. Maybe. They were in my dream, the handcuffs and the drunk guy. How did you get them off the bed? Did you find the keys?"

"I picked the locks." Andy sat down beside Alia.

"Why do you know how to pick handcuff locks?" Alia asked.

"You have to tell her the story," Shelby urged. She got three bowls from another cabinet and set one each in front of Alia and Andy and the empty place next to Alia.

"Is this the story you mentioned a couple of weeks ago that you would only tell me if I came here?" Alia asked.

"Yeah."

Shelby continued to gather breakfast items as Andy talked.

"A few weeks ago – it was a Monday morning – I heard Ella calling for help. Not like an emergency or anything. She was shouting, 'Is anyone home? I'm stuck. I need help!' Shelby had left early for some sorority thing and David had gone to class, so I was the only one home besides Ella."

"I walked in and there she was…."

"Naked," Shelby finished.

"Well, she was wearing panties, but that was it. The covers were bunched up at the foot of the bed. Her hands were cuffed to the headboard, but she was kind of twisted to her side, with her knees pulled up close to her body. I *noped* right out as soon as I saw her."

Alia looked at Andy in disbelief, wondering if this was just a tall tale he made up for laughs. "I can't believe you didn't tell me about it as soon as it happened."

"Well, you know, it happens so often, I just didn't think it was worth mentioning."

Shelby snorted before commenting, "Yeah, right. Girls are just throwing themselves at him all the time."

Andy ignored the comment and continued the tale. "Then she called me back. 'I need help. I need to pee.' Anyway, after an appropriate amount of staring, I covered her with the sheet."

"Appropriate amount of staring?" Shelby asked. She'd heard the story before but liked teasing Andy about it, especially in front of Alia.

"Hey, it took some time to get over my shock," he defended, looking at Alia rather than Shelby.

"Who put the handcuffs on her?" Alia asked.

"Her boyfriend. He'd slept over. That morning he put the handcuffs on her and then he went to class. She said that he told her he liked her submissive...."

"Which I can understand, because she's a bit overbearing," Shelby interjected.

"And he told her he would be back after class to let her go. The kinky part is...."

"The handcuffs weren't the kinky part?" Alia interrupted.

"The kinky part was that she let him do it," Shelby added.

"Hey, I'm telling this story," Andy said.

"So, you picked the locks and got her out?" Alia asked.

"Yeah, eventually. Ella found the keys a couple of days later on the floor behind the bed. Anyway, the whole time I'm looking for the keys, she's saying 'I gotta pee. Hurry, I gotta pee.' I got a paperclip and started trying to pick the locks when she just suddenly yelled out, 'I gotta go now! It's about to come out!' I just yelled back to hold it a little longer."

"Did she pee on the bed?" Alia asked.

"I'm getting there. Let me tell the story," Andy complained. "I finally looked up a video and found out how to pick the locks. I still used the paperclip, but there's a trick to it. You have to first turn it one way until you feel a click, then turn it the other way. Do you want me to show you?"

"Not now; you're supposed to be telling the story," Shelby reminded.

"Yeah, did she pee on the bed?" Alia asked again.

"You know, I should have asked for a discount on my rent," Andy said, more to himself than to the girls.

"Get back to the story," Alia said. "Did she get free in time to go to the bathroom or did she pee in bed?"

"Okay, okay. As soon as the cuffs were off, she ran to the bathroom, dragging the sheet with her, as if she didn't want me to see what I already saw. After that, I went back to my room. That was it."

"She hugged you," Shelby reminded Andy. "That's when I got back home."

"Oh, yeah. When she got out of the bathroom, she called my name, so I went out into the hallway and she thanked me and hugged me."

"While naked," Shelby added.

"She was wrapped in the sheet," Andy corrected.

"And you think she's hot," Alia stated. "That's what you said a couple of weeks ago."

"Yes, my landlord's hot, psycho daughter hugged me. That's all. Just a hug."

"A naked hug," Shelby reiterated, looking at Alia for her reaction.

"She was wearing a sheet," Andy said again, more emphatically. He placed his hand on Alia's and looked at her. "I prefer hot and normal."

Alia smiled. While other girls might have picked up on 'hot', Alia focused on the other adjective. *He said 'normal'. He thinks I'm normal.*

Chapter 28
~A good night's sleep~

Previous June – vacation day six

In the wee hours of the morning after the skunk ordeal, the beverage from the late-night meal made its way through John's system and he got up to use the bathroom. He quietly felt his way to the bathroom without the light. Upon taking care of business, he returned to his usual spot in the bed by the window and quickly drifted back to sleep.

Lizzie stood behind John in the line for movie tickets. She wrapped her arms around his waist and pressed her face into his back. As he stepped forward in the queue, she stepped with him. He put his hands on her arms and smiled at the closeness. He liked when she did that. Not as much as a real hug from the front, where he could sneak a kiss, but this was the next best thing. Once they reached the cashier's booth, he was forced to change his focus from Lizzie to the unusually bright computer monitor showing the available seats in the movie house.

As the morning light found its way through a narrow opening between the two panels of curtains over the window, John unconsciously shifted his face on the pillow to avoid the glare, and his groggy mind slowly awakened. He felt the body pressed against his back and the arm across his torso and smiled at the thought of Lizzie. He opened his eyes to see, not a movie theater, but the curtains of a motel room. It took a moment to remember he was in Arizona and Lizzie was thousands of miles away. And if Lizzie wasn't snuggled up against him, who was?

The light was enough to see that the arm was pale, not as dark as his own or as his sister's. That meant it was either Alia or Annie.

Please don't let it be Annie, he thought. *I'll be in more trouble if it's Annie than if it's Alia.*

He reached back to gently touch the girl's thigh. The girl hummed at the touch. He felt smooth skin, not basketball shorts. It was Alia. Her shorts weren't as long as the basketball shorts Annie "borrowed". He remembered now. This was Alia's bed, not his. He had changed rooms due to the smell.

I went to sleep on the floor. How did I end up in bed?

He very slowly shifted his body away from Alia and slid his legs out of the bed and onto the floor. Alia stirred slightly as if trying to find the body she had been snuggled up to but did not awaken. John stood up and walked towards the bathroom, stopping between the beds to look at the bed covers and pillow on the floor.

Emi stirred in her bed, drawing his attention. She was awake and staring at him. When their eyes met, she glanced over at Alia, then back at John, and shook her head "no".

He replied with a shake of his own head before continuing to the bathroom.

* * *

The rooms opened directly to the parking lot. Upon exiting the girls' room with his armload of bedding, John found Ty outside talking with Kumiko, explaining the events of the previous night. She was leaning on the van, her crutch visible through the open passenger door, on the floor behind the driver seat. John noticed her nose twitching. As he approached, he understood why. Although the skunk smell had greatly diminished, he could still smell it on Ty.

Mrs. Yunohara was already seated in the front passenger seat of their van and the boys were in the second row.

"Hey, Kenji, Jun," John greeted. He waved at their grandmother. "Are y'all going home today?"

"Yes," Kenji answered.

"Did you guys have fun on the trip?"

"Yes, but now is good to go home."

"Do you miss home?"

"No, but Mr. Ty stinks," Jun explained.

"Do you stink, too?" Kenji asked.

John got close enough to put his head into the van. "What do you think?"

"You're okay. Mr. Ty smells bad."

Ty got Sophie and the girls to come outside to say goodbye to Kumiko's family before they left.

Once the Moriguchis had gone, Ty implored his group, "Y'all get dressed so we can go get breakfast or brunch or whatever they're serving now."

"How did everyone sleep?" Sophie asked.

"I don't know if it was the bed or what, but that was the best sleep I've had all week," Alia stated. "I dreamed I was snuggled up with Emi's giant teddy bear."

Emi looked at John and slightly shook her head.

"Nothing happened," John mouthed silently. He put his forefinger against his lips to indicate silence on the matter.

"Hey, Annie," Ty called. "John has a shirt just like that."

She smiled and returned to the room to change clothes, careful to hold up the shorts as she walked.

Chapter 29
The rumor grows

Alice McGee entered the office she shared with two other English teachers and a set of filing cabinets and announced, "I've got more info."

"What are you talking about?" Jennifer Salazar asked.

"That rumor the kids were talking about at the dance," Mrs. McGee answered. "The boy is Annie Bates' boyfriend. I don't know his name, but we can probably figure it out."

"The girl's name is Annie?" Breanna Jacobs asked.

"Not the victim. Annie is the boy's girlfriend. She's a freshman."

Mrs. Salazar rolled her chair back and swiveled around to face the other teachers. "What's the rumor?"

"That Annie's boyfriend sexually assaulted another girl," Miss Jacobs stated. "And now another conversation I overheard makes more sense."

"What's that?" Mrs. McGee asked.

"I heard the Halloween sisters talking about…"

"Halloween sisters?" Mrs. Salazar interjected.

"You should have chaperoned with us," Mrs. McGee stated. "The emo girls looked like they got their homecoming dresses from the set of *Hocus Pocus*."

"What's *Hocus Pocus*?"

"It's a classic Halloween movie. Where've you been?"

"Sorry. I don't watch horror movies."

"It's a comedy. Anyway," Miss Jacobs continued, "I heard them say something like, 'whether whatever happened to Sienna is true or not, I feel sorry for Annie.' I didn't think much of it and didn't connect it to the rumor you heard. But if the Annie that they were talking about is Annie Bates, then Sienna must be the victim."

"We need to find Sienna's last name and find the identity of Annie's boyfriend," Mrs. McGee pointed out.

"Why?" Mrs. Salazar asked. "If she didn't report it, why should we get involved?"

"You're so sheltered. We have an obligation to report things like this," Mrs. McGee replied. "The kids don't like to snitch, so they won't do it. But if there's a predator at our school, we need to prevent him from hurting anyone else and we need to help his victim."

"Annie Bates is in one of my classes," Miss Jacobs said. "I'll chat with her about homecoming and see if I can get her to tell me who her boyfriend is."

"Good," Mrs. McGee responded.

"I've got a Sienna in one of my classes," Mrs. Salazar volunteered. "I can try to discreetly find out if she was involved."

"Yes. Discreetly," Mrs. McGee agreed.

* * *

"I checked the records for sophomore transfer students named Joel," Principal Bret Holton said, scratching his bald head. "The only one is Joel Vaclavik. I'm not sure if I'm pronouncing that right. It looks like *Vak*-la-vik, but Kendra said it might be pronounced *Vas*-la-vik." Kendra was the school secretary.

"I know that name," Adriane Sanders, the school counselor stated. "I saw his records when he registered this summer. He lives with his sister because his parents are in jail."

"Bad parental influence," Principal Holdon noted. "That says a lot. Anyway, I have the girl coming in next period. I want you involved in case she's reluctant to discuss the attack with me. She might rather open up to a woman than to an old man like me."

* * *

After Principal Holton stepped out of his office, Mrs. Sanders pulled his desk chair around to the side of his desk and sat down. It was her strategy to be closer to Sienna without the imposing desk in between. "Did Joel attack you?"

"No," Sienna answered simply.

"Look. We're on your side. You didn't do anything wrong. When we hear a student is in trouble, we want to help. I want to help. And if one of the students caused the trouble, we need to deal with that, too."

"It's nothing. Rumors get blown out of proportion."

"Well, what part of the rumor was true?"

Sienna shrugged her shoulders.

"Did you go with him to his apartment?"

"Yes."

"Was anyone else there?"

"No."

"Just you and him?"

"Yes, Ma'am. Just me and him."

"Have you been to his apartment before?"

"No. I hadn't done anything with him before. I've seen him around school and that night I saw him at Bullseye and we started talking."

"How did you end up at his apartment?"

"I asked him for a ride home."

"And he took that to mean his home." Ms. Sanders said it as a statement, not a question. "What happened at the apartment?"

"Look. It's no big deal. He took me home; to *my* home. End of story. I don't want to get him in trouble."

Mrs. Sanders leaned toward Sienna, with one arm on the side of the desk.

"Sienna, sexual assault *is* a big deal. I understand the trauma. I was assaulted by a boy when I was in high school, too. For the longest time, I told myself it was my fault, that I must have led him on. I didn't tell anyone because I was ashamed."

As if she wasn't close enough to Sienna, she leaned even closer but lowered her voice. "A few months later he raped a girl. I finally told a teacher what happened to me. I regret not telling someone sooner, because maybe then he wouldn't have attacked that other girl."

Sienna glanced at the door. "I need to get back to class."

Ms. Sanders sighed and gave up trying to get anything more out of Sienna. She leaned back in her chair and jotted something on a notepad, tore off the sheet, and handed it to Sienna. "That's my number if you decide you want to talk about it." She scribbled again on the notepad and handed Sienna the second sheet. "That's a hall pass to get you back to class."

* * *

"Hey, Moped Guy," Gretchen greeted as she and Joel both arrived at the apartment complex at the same time after school.

"Hi, Gretchen," Joel responded without enthusiasm.

"You didn't call me Sandwich Girl. Is something wrong?"

"Your friends were right. People think the rumor is about me. But I didn't do anything."

"I know. If it's really about that girl you took to your apartment, I know you weren't there long enough to do anything, and she didn't act like anything was wrong when you came out. Everyone will forget about it in a couple of days."

"Thanks. But the principal wants to meet with me and my sister tomorrow morning."

"Dude, that's crap."

* * *

Joel sat on the sofa, leaning over the phone in his hands. After a moment of thought, he began tapping out a message.

Joel:
The principal wants to meet with me and Ryn tomorrow morning

Annie:
About what?

Joel:
That stupid rumor

Emi:
No one takes that seriously

Joel:
The school does. They said I did something to a girl. And I don't think you two would have anything to report

Annie:
Who?

Joel:
They didn't say. Just a girl

Emi:
You think Sienna said something?

The Lingering Scent

Annie:
If she did, wouldn't they say it
was about Sienna, not "a
girl"?

Joel:
Did you ever feel scared around
me?

Annie:
Scared of what?

Emi:
I was scared when the tires
blew out

Joel:
That's not what I mean. Did you
ever feel scared I would do
something to you?

Annie:
No

Emi:
No. That's crazy

Annie:
It's probably just a step they
have to do. They heard a
rumor and have to say they
checked it out. They'll talk to
you, find nothing. Case
closed

Emi:
A formality

> Joel:
> But why do they want Ryn to
> come?

Emi:
Another formality?
I can be your character
witness if you need me

Annie:
Me too

Joel set his phone down on the sofa and stared at the teddy bears on the cabinet under the TV. Then he picked up his phone and scrolled through the photos. He finally found the one he was looking for and clicked it to view full screen. It was a couple of years old but was the most recent photo that had his whole family: mom, dad, Ryn, and himself.

Chapter 30
The accusation

"I told you not to bring anyone here when I'm not home," Ryn scolded as she stood in the kitchen, checking whether the stew was done.

"I didn't invite her in," Joel defended. "I told her to wait in the car, that I would only be a minute."

Ryn dished stew out of a pot and into two bowls. "Is she cute?"

Joel paused his effort of putting ice cubes into their two glasses. "How does that matter?"

"Was she worth it?" Ryn asked as she carried the bowls to the table.

"Nothing happened! She followed me in. I got the jewelry cleaner and then we left. I never touched her. Oh, and she decided she didn't want the jewelry cleaner after all."

"Then why did Mr. Holton call me to come to a meeting tomorrow?"

"I don't know."

"Did you make enemies at school? Is someone making up stuff to get back at you?"

"No. Most people don't even know I exist."

* * *

Ryn and Joel stood in the waiting area outside of the principal's office, waiting to be called. A couple of students sat in chairs looking at their phones. Ryn and Joel didn't feel like sitting.

"This meeting can't last long if these other students are meeting with Mr. Holton, too," Ryn observed.

"I hope so," Joel replied.

A school district police officer – resource officer – walked in and everyone turned their attention to him. When he began discussing car models with the secretary, the students resumed checking their phones. Another woman walked in and joined them in their conversation.

"Good morning, Adriane."

"Hi, Aaron. Flirting with Kendra, again, I see."

"Just talking about cars."

One of the assistant principals came out of his office and called for one of the sitting students.

Upon realizing the boy was not waiting for the principal, Joel said, "So much for your idea about a short meeting."

The door to Principal Holton's office finally opened and a teacher emerged.

"Joel, you and your sister can go in now," the secretary stated.

The resource officer and the woman named Adriane followed them in.

* * *

Minutes after the bell rang for the end of the school day, the bus riders gathered at the covered walkway outside the back entrance of the school to find their bus for the ride home.

"Hey! Bailey!"

Bailey looked around to see who was calling her. A heavyset girl with dark purple lipstick, black nail polish, and wearing black military-style boots approached her at the bus pickup line. As if her outfit was not intimidating enough, her scowl completed the mood.

"Me?" Bailey responded.

"Any other Bailey around here?"

Bailey looked around again and then gulped. Other students who had paused momentarily at the call to Bailey moved on after the caller looked at them with squinting eyes.

"I want to talk to you about your friend Sierra."

"You mean Sienna?"

"Yeah. Whatever. You and Sienna were in my sandwich shop a few weeks ago."

"Oh, yeah. That's where I recognize you from."

"And y'all were talking about finding a way to break up Annie and Joel."

"That was mostly Sienna venting and me listening."

"So, what was the plan? Frame Joel for attempted rape so Annie would dump him?"

Bailey gulped again before answering, "That was just a rumor."

The girl with the purple lipstick stepped forward, backing Bailey up to the wall. "And Sienna started that rumor."

"I wasn't involved in that."

The girl leaned forward, her face mere inches from Bailey's. "You are now."

* * *

Bailey was the last student to enter the school bus before the driver closed the door. The second she took her usual seat next to Sienna, the bus started moving. "I guess your plan to split up Annie and Joel involves getting Joel kicked out of school and arrested for assault," Bailey said. "You're getting your wish."

"I didn't mean for it to go this far," Sienna stated. "But I can't stop it now. Look, if the police start asking me about it, I'll just tell them I don't want to talk about it and I don't want to pursue anything. They'll have to drop the matter."

"But you're not denying it happened," Bailey noted. After three seconds of silence, she added, "I'm done with you." At the first stop, she got up and moved to a seat vacated by a rider who had gotten off.

"Hey, it'll blow over and everything will be fine," Sienna called after her.

Bailey ignored her and gave her attention to her phone.

"Everything will be fine," Sienna repeated to herself.

* * *

> Emi:
> Where were you at lunch?

Joel:
Ryn took me home after we
met with Mr. Holton AND THE
POLICE.

I felt sick after that

> Emi:
> Calling

Emi made the FaceTime connection to Joel from the privacy of her bedroom.

"Why were the police there?"

"It was that cop I always see at school. The one who looks like a soldier but also like he doesn't want to be there."

"So, it wasn't like a real police investigation," Emi said.

"It was close enough. And they confirmed it was about Sienna."

"Did they meet with Sienna?"

"Yeah, without the police, though."

"What did she tell them?"

"They wouldn't say. But they wanted to hear my side of the story. That got Ryn pissed off. She said if they can't tell us what Sienna is accusing me of, then we don't know what 'story' they're talking about."

"The cop said they don't need the victim's cooperation to press charges because sexual assault is a crime against the state."

"So, I'm like, 'Sienna accused me of sexual assault?' I said that because I hadn't heard anything official, only that rumor that Gretchen's friend told us about. And they won't tell me what Sienna said."

"That's crap. This is America," Emi protested. "They have to tell you what you're accused of."

"Ryn thinks they're just bluffing. That they have to look like they're doing something about the rumor and they're just trying to scare me. Well, it worked. It scared me. I still told them about meeting Sienna at Bullseye and taking her to get the jewelry cleaner. That's the only time I've done anything with Sienna."

"What are they planning to do?"

"They said they're still investigating. Oh, and the counselor said she's dealt with boys like me before. I don't even know what that means. The principal brought up that my parents are criminals. It's like they expect me to be a criminal because of what they did."

"I'm so sorry this is happening. I can go talk to Mr. Holton if you think it will help. After all, we practically spent the night together and you didn't do anything to me."

"Thanks. Maybe wait a couple of days to see where this goes."

After the call ended, Alia walked through the bathroom to Emi's room. "Is Joel in trouble?" she asked.

"Yeah. A girl spread a rumor about him, and the school is taking it seriously." At Alia's pressing, Emi explained the rumor and how Gretchen's friends identified Sienna as the source.

"Do you think there's any truth to it?"

"No," Emi replied with conviction. "It doesn't make sense. That night we were stuck in the Walmart parking lot," Emi paused and lowered her voice, "we kissed. If he was the kind of guy that would try to get in a girl's pants, that would have been the time for him to try it with me. But he didn't. We just fell asleep leaning on each other until Sophie and Ty came. I trust him."

"Then I trust him, too. I'll ask Gretchen about it in class tomorrow," Alia stated. "I want to find out what else she or her friends know."

* * *

Thursday morning, the walk to first period was uneventful and Joel thought maybe the whole rumor would blow over, as Gretchen suggested. The administration could say they took the rumor seriously, investigated it, and found nothing. All boxes checked off. Case closed.

As he took his seat, he said his usual "Good morning" to the girl in the adjacent seat. She merely nodded in acknowledgment, then quickly turned her attention to review an essay due in her next class. It was not her typical cheerful behavior. Only later in the class did Joel suspect her attitude was due to himself. Her pencil rolled off her desk and clattered to the floor, closer to him than to her. He leaned over to pick it up, but she stuck out her foot and kicked it so that it scooted across the floor, stopping at the desk in front of her. She leaned forward and whispered to the boy at that desk, "Can you hand me that?" He picked up the pencil and passed it back.

After class, Joel headed to his locker before his next class to put away his jacket. As he approached, he noticed a white rectangle against a line of pale green lockers. Students glanced at it as they passed. A few steps more and he realized it was a sign and that it was attached to his locker. It said, "Warning! Beware of molester."

Joel's face reddened. He grabbed the sign and wadded it up before anyone else could read it. He stuffed the wad into his jacket pocket and looked around to see who might have seen it. A couple of students looked at him and quickly turned away. He stowed his jacket in the locker and headed to class.

In his third-period class, someone left a news article on his desk. It was a printout of an article published after his mother was sentenced to prison. The article summarized both parents' criminal trials and subsequent sentencing. A handwritten note on the top said, "This explains a lot."

* * *

In the afternoon, Joel's phone vibrated with a message.

> Annie:
> Why weren't you at lunch?

> Joel:
> Not feeling well. Went home

Chapter 31
The unraveling

Friday morning, Gretchen knocked on Joel's door. "I need a ride to school."

"I'm not going."

"Yes, you are," Ryn said from the kitchen. "Do I need to drive you?"

"No. I'm not a kid."

"Is that your backpack?" Gretchen asked, pointing to the pack on the sofa.

"Yes, but..."

Gretchen pushed past him to enter the apartment and went straight for the backpack. "Since you're going to school, you can give me a ride." She picked up his backpack and carried it out the door.

"If I have to go, I'm taking the moped," he pointed out. "And I don't have an extra helmet."

"I'll risk it. It's less than two miles and everyone's driving slow."

Not finding any further excuses, he reluctantly muttered, "Okay. Fine."

Joel took his backpack from Gretchen and put it on backward; that is, with the pack in front. "Hop on."

Gretchen tapped out a message on her phone. After she put away her phone and positioned herself on the back of the saddle, Joel climbed on and started the engine.

When they reached the slow-moving traffic near the school, Joel asked, "What made you want a ride today? Tired of the bus?"

"It's all part of the plan. What classes are you taking?"

* * *

Joel and Gretchen entered the school and were met by the girls Joel had jokingly called 'the coven', Gretchen's friends who seemed to favor dark colors in clothes, makeup, and nail polish.

"You remember my friends, don't you? Rampage, Esmer and Sarah."

"Hey," Joel greeted.

"Esmer, you're up first," Gretchen announced. "Science hallway."

"That's where I'm going," Joel stated. "Chemistry."

"I know," Esmer stated. "Walk with me."

"You know?"

"I've seen you in the hallway. I've got Chem 2."

* * *

"Jalen's been texting me," Annie told Emi as they waited at the edge of the cafeteria for Joel to join them for lunch. "Are you okay with that?"

"Why would I not be okay with it?"

"Because he was your date for homecoming."

"Please," she said, drawing out the word. "It was a group thing. I think he was more like *our* date. And I'm happy for you. That is, if you like him. If you don't like him, then I won't be happy for you."

Annie smiled and continued to scan the hallway as she talked, "Thanks. If he asks me out, I wouldn't turn him down. Oh! Joel's coming."

"I've got to go," Emi stated. "I'll see you later today."

"Hey!" Joel called as he approached Annie. He had been talking with a girl who walked next to him, nearly shoulder-to-shoulder. The girl smiled and appeared to say "Bye" before turning and walking back the way they came.

"This has been a weird morning," Joel stated.

"How so?" Annie asked, sliding her hand into the crook of his arm.

Joel looked at her curiously before answering. "Someone's met me at every class and walked with me to my next class."

"Yeah, that's strange," Annie replied, patting his shoulder.

"What's going on?" Joel asked.

"I know yesterday was rough. I'm just glad you showed up again today. Let's get in the lunch line before it gets too long."

"Where's Emi?"

"She's skipping lunch today to help someone with a video project. She's got experience in video editing, you know, due to her hair videos and all."

After lunch, Annie walked Joel to the stairway where he would go upstairs for his next class and Annie would continue down the hallway to hers. Alia met them at the foot of the stairs.

"Are you about to head up?" Alia asked Joel.

"Yeah."

"I'm heading that way, too."

"Don't tell me. You're walking me to class."

"I'm going that way anyhow," Alia pointed out. "Why not?"

Joel shrugged his shoulders. "Let's go."

* * *

Joel:
What's the deal with people
walking me everywhere
today?

Emi:
Did you notice they were all
girls?

Yes. Did you have something
to do with it?

A little

Why? To make me look like a
player?

> No. To let everyone see that girls
> trust you and aren't bothered by
> the rumor

* * *

"My name is Bailey Hutchins," Bailey stated at the beginning of the video. A poster advertising the latest sub-shop special could be seen in the background.

"Why are you here today?" the interviewer asked, off-camera. She sounded a lot like Gretchen.

"Because you…"

The video wavered a bit and it picked up the sound of someone clearing her throat.

"Sienna is my friend. We've been friends for years," Bailey said on the video. "But she's gone through some difficult times lately."

"Get to the point."

"She's jealous of Annie Bates."

"Why does that matter?"

"Sienna doesn't realize her potential; that she has so much to be thankful for and so much to look forward to."

"Get back to how this relates to Annie Bates."

"Sienna, I love you like a sister," Bailey said directly to the camera. Then moving her eyes slightly above the camera, she continued, "Sienna got so messed up about her declining social status …."

"Get to the point," the interviewer commanded again.

Sienna looked up and said, "I'm getting there. Let me tell it my way." She looked at the camera again to continue, "Sienna feels her, uh, social status has been going down, and Annie's been getting more popular. So, she's jealous and wanted to do something to… uh…burst Annie's popularity bubble."

"Popularity bubble?"

"Did I mention that Sienna's parents divorced a couple of years ago and her dad remarried last year?"

"Focus."

"Sienna planned to do something to cause Annie to break up with Joel."

"Why?"

"You know, the bubble thing. I guess to deflate her ego."

"Do you think Annie has an inflated ego?"

"I don't know. I never talk to her or have any interaction with her. She smiles a lot and hangs out with the basketball team and has a boyfriend."

"Did Sienna tell you how she was going to get Annie and her boyfriend – Joel – to break up?"

"She was going to try to get Joel to like her – Sienna – instead of Annie. But if that didn't work, she would try something else. She would just look for an opportunity. We didn't talk about it after that. I thought she was just venting.

You know, not really planning anything, just talking through some dumb fantasy."

"Well, it looks like she made that fantasy happen."

"Are we done now?" Bailey asked the unseen interviewer.

"Yes."

"Sienna, I love you! We're still friends, okay?" The clip of the interview ended abruptly.

But the video didn't end there.

The scene changed to a view of Joel's apartment building at night, taken by a security camera. A yellow circle appeared around one of the doors in the apartment building, somewhat distant from the camera. "That's Joel's apartment," said the narrator who still sounded a lot like Gretchen.

Another circle appeared around a white SUV in the parking lot. The doors opened and two people got out. "That's Joel's car," the narrator said. The scene froze. An arrow appeared over the driver. "That's Joel." The arrow above the driver disappeared and another arrow appeared over the passenger. "And that's Sienna." The scene unfroze and the two people from the SUV walked towards the apartment that had been circled earlier.

The scene switched to a different camera. This one had a closer view of the door. Joel unlocked the door and pushed it open. Sienna stepped across the threshold just before the scene froze again.

"Let's start the clock," the narrator said. A stopwatch icon appeared in the lower-left corner. The video resumed playing and the stopwatch started counting.

Joel followed Sienna into the apartment. He left the door open. The two disappeared from view. After 30 seconds, Joel could be seen just inside the door, holding something. A couple of seconds later, he disappeared from view again. Another 28 seconds passed and Joel could be seen just inside the door again. Not a full view, but the person's clothing matched Joel's. He had been wearing beige shorts, whereas Sienna had been wearing jeans.

Another few seconds passed and Sienna came into view, holding something. A box. They appeared to be talking. She handed the box back to Joel several seconds later. They both disappeared from view again, only to return about ten seconds later. Both were empty-handed when they returned to the doorway. Sienna walked out first.

The clock stopped counting, but the scene continued. Joel stepped out and locked the door. They both began walking toward the SUV. The scene switched back to the camera that had a better view of the SUV. They got into the SUV and a few seconds later, it backed out of the parking space. Shortly, the vehicle drove out of view and the scene froze. The stopwatch remained on the screen the entire time, even after it had stopped counting.

"92 seconds," the narrator stated. "That was 92 seconds from entering the apartment until leaving it."

The scene fast reversed to the 30-second mark, where Joel reappeared inside the doorway, holding something.

"Did the alleged attack happen during these 30 seconds?" the narrator asked.

The scene fast-forwarded to the second time he appeared at the door. "Or did the attack happen in the twenty-two seconds before his second appearance at the door?"

The scene fast-forwarded to the point of Sienna walking out of the door. "Or did it happen during the ten seconds just before they both came out?"

The scene forwarded again a few frames to a point where Joel and Sienna were walking back to the car.

"Or did the attack happen at all?" The scene was frozen at the point that Sienna's head was turned towards Joel and her hands were out, palms up as if she was moving her hands to emphasize a point of conversation.

"They're walking together, side-by-side. Does she look upset to you?" the narrator asked.

"No. It looks like they are having a normal conversation," another voice replied.

* * *

Around one o'clock, the video was uploaded to a little-known YouTube channel called "JentlerHair", which mostly had videos about hairstyling. By the last school period, the link to the video had been disseminated throughout the student body of Cypress Grove High School. By the time the school staff left for the day, the link had been forwarded by multiple students to the email addresses of the Cy Grove principal, vice principals, and counselors.

* * *

Jalen:
Were you involved in that
vidco?

Annie:
Not much. It was a collaboration
with Emi and some others

Are you and Joel a thing?

Take me to get boba tea after
school and I'll let you know

Deal! But it'll have to be after
practice

I'll wait

* * *

"Thanks for the ride," Gretchen told Alia as she got out of Alia's pink art truck in front of her apartment building.

"No problem," Alia smiled. "Thank you for taking the lead in our little project." The smile disappeared. "I know what rape is, and to have some snobby brat fake a rape claim just to mess with people really pissed me off."

Gretchen twisted her mouth. "Joel's one of the few people who treat me like a person; most guys look at me like I'm furniture. Annie's lucky to have him. Besides, I kind of felt like we were sticking it to Holton and Sanders. I think they thrive on these power trips, and I love the idea of proving them wrong. That's what got Esmer and Rampage on board. Anyway, see you Monday."

"Maybe we can do a project together for shop class," Alia called out to Gretchen.

Gretchen gave Alia a thumbs-up sign as she walked away.

Alia continued watching Gretchen until she disappeared around the corner of the building. She looked up at the security camera attached to a light pole in the parking lot. Footage from that camera and another were used in the video that Gretchen and Emi made.

This is a good place for a surveillance camera, Alia thought. *Not like in a bedroom.*

Alia took out her phone and tapped out a message.

> Alia:
> Why didn't you tell me the story about Ella and the handcuffs when it first happened?
>
> I want real reason, not a joke

> Andy:
> I wanted to tell you so bad, but it ranked pretty high on the humiliation scale

> What do you mean?

> There's a line between embarrassing and humiliating. I didn't want to say anything that might

humiliate her in front of
anyone who knew her

I don't know her

I was always hoping you
would visit. Then you might
meet her

Are you done with classes
today?

Yes

I'm about to leave for college
station. Do you have time to
meet up?

Sure. Anything wrong?

Take me to that big tree on
campus

Which tree?

The old tree that Shelby pointed
out last week. Near that statue of
the old guy with the goatee

Do you mean the century
tree?

Yes. I want to take pictures
there.

> With you

> No more texting. I'm about to
> drive

Alia's phone vibrated with a call as she was tapping out a message to Sophie and Ty to let them know she would be home late.

"Alia, do you know what the Century Tree means?"

"Yeah. Shelby explained it last week," she said as she finished her text message to Sophie and Ty. "It's a romantic place for couples."

"It's more serious than that. People will think…"

Alia interrupted him with, "Do you want me to come or not?"

He couldn't tell from her tone if she was teasing or annoyed. "Yes. I want you to come."

"Good, because I'm on my way," she said, pulling out of the parking lot and onto the street.

The significance of Alia's plan finally reached Andy's consciousness like someone who took a few seconds to get the punchline of a joke.

"Do we get to call each other pet names?" he asked.

"Like what?"

"Like Snuggle Muffin," he said.

"Is that for me or you?"

"For you. I'm Andy Bear."

"Let's see what else you can come up with, Andy Bear. I'll be there in about an hour."

* * *

As Shelby walked down the hall to her bedroom, she saw Andy's door was open. She glanced in to see him pumping his fists in the air and shuffling his feet as if he had just scored a touchdown.

"I'm not even going to ask," she muttered as she shook her head. "Probably another stupid stunt for the next football game."

She hurried on to her room.

* * *

At Annie's request, Joel and Emi rendezvoused with her by the bus pickup lines when school was over, hurrying to get there before it became crowded. As soon as they saw Sienna, they blocked her path.

She looked around for an escape, but Bailey rushed up behind her and put an arm around her shoulders, causing her to flinch.

"I did what you wanted," Bailey said to Annie, "that should be enough."

Annie ignored Bailey and spoke to Sienna. "The problem, Sienna, is that you got it all wrong."

Sienna remained silent.

"Joel was never my boyfriend," Annie clarified.

"What!?" Bailey responded.

"He's Emi's boyfriend," Annie answered.

The group looked at Emi, who raised her eyebrows and opened her mouth as if to speak, but nothing came out. When she got her voice back, she whispered to Annie, "That's not what you said you were gonna tell her."

"Come on, Emi," Annie replied in her regular, non-whisper voice. "You know it, I know it, and Joel knows it."

Emi looked at Joel.

He smiled sheepishly and shrugged his shoulders. "As much as I like Annie," he reached out and took Emi's hand, "I can't stop thinking of you."

Emi looked at him, unsure how to respond.

"Joel," Annie said, getting his attention. "How do boyfriends greet their girlfriends?"

Joel leaned forward and kissed Emi on her cheek.

"Not fake girlfriends, real girlfriends," Annie reiterated.

Joel released Emi's hand and leaned in.

"Are you sure?" Emi asked, their noses touching.

"Are you?"

She closed her eyes and nodded almost imperceptibly. But Joel felt the motion. He tilted his head and kissed her. Eyes still closed, Emi smiled, then felt his hands slide across her waist to the small of her back, pulling her closer. She put her hands on his shoulders and felt a thrill of excitement as he kissed her again. The warmth spread from Emi's face, down her neck, and throughout her body.

Oblivious to Emi and Joel's activity, Jalen called out loudly as he approached, "Hey, Annie! How's it going?"

Annie put her hand up and waved.

When he got closer, he added, "Practice was canceled. Something about the A/C in the gym."

Annie placed her hand on Emi's shoulder, interrupting her moment with Joel. "I guess this means I've given up my fake boyfriend for your fake homecoming date."

Sienna and Bailey slipped away, unnoticed.

"Where'd they go?" Annie asked the group after realizing Sienna and Bailey were gone. "Do you think Sienna will be punished?"

"I doubt it," Jalen said. Then he pointed toward a bus. "If you're looking for her, she's over there getting on a bus. I don't know if she'll ever be punished, but she'll have consequences."

"Like what?" Annie asked.

They watched the bus close its door in preparation to drive away.

"Like, no guy will ask her out after this. Who wants to risk getting accused of something if she's in a bad mood?"

Epilogue

Previous June – vacation day eight, home again

When the Jentler family rounded the corner onto their street, completing the journey from Arizona, they saw a familiar car parked in front of their house. Lizzie sat inside, looking at her phone. She looked up at the SUV turning onto the street as she had with every vehicle that approached. As the Cadillac pulled into the driveway, she ran up behind it and followed it up the driveway to the back of the house. After seeing the seating arrangements within the vehicle, she went to the back door on the driver's side.

John emerged from the car and immediately embraced Lizzie with a bear hug that lifted her off her feet.

"I missed you!" he said as he set her back on her feet, but without releasing the hug.

Lizzie kept her arms around his neck and kissed him for several seconds.

Ty loudly cleared his throat. "We're all watching."

"I missed you, too," Lizzie said after their lips unlocked from each other. She then lightly kissed the bandage covering the cut on his chin.

Looking at Ty, Lizzie added, "My Dad makes that same throat sound. I ignore him, too."

Ty chuckled.

As the other passengers climbed out of the vehicle, Annie whispered to Emi, "I wish he didn't have a girlfriend."

"Yeah, well, you'll have to get in line behind Alia."

"I thought she was dating that guy in Arkansas?"

As she was saying it, a red Camaro pulled into the driveway. Andy stepped out of the sportscar and headed for Alia, who now stood at the back of the SUV, waiting to retrieve her suitcase.

"I guess we'll see," Emi commented.

Andy spread his arms as he got close to Alia. Alia hesitated for a moment before hugging him.

"I wasn't sure if you would be mad at me," she said.

"Are you kidding? Why would I be mad at you? You may have found the skeleton in the Crenshaw closet, but you didn't put it there."

Emi elbowed Annie. "Short hug; lots of talk; no kiss."

Andy looked at Alia as if trying to read her mind. "As I told you before: you don't disappoint me. You're the one who has a right to be mad." He reached out to hug her again, this time kissing her lightly and quickly on the lips.

"Thank you," she responded, hugging him tighter.

Annie leaned her head to Emi's and whispered, "It wasn't like John's kiss, but it was still a kiss."

"It looked more like a friend kiss than a boyfriend kiss," Emi whispered back.

"I wish I could have a boyfriend for my birthday," Annie stated.

"Your birthday just passed, so I guess you'll have to wait 'til Christmas," Emi pointed out. Then she added, "But my birthday's coming up in a couple of months."

"Fine. I'll order you a boyfriend online for delivery on your birthday."

* * *

November - Thanksgiving

Grandma Jensen seemed a bit confused at the Thanksgiving meal. John invited Lizzie over for the meal and Grandma kept calling her "Alia". Perhaps the confusion would have been alleviated if Alia had been there. But Alia was at Andy's family meal, showing off the heart pendant necklace Andy gave her to celebrate their new relationship.

Each time Grandma said "Alia", one of the family members would respond with "Lizzie".

"Who's your friend, Emi?" Grandma asked upon Joel's arrival.

"Grandma, this is Joel."

"At least she got my name right," Joel whispered to Emi after the third reference to Alia.

"Do you think your mom will confuse me with anyone?" Emi asked.

"There's no one remotely like you," Joel responded. "But we'll find out when we visit with her this afternoon. Are you ready for that?"

"Can I bring a cake with a file in it?"

"Don't do that. The guards will just eat the cake themselves and lock you up with Mom. And that would be scary for me."

"For you?"

"Yeah. She'll spend hours telling you all the embarrassing stuff I did as a kid."

"Hmm." Emi walked away.

"Where are you going?"

"To get the cake mix."

The End

Acknowledgments

I want to thank my wife Wendy for her feedback on the story and encouragement to continue this writing project and my daughter Katie who was my first reviewer and provided the earliest advice.

My appreciation goes to Miki T. for her translation of the Japanese phrases and for jogging my fading memory of the Japanese phrases I once knew. I also want to thank Ruth M. for her review and feedback on the manuscript and the Cypress Authors Group for their general writing advice.

About the Author

Todd H. Davis is the father of three kids (two girls and a boy) who were older teenagers at the time of writing *The Trailer Behind the Garage*, its sequel, *The Gas Station Girl*, and at the start of this novel. He lives with his "smarter-than-me" wife in the Houston, Texas, suburb of Cypress, which is the setting for his novels.

Todd spent most of his life in the Houston area, except for the two years in Japan as a young man, teaching English in churches in the Nagasaki area. While he was getting used to Asian culture, his wife, who had recently arrived in the US from China for studies, was getting used to American culture. They have spent the time since then getting used to each other.

You can contact him through his website:

www.toddhdavis.com

Books by Todd H. Davis

The Trailer Behind the Garage

The Gas Station Girl

The Lingering Scent of Wrong Assumptions

The DollarFly Girls
a prequel to The Gas Station Girl

The Kennedi Identity

Made in the USA
Columbia, SC
02 March 2024

32564585R00193